DANIEL DEPP
BABYLON NIGHTS

SIMON &
SCHUSTER

London · New York · Sydney · Toronto

A CBS COMPANY

First published in Great Britain by Simon & Schuster UK Ltd, 2010
A CBS COMPANY

Copyright © Daniel Depp, 2010

A CIP catalogue record for this book is available
from the British Library.

ISBN 978-1-84737-409-7

Printed in the UK by CPI Mackays, Chatham ME5 8TD

AUTHOR'S NOTE

Astute readers will see that the Author has shamelessly taken liberties with Los Angeles, Cannes, Nice, and that famous film festival occurring yearly at you-know-where.

In fact, the Author has taken liberties with just about everything he can think of, not the least being the readers' willingness to suspend disbelief and enter into the fun of it all.

There is, for example, no Coren Investigations on Sunset. There is no Le Vent Provençal on the rue d'Antibes in Cannes, and as far as the Author knows there's no old vinegar factory anywhere in the city limits of that lovely Mediterranean burg.

There is no Anna Mayhew, there is no Andrei Levin, and, while we're at it, the Author lied about the members of the Cannes jury as well. None of them exist.

While there are bound to be some accuracies in this book in spite of how hard the Author worked against it, the Author still asks the international film community to quit seeing themselves in every character and stop irritating the hell out of him at parties.

Once again, You are not You, They are not They, etc., etc.

On the other hand, Cocteau says somewhere that all art is a lie that tells the truth.

In that case, the book you hold is, hopefully, a big fat lie.

The author would also like to thank Mr. William Goldman, patron saint of screenwriters, who's penned the best books on Hollywood and Cannes that anyone will ever write, period, present company included.

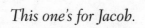

This one's for Jacob.

*Daughter of Babylon, who is to be destroyed; happy shall be
the man who serves you as you have served us.*

PSALMS 137:8

*Popular culture is the new Babylon, into which so much
art and intellect now flow. It is our imperial sex theater,
supreme temple of the western eye. We live in the age of
idols. The pagan past, never dead, flames again in our mystic
hierarchies of stardom.*

CAMILLE PAGLIA

BABYLON NIGHTS

PART ONE

LOS ANGELES

1

THE NUDE PHOTOS OF HER WERE SPREAD ALL OVER THE floor. Thirty or forty eight-by-tens, arranged carefully side by side, touching each other so that the images of her lay before him like a carpet. A magic carpet, up here in his hideaway. Up here in his world.

They were computer prints, not particularly good, copied and digitized from the originals, wherever they were. Perec didn't care. They'd cost him two thousand dollars and months of searching, but he'd found them. Perec had heard they existed and searched the Internet, right here in his room, until he found someone who had them. A guy in San Diego. Perec couldn't allow them to be mailed to the house, Maman would have needed to see, she'd have taken them from him, ripped them open, read his mail, looking for whatever filth was meant for his eyes. So Perec had driven to San Diego and given the man his money. On the way home Perec kept touching the package, over and over, as it lay in the passenger seat.

The Internet was wonderful. You could find anything on the Internet, provided you looked hard enough.

Now she lay there, over and over again, pouting, smiling, gazing at him, her bubbies showing and in most of them her Down There showing too, and it made Perec at once sick but excited to see them. He felt like his heart was being torn from his body, but the pit of his stomach ached and his own Down There felt a way he'd never felt before.

Perec took off his socks and slowly, hesitantly, ventured barefoot onto the ocean of her, floating on a raft of her. He could feel her body under his feet, her warmth rising through his soles and up into and through him. He was dizzy. He took a breath and moved another step. A nipple peeked between the toes of his left foot, the edge of his right snuggled her hip like a lover's body. Perec thought he might pass out. Perec thought he might go mad.

He didn't want to do it. He swore he wouldn't do it. But he stepped off the photos and undressed until he was as naked, as shameless, as helpless as she was. He moved back onto the photos, stepping across them slowly, stepping from one to the other like stones across a stream. She entered his body in a wave, a great rush from the floor up through him, and Perec felt that stirring he could not name, his Down There hard and aching, and he lowered himself onto her, the infinite numbers of her, and he found he could hardly breathe.

He thought about doing that Thing, the one he sometimes had to do after certain girls came into the shop and teased him. Perec knew that it was ugly and it was dirty and he hated himself whenever it happened. He wanted to do it now so bad, the filthy devils in his body screamed at him to do it, but Perec refused. Perec fought them. No, said Perec. No, I will not. It wasn't the sort of thing you did to someone you loved, and Perec loved her with all his heart.

Instead he got to his feet and went over and took the razor

from his drawer. His father's straight razor, ivory-handled Solin-gen steel, when his father died the only thing he could grab before his mother threw it all away and forbid that his name be spoken again. Perec made a small incision on his forearm. It was small but just enough. Perec knew how to do this, he'd done it often over the years, his body now a map of tiny puckered scars. He watched the blood trickle slowly down his wrist and into his cupped palm. Perec moved again among the photos, dipping his other thumb in the blood, kneeling at each picture, carefully leaving a crimson print on each breast and between her legs, at once clothing their shameful nakedness and offering a benediction, just like the priests his mother hated now, the ones who used to touch his forehead and tell him his sins were gone forever. Perec's heart quickened, his hands shook, he feared he would spill blood all over the photos. He stepped off the pictures just as it happened, he couldn't stop it, his body quivered and he cried out. He felt no guilt now because he had not done it himself, she had done this for him, and it was fine. She had given this to him, she had shown she loved him as well.

Perec sat down and looked at his work and was filled with a greater love than he could ever have imagined. Even in the days when he loved God, there was nothing like this. Perec knew he must show her his love. He must find her and give her his gift.

Perec, for the first time in his life, knew joy.

2

KENNY KINGSTON STOOD ON TOP OF THE BEVERLY CENTER
in Hollywood, California, thinking about Life, Love, and Disease
in America during these early days of the twenty-first century.

To be more specific, he was thinking about genital herpes. His
own were acting up this morning, as they always did when he was
stressed. He scratched his crotch through his jeans and shifted
uneasily. To the east a lemon-colored sun cleared a pinkish L.A.
skyline, a scene not devoid of beauty until you thought about the
sheer number of airborne carcinogens that made this possible.

Kenny was slightly below-average height for a California
male. He had dirty shoulder-length blond hair, and wore a black
T-shirt featuring the Jägermeister stag. His blue jeans had been
worn for a week and the knees were gone. He wore Birkenstocks
on his bare feet, and if you got close enough there was a fungus
beginning under his left big toenail. Kenny looked much like the
talented and extremely dead Kurt Cobain, a fact not lost on him.
This too made him popular in certain circles. That and his access
to many amusing chemicals.

It was seven-thirty in the morning and Kenny's twenty-year-old green Porsche was the only car yet parked on the top tier of the structure. Kenny leaned on the short concrete wall, gazing downtown and smoking a cigarette. He'd read somewhere that one out of three people in Los Angeles had herpes, making L.A. a garden spot for the disease. Meaning that out of ten million people in L.A. County, over three million had it, and maybe a million of those didn't know it yet. Meaning that, unless you were of a very cautious nature, if you didn't have the herp by the time you got to L.A., you'd probably have it by the time you left. Of course, once you had it, an entire world of unprotected sex opened up, given all those diseased people who were grateful to find an equally diseased partner. Kenny had even joined a club, which eliminated that awkward prefuck "Do you or Don't you" question, since, of course, they Did. And there were online dating sites as well. In the three years Kenny'd had the disease his social life had improved enormously. He hadn't even gotten laid until his junior year in college, and now he got laid all the time. Kenny sensed that there might be something a little weird about living in a world where it was better to be diseased than healthy, but who was he to complain?

He had to be in the lab by nine, working on a project that was going nowhere, since Kenny could not get the results they wanted. By eleven o'clock his supervisor, who also happened to be his graduate sponsor, would be yelling at him again and Kenny's schlong would feel as if it had been bathed in acid. In all likelihood the project wasn't going to get funded for another year, depriving Kenny of incomes both legal and illegal and the American covert intelligence community of one more nifty way of assassinating foreign politicians. There was also the matter of Kenny's doctoral dissertation on nonsoluble alkalids, which had ground to a halt. Kenny seriously needed the money he was about to make.

Kenny turned to watch a large black Lincoln Navigator pull up onto the deck. It didn't park next to his car but stopped in the middle of the deck, straddling the spaces and lines, as if making some kind of statement, which is exactly what it was doing. Her making a fucking entrance, thought Kenny. He took a last drag off his cigarette and dropped it over the parapet and down onto the hood of a Mercedes, where it lay sizzling.

She took her time getting out of the car, but when she did you had to admit it was worth the wait. She was no spring chicken anymore, but she was tall and blond and that famous body was still tight. She wore a pale silk blouse that drew attention to the gentle motion of her breasts as she walked, and designer jeans that did what an expensive pair of designer jeans are meant to do. The high heels made her taller than she was, and she was already a tall woman. And sunglasses, for chrissake, at this time of the morning. She smiled and walked toward him like a goddamn Amazon. She meant to impress him, and Kenny had to admit she damn well did.

"This is a great city until people actually get up," said Kenny. "Then it sucks."

She leaned next to him and the wall and pretended to take in the view.

"Everybody slams L.A.," she said. "Me, I love the place. I always have."

She turned to face him.

"I came out here from Texas once when I was a cheerleader in high school. You know, those competitions they have. Rah-rah, you get all psyched up, they treat it like the well-being of the nation depends on it. Anyway, once I got out here I didn't want to leave. Screw cheerleading, screw Dallas. I saw the light. I saw Faye fucking Dunaway coming out of Spago."

She paused, turned back to the view. Get on with the fucking story, thought Kenny.

"We'd all lined up out front to see the stars—no goddamn idea what sort of place it was, I'm not even sure if I knew it was a restaurant, just that this was where stars went. Sure enough, we're waiting there, watching people go in and out, can't recognize anybody, then—Faye fucking Dunaway strolls out. And she's gorgeous. She sort of floats out. Even in the middle of the day, coming out to eat a hamburger, she looks like a goddamn million dollars. A goddess. A car pulls up, a guy gets out and opens the door for her. She drives away.

"And I'm standing there on the sidewalk in front of Spago with a bunch of giggly cheerleaders and not one of them had an idea of who she was. But my life had changed. I knew that was what I wanted. I wanted to be like that."

"Faye Dunaway," repeated Kenny. "She's like fucking how old now? And she's got this thing with her teeth. I mean, in *Bonnie and Clyde* her teeth didn't look like that. What the fuck is up with her teeth? She got dentures or what?"

She stared at him.

"I think you're entirely missing the drama of the story, Kenny."

"You ever meet Monica Bellucci? Now there's a hot babe."

"And I hear her teeth are in pretty good shape. You want to hear about Harrison Ford's bridgework?"

She did that, the superior number, the little dig to remind you of who she was. Kenny felt it was time to level the playing field, so he went to the Porsche and took out a tiny cardboard box about the size of a wristwatch package. Then she let him stand there holding it while she dug around in her purse, like she might not be able to find the money. He'd sold stuff to popular actors before, and it irritated Kenny that these goddamn people always seemed to think they were still being filmed.

She took out a wad of bills and put them in his free hand.

"Count that."

Kenny put the box on the hood of the Porsche and counted the money. "Fifty-five hundred."

She dived back into the purse and came up with another wad.

"That's sixty-five hundred," Kenny said.

One more dive like a fucking cormorant.

"Seven thousand even," she said, as if she was waiting for a fucking pat on the back.

"You always this organized?" Kenny asked her.

He handed her the box. She opened it carefully. There was a tiny vial resting in a nest of tissue. She started to pick it up but Kenny stopped her.

"Whoa! You want to play with it, you take it home, not with me around. Lady, that's a synthesis of five of the ugliest fucking toxins on the planet. It ain't no Coca-Cola."

"I thought you said it only worked if you swallowed it?"

"I said ingested. You fucking drop it and it breaks and one drop, just a single lousy drop, splashes in your eye or on your lip or something and you're as good as dead. You get it on your skin, you wash it off real quick. You got an open cut and you're fucked. Any way it can get inside your body, that's it, good night, nurse, you got maybe fifteen seconds, max. And you got enough there to kill maybe thirty people if you give it to them with an eyedropper. A hundred, you want to pour it in their Kool-Aid and you don't mind waiting."

"And not painful, right?" she asked, for probably the millionth time since they started all this.

"You black out," said Kenny. "It's like somebody switching off a light. Then the nervous system shuts down, only by then you don't know it."

"You sure? How do you know?"

"Because," said Kenny, "the fucking U.S. government paid for tests on ninety-pound apes, that's how I know. I read the reports, they got the files locked up in the lab. Us grad assistants aren't supposed to see this shit, they'd bury my ass *under* a cell in Leavenworth they found out I stole this. Look, I don't want to know why you want this stuff. I don't care. I just want to finish my degree and get a nice safe research job somewhere and not starve in the meantime."

She smiled. "You sure you don't want to know?"

"Rats," said Kenny. "Fucking moles in the backyard. The neighbor's barking dog. That's what you'll use it for. By the way, we never meet again."

"Oh, I don't think that's going to be a problem, sweetheart," she said dreamily. "Not really."

Kenny got into the Porsche and drove away. She stood there with the box, looking out over Los Angeles as if she were deciding whether to move it or just leave it where it was. She plucked the vial out of the box, tossed the protective box on the ground, and gingerly dropped seven thousand dollars' worth of neurotoxin into her cute little Gucci handbag.

3

ANNA MAYHEW, OSCAR WINNER AND ONETIME TABLOID fodder, sat in the dining room of a large Beverly Hills restaurant. She was thinking of tits and ass, and how many days should be allowed before she killed herself. She fingered the tiny vial of poison like a talisman. For some reason it made her feel better, holding it.

It was kind of a clinical study, really, as Anna surveyed the room from a table surrounded by fifty-odd well-heeled Beverly Hills matrons, who in turn sat gossiping over their salads as the Mexican waiters tried to serve them unscathed. It was a useless attempt. The ladies pelted the Latinos with critiques like Roman Christians being stoned to death. The waiters went about their jobs with heads bent, trying not to make eye contact, which would only have earned them a report to the manager for insolence. They were all, to a man, illegal as hell, and endured it. But if they'd somehow been able to move the room to Tijuana, it would have been a gleeful bloodbath.

Anna had pretty much worked out the suicide aspect of

things. She was just having trouble making up her mind when. Meanwhile, in her darker moments, she liked to roll the vial back and forth in her fingers. It relaxed her, knowing that death was just a couple of seconds away.

"You know, Attila is my husband," said the woman next to her.

"Pardon?"

"Attila. Attila Boyagian. He produced one of your movies. I forget which one. You don't happen to remember, do you?"

"No, sorry."

"Well, no matter," said Mrs. Boyagian. "It was ages ago. I'd ask Attila but he's three-quarters senile himself at this point."

Mrs. Boyagian looked at her watch, then stood up and went to the lectern at the front of the room. "Everyone! Everyone!"

The ladies stopped their ritual torment of the waiters and gave Mrs. Boyagian their attention.

"Thank you all for coming," said Mrs. Boyagian. "We're having such lovely weather—hasn't it been just the best spring?—and I know everybody wants to be outside, working in the garden or playing tennis. But I'm sure you're all excited about today's guest. I know I am. We're fortunate to have with us today a legend, and one of the finest and most influential actresses—oh my, can I say 'actresses' these days?—of the last few decades."

Oh, that "last few decades" hurt. Anna made a note to insult the bitch somehow. Mrs. Boyagian stood there in her thousand-dollar pant suit while Anna examined the woman's ass, which wasn't bad for a woman in her fifties. Tuck job, of course, and maybe some kind of insert? The trouble with the asses in this room is that you couldn't find a pristine one among them. Tits either, for that matter. The place caught on fire and knockers and derrieres would be melting like Vincent Price in the last scene of *House of Wax*.

The day had started badly. Anna was going through one of those blue periods that seemed to get longer and longer. This one threatened to outlast Picasso's. Coming out of the shower, she'd examined her face in the mirror, and had to admit it still wasn't bad. She didn't look her age, which was forty-three. I could pass for thirty-five, she reasoned, which was a good bet since she'd done it for the last eight years. This had made her brave, and she'd done the foolhardy act of placing a pencil under her left tit. The pencil remained as firm as Super Glue. Anna bounced up and down a little and the fucking pencil clung like a mountaineer. Same for the other tit. This was when she made the really serious mistake of trying it with her ass. Jesus God, you could have wedged a salami down there and gone jogging. So far she'd put it off, the cosmetic engineering, but her time was coming. Maybe she'd just stop all this crap, relax, and grow old gracefully. There was enough money. She didn't have to act anymore, not really. She could do her charities and her garden and maybe write her memoirs. She had a fleeting vision of her gray-haired, saggy-assed future self. No, fuck that. I'm in this till the bitter end. I've made a couple of good films that people might remember. I do it now and I never age.

"We've all admired her work for years," said Mrs. Boyagian and her plastic ass, "and she won a Best Actress Oscar for her role in *The Lady from Barcelona*—I still get teary-eyed when I think of that scene with her mother, don't you?—and certainly she's been an outstanding role model for a new generation of, um, women actors. The West Hollywood Arts Society would like to introduce . . . Anna Mayhew!"

Applause, and Anna walked to the lectern feeling fifty-odd pairs of eyes focused on her own massive hams.

"Thank you, Shirley," Anna enunciated to the room, "for that kind introduction. And I'd like to thank the West Hollywood Arts Society for inviting me here today. I know it's hard to remain indoors in such lovely weather, but I'd like to speak to you about something that's dear to my heart."

Mrs. Boyagian beamed at Anna as she spoke, and noticed the small vial Anna had left by her plate. It looked like a perfume sample, probably something French and expensive. Mrs. Boyagian leaned forward a bit and sniffed. Nothing. Well, shit.

"If someone suggested we stop taking care of the Lincoln Memorial in Washington, D.C., or allow the works in New York's Metropolitan Museum of Art to decay and disappear from the face of the earth, we'd all be up in arms about it, wouldn't we? I mean, that sort of thing would never be allowed to happen, would it? There'd be a public outrage, nobody would ever consider letting our national treasures die and fade away forever."

Mrs. Boyagian continued to smile and look respectfully at Anna, but poked the vial with her finger. It rolled a little on the tablecloth and Mrs. Boyagian was terribly happy when it didn't go off the edge. She inched her hand across to pick it up.

"But the ugly truth is, that's exactly what we are doing. Oh, not to the Lincoln Memorial or the Met, but to our own treasures right here in Los Angeles. Hundreds of buildings in L.A., beautiful works of art constructed in what can only be called L.A.'s golden age of the early first half of the twentieth century, are being allowed to fall into neglect, to be torn down in favor of—"

Anna saw Mrs. Boyagian pick up the vial and the pit of her stomach fell through her sphincter. Her vision went a little gray as she foresaw the end of the world, at least for fifty-odd Beverly Hills housewives, three Mexican waiters, and one washed-up actress with a droopy ass. She tried to struggle on.

"Of, um, of strip malls and fast-food restaurants. They, um . . ."

She could feel it all going sideways, like a pig on ice. Mrs. Boyagian squinted at the vial, examining its odd color. She definitely didn't know this one.

"They, ah, they . . ." Put it down, you stupid bitch, oh, please don't open the thing. "Every year, dozens of architectural works of art get demolished to make way for objects that not only lack any kind of aesthetic pleasure but grow like a blight on our landscape . . ."

Mrs. Boyagian sniffed the vial and resisted the temptation to just have a little snort. I'm going to puke, thought Anna. She went on, rushing, falling headlong through the speech.

". . . adding nothing to the natural beauty we are blessed with here in Southern California. Why I am here today is to ask you—"

She wouldn't mind me having just the littlest sniff, said Mrs. Boyagian to herself, and started to open the cap.

"MRS. BOYAGIAN!" cried Anna.

Mrs. Boyagian dropped the vial. It fell in her lap, caught in a fold of cloth. Mrs. Boyagian became rapt.

"—and the rest of the West Hollywood Arts Society, to work with me and my friends as we endeavor to save as many of these wonderful old buildings as we can. Thank you."

Mrs. Boyagian alone stood up to applaud, like she was giving the floozy—God knew that Anna Mayhew had slept with everybody—her own mini-ovation. She let the vial drop to the carpet. It just rolled onto the floor, blame the goddamn beaners.

Anna rushed to the table. The vial was gone. The fucking old cow didn't have it in her hand. The bitch has stolen it, she'll open it when she gets home, she and her fucking senile producer husband and their maids and gardeners and fucking cats and Sharpeis are all going to meet in heaven relatively soon.

"Inspiring," said Mrs. Boyagian, and went back to the lectern.

"Thank you, Anna Mayhew, for reminding us of one of our primary civic duties, that of preserving our architectural heritage."

Anna looked around frantically. She bobbed under the table, well aware that people were staring at her but at the moment she didn't give a shit.

"Let's give Anna another round of applause for a job well done, shall we?"

She saw it, her tiny bit of Armageddon, between the tables a few feet away. She felt a great wave of relief until she saw one of the waiters, carrying a tray of lobster thermidors, about to tread on it.

There are defining moments in life and Anna knew this was one of them. She threw herself at the vial, flat on the carpet, her hand just managing to grasp the tiny container. The Mexican waiter hit her, went flying himself, and sent bits of Maine crustacean and Wisconsin cream sailing toward the windows. Anna and the waiter disentangled themselves, the waiter painfully aware his ass was now fired and Anna relieved she had just given half of Beverly Hills society a fresh chance at life.

"Oh dear," said Mrs. Boyagian as Anna got to her feet. "These waiters . . ."

"I caught my heel on the tablecloth," said Anna. "How stupid."

"They don't know how to hang them properly," said Mrs. Boyagian. "They can't even set a table, these people. You're all right, then?"

"Yes, I'm fine now, thank you."

"You know, I couldn't help noticing that wonderful scent you're wearing. May I ask what it is?"

"Thanatos," said Anna.

"Thanatos?" repeated Mrs. Boyagian. "What an odd name. It smells amazing."

"Yes," said Anna. "It's a killer."

"Oh, how cute," said Mrs. Boyagian.

She made obligatory nice-nice for a while—she was, after all, picking their pockets for a good cause—but the single thing that occupied her mind was getting out of that room, out of the door, into the car, home. She stood around, answering the same stupid questions she'd answered for years, nodding as if she cared, making use of all that expensive dentistry she'd invested in. There was a lull and she shook hands with that bitch Boyagian and made her way out the front door. Chandler, her driver, was waiting at the curb. She pulled on her sunglasses and threw the Hermès scarf over her shoulder and made a beeline for the car. Then someone stopped her on the sidewalk, goddamn it, one of the women, another lame question she had to answer. Someone brushed by her and she moved out of the way to finish the conversation. She flashed a final smile and hopped into the black Navigator and shut the door. Safe.

"Where to now?" asked Chandler. He was a large, handsome black man, a bit of a Romeo who'd knocked up her young Iberian maid. Anna was going to have to fire somebody, but she liked Chandler and it would be worth the six months' wages to the Portugee, as Anna thought of her, to keep him. Anna envied the maid, and sometimes when drunk thought about climbing Mount Chandler herself. She'd done far less dignified things. But then she really would have to fire him.

"Home, I guess," Anna said to him. "Is Pam there?"

"You want me to call and check?"

"No, to hell with it. Just get me home."

Anna sat back, took a deep, relaxing yogic breath, just like

Shakti, her gay Ayurveda instructor from Brooklyn, kept show-ing her. She took off the sunglasses and pulled the scarf from around her neck. As the silk drifted through her fingers, they caught on something. She looked at it. Nearly half the scarf had been cleanly sliced through. Shit, she liked this scarf. She tried to remember where she could have snagged it. She'd had it with her the whole time. Then she remembered the bump on the side-walk, and thought, that's silly, but she realized it was the only place it could have happened, a cut like that. She told Chandler to pull over, pull over now, and he did and then watched her fi-nally puke salad and lobster thermidor all over the curb in front of the House of Blues.

4

THE CEMETERY WAS IN THE DESERT OUTSIDE OF PALM Springs, an obnoxious spot of greenery in the sand, where the headstones and monuments looked like they'd been planted in a golf course. It was hot and all the granite glowed and shimmered in the sun, as if the souls of the smoldering dearly departed were fed up and making a break for it. The place looked absurd and gaudy, but then Hollywood was absurd and gaudy and this is where they liked to bury their dead.

David Spandau stood to the back of the crowd that kept nudging ever forward, until the minister, worried the corpse was about to have company, warned them away. There was a brief shuffle away from the center of attention, and the minister picked up the eulogy again. The minister was from Ohio, the home of the deceased, and he felt he had no business in this godforsaken place. He was sweating like a pig and there were TV cameras on him and all he could think about was looking like a rube on the *Today* show. But the family of the deceased had paid him good money to come out here, put him up in a nice hotel with room service, and being an honest man, he was determined to give them their money's worth.

"It is said that Robert Leonard Dye was the finest actor of his generation, and there are few who would dispute this. Certainly not the millions of fans who idolized him, and certainly not his friends and colleagues, who knew him for the kind and generous friend that he was . . ."

Bobby Dye's mother stood at the foot of her son's grave, crying. They were real tears, which is something this particular cemetery didn't see all that often. Her oldest son, Harry, Bobby's only brother, stood with his arm around her. He wasn't crying, but then he'd just inherited several million dollars and a house in Malibu. Behind them were Bobby's longtime agent, Annie Michaels, and big-shot producer Frank Jurado, producer of several of Bobby's films. Bobby's girlfriend, Mila-just-the-one-name-like-Cher, the Russian starlet of *Galaxy Invaders III*, was with them. Like a jockey spotting an opening at the fence, she tried to edge her way forward, but Bobby's brother gave a high sign and they closed ranks. Poor Mila, she was suing the estate and nobody liked her.

". . . Ashes to ashes, dust to dust . . ." said the minister, and hoped he'd said it dramatically enough for the media.

A group of musicians launched into Led Zeppelin's "Stairway to Heaven" as somebody kicked a switch and the coffin sank into the ground. Good-bye, Bobby, you poor son of a bitch, thought Spandau. He followed the line past the grave, picked up his handful of earth, and dropped it on the casket. He saw Frank Jurado glaring at him. Annie wouldn't look his way. As he started toward the parking lot, a small red-haired man grabbed his sleeve.

"Hello, Ginger," said Spandau. Ginger's eyes were raw from crying. He'd stood nearly as far back as Spandau, being merely Bobby's personal assistant, and no longer warranting inclusion.

"He'd've hated this, you know," said Ginger. "He wanted 'Siegfried's Funeral March.' Tasteful, just like he was. The Led Zeppelin is just tack. Oh Lord, as far as I know he didn't even like Led Zeppelin. That's Mila's doing, the bitch. Right now he's in heaven, swearing like a sailor. You're not mad at me too, are you? I don't think I could bear it."

"Why should I be mad at you?"

"That whole business, after all you'd done for him, and he refused to see you again . . ."

"I never blamed that on you."

"They fired me too, you know," said Ginger. "Just after he won the Oscar for *Wildfire*. Mila came in and cleaned house, got rid of anybody who meant anything to him. I'd been with him through it all, then he has Annie come in and ask me to leave. He couldn't do it himself. He knew it was wrong. He was afraid of Mila, though, afraid she'd leave him. And she did leave him too, didn't she, the bitch. They didn't want to let me in here today. But I told them I'd make a scene. Fuck the hush contracts, I'll go to the fucking papers, I said. I'll go to fucking CNN. They let me in. I was lying, though. If they knew me, if they knew anything, they'd know I couldn't do anything like that. I'd never do that to him, never."

He began to cry again.

"You were his friend," said Ginger. "He knew that."

"He had a funny way of showing it."

"I never knew anybody so afraid. They pushed him around, ran his life. Took it from him, in the end, didn't they? He liked you. They made him do what he did."

"He was a grown man, Ginger. Nobody put a gun to his head. Anyway, I was just the hired help. He got into a mess and paid me to get him out of it, that's all."

"You know that isn't true."

"I don't know anything," said Spandau. "I wish I did, but I don't."

Ginger embraced him. Spandau put his hand on the little man's shoulder. Ginger had loved Bobby, but Bobby Dye had a hard time with love. It wasn't something you could pick up and fondle like a pretentious French wine, a sports car, or a girlfriend he'd selected from the Victoria's Secret catalog. People loved Bobby at their own risk, and he ran them away when he could. All that was left were the cynics, who, like Oscar Wilde once said, knew the price of everything and the value of nothing.

"Take care of yourself, Ginger," said Spandau.

"Oh, I will. Keep your pecker up, I always say." Then he giggled. "He always laughed when I said that, said it didn't mean the same thing here." He turned away, crying again.

Spandau had reached the parking lot when the long black Lincoln Town Car finally pulled up and blocked his path. He'd seen the car waiting all through the service but hadn't been sure until now it was for him. The tinted black window went down and Salvatore Locatelli leaned forward. Locatelli was a very busy man, but he dearly loved driving around town and scaring the shit out of people like this.

"Get in, Texas," said Locatelli.

Spandau ignored him and tried to walk around the car, but the driver moved it to block him and they did this several times.

"Don't be a hard-on, Texas. All this rocking back and forth, I get seasick."

Locatelli pushed open the door. Spandau climbed in. The air-conditioning was a shock after the desert heat. Locatelli took his time unwrapping a Havana cigar, clipping it, lighting it with a long match. Locatelli liked his little theatrics.

"What'd you think of the ceremony?" Locatelli said finally, around puffs of smoke.

"You drag me in here to exchange funerary critiques?" said Spandau.

"I thought it lacked gravitas. A man dies, it ought to be treated with gravity. Even if he was an opportunistic little prick."

Spandau reached for the door, but Locatelli stopped him.

"Okay, sorry, I know you liked the little bastard. God knows I could never figure out why. He treated you as shitty as he treated everybody else. Maybe worse, because you actually liked him. Very few people did, Texas, we have to admit this. I produced three of his films and I couldn't stand the sight of him."

"That never stopped you from making a good buck off him."

"Yeah, yeah, he was a poor innocent kid from Ohio, kind to his mother, the new James Dean. Tell that bullshit to the family of the dead girl he let die on his toilet and had Richie Stella's goons bury in the desert. You helped him get out of that one too, I seem to recall."

"Which you promptly used to blackmail him into working for you."

"Oh, you got that wrong. I didn't have to. Like every other swinging dick in this town, Bobby Dye was for sale. I just happened to have enough money to buy him. That's it, plain and simple. As usual, Texas, you got your villains mixed up."

"As much as I enjoy catching up on old times, would you mind cutting to the chase? I have an appointment."

"I like you, Texas. I think you're an idiot, but you've got balls and a certain sense of honor. If you dressed better you could almost pass for Italian, which is why I would hate to find you bobbing with the condoms under Santa Monica pier early one morning."

"I can't think of the last time anybody threatened my life so poetically."

"I want to lead a quiet life, Texas. I have a nineteen-year-old Argentine mistress and a variety of business associates who think they're Sonny Corleone and that cement shoes are still a swell idea. These will send me to my grave soon enough. I don't want to have to worry about you too."

"So this is you looking out for my welfare? I already got a Saint Jude's medal hanging around my neck. Sorry."

"Very funny," said Locatelli. "And I'll be laughing right up to the point where I have Louis here break your fucking kneecaps with a sledgehammer. You know what I mean. I don't want any trouble out of you. No heroics, no revenge fantasies. I didn't kill your pal. Your pal killed himself, with a little help from the American Medical Association. Those were all perfectly legal drugs he ate. I had nothing to do with it. You want a real culprit, talk to that bimbo he was engaged to. He's not the first guy to walk cunt-struck off the edge of a cliff. He was a business investment for me, Texas. I didn't like the little shit, but he's no good to me dead. Even you ought to be able to see that."

"We're just awash in sentiment here, aren't we? You mind if I go now, or is Louis up there determined to run over my cowboy boots again?"

"A fucking grown man, wearing those things. I could never understand it."

"They correct my pigeon toes. Otherwise I walk sideways like John Wayne."

"A sense of humor in the face of serious physical harm," said Locatelli. "I like that."

He reached over and pushed open the door. The desert rushed into the car and Locatelli winced. He disliked sand and heat and anything else that interfered with the crease of his Savile Row trousers. Spandau climbed out. He waited for Locatelli to have the last word, which he would do if he had to spend the afternoon chasing Spandau around the parking lot.

"Take care, Texas. Like the man says, these are mean streets."

The door closed and the Town Car whirred away. Spandau wondered for a moment if the biggest gangster in Los Angeles actually read Raymond Chandler, then realized Locatelli was quoting Martin Scorsese.

5

SPANDAU DROVE THE BLACK BMW EAST DOWN THE SUNSET Strip, past the Hollywood icons, the clubs, the restaurants, the unbearably hip, the tourists, the street people. He turned up onto a narrow street that rose steeply and became a series of sharp, blind turns. A delivery van nearly hit him, head-on, and he had to pull over and let the guy inch past. It was a short climb until the street opened up into a cul-de-sac and a large green gate that guaranteed its owner protection from the barbarian hordes. Instead of pulling up to the gate, Spandau pulled over and parked and dialed a number on his cell phone.

"Hi, you've reached the cell phone of Delia Macaulay. Please leave a message and I'll return your call."

Spandau hung up, then realized she'd see his number on her phone. Goddamn modern technology, thought Spandau. There was something horribly wrong with a country where you couldn't make an anonymous call to stalk your ex-wife. She'd said "Macaulay," her maiden name. At least she wasn't using the new one. That was a good sign. She was clearly beginning to see she'd made a mistake marrying that geek Charlie. Spandau felt a tiny ember ignite in his heart, but the part of him that still retained any sense knew it was desperation, like some Jack London character about to die of exposure. He drove up to the gate, buzzed, and hung his head out the window so they could see him.

"Yes?" said a woman's voice.

"I'm David Spandau. I have an appointment."

"Just a minute . . ."

The gate creaked and eased open. Spandau pulled through, half expecting, as he always did, for Saint Peter to come rushing up and demand his résumé. In the courtyard a large black man was washing a new Lincoln Navigator. There were tall ancient palm trees, cobblestones, and an Italianate fountain that just lacked Anita Ekberg prancing through it. The house itself was a great gray Norman thing, a castle really, that sat uncomfortable among the California splendor like a bull mastiff at a tea party. Birds cawed from above. Spandau parked beneath a palm tree out of the sun, risking the birdshit in favor of upholstery that didn't feel like a frying pan.

A small businesslike blonde came out of the house and walked up to the car. All six feet two inches of Spandau unrolled from the BMW and stood towering above her. She held out her hand and gave him a look that implied she ate hulks like him for breakfast. She was fair and blue-eyed and pretty, but there was something undeniably fierce about her, like a peculiarly attractive marmot.

"I'm Pamela Mayhew. I'm Anna's sister and her personal assistant."

"David Spandau," he said, taking her hand, "from Walter Coren and Associates."

"This way," she said, and marched back toward the house. Spandau lumbered behind her. He hated crisp people, especially in hot weather. He felt sweat trickle down his backbone and into his belt. Luckily inside was cooler. It was dark, and the two-foot-thick stone walls and slight hum of air-conditioning did a fine job of blocking out the rest of the cruel world. Spandau often dealt with the rich and famous, and what he envied was not the wealth or renown, but their ability to enclose themselves in a shell of real estate like giant armadillos. It was an illusion, of course. They were even less protected than most people, and Spandau's profession—a private detective specializing in the Hollywood elite—had taught him that various kinds of nastiness managed to get at them anyway. Still, you couldn't help but feel safe here, and Spandau thought of his own small, lonely house in the Valley, his own frail shell, where reality kept pouring in through all the cracks.

"I don't think I've ever met a real private eye before."

"Thrilling, isn't it?" said Spandau.

She laughed. It was a good, genuine laugh. "I take it you're the wisecracking sort who shoots the bad guy and kisses the girl in the last scene."

"Usually it's the other way around," he said, "but I keep my hopes up."

"Are you familiar with Anna's work?"

"Sure. She's not done anything in a while."

"I'd appreciate your not mentioning that."

Spandau nodded.

"Can I have a look at the scarf? And the letters?"

"I'll get them for you. Anna's up at the pool. I'll go and tell her you're here. Would you like something? Coffee? Water?"

"No thanks."

She left.

Anna was doing laps in the pool when Pam came out. She

stood there waiting for Anna to finish, then Anna climbed out of the water and Pam handed her a towel. She stood there some more while Anna dried herself.

"The detective is here," Pam said.

"Look, I don't want to deal with this right now. I've got this fucking speech to write for the theater opening and Cannes is coming up. Did you find us a place to stay?"

"Everything's all set for that lovely old place up in the hills."

"Maybe I shouldn't do this."

"You've already accepted and you're officially on the panel."

"It's going to be a jugfuck."

"It's been a jugfuck every May for the last fifty years, but it's an entertaining jugfuck. You go there, they treat you nice, you watch some films and pick out the ones you like. How hard is this? Come on, you know it's an honor to be asked."

"The politics are shit and I don't feel like spending all day every day arguing with the fucking French, which is what happens. I'm still trying to figure out the reason they asked me. There's always some ulterior motive. Andrei's got his film there. They fucking love Andrei, he's their fucking Russki poster boy. Him and those fucking interminable, boring, pretentious films he makes."

"You didn't think they were interminable, boring, or pretentious when you were doing them."

"I made two films with the bastard and never understood either one of them. Everybody else said their lines in Russian and he'd feed me mine in English off camera. The fucking script was in Cyrillic. I never had a clue and I don't think anybody else did, least of all Andrei. Andrei's secret is to make films so confusing you can read in anything you want. Andrei's only talent is to act like he knows what he's doing, so everybody else just goes along.

God, he was an amazing fuck, though. Who else is on the jury? Other women?"

"Kat Barrows, I'm pretty sure."

"That limey twat? Andrei fucked her too. Jesus, you know what they're doing, don't you? They loading the jury. Fucking frog bastards, they know his reputation. They think because he fucked us we'll vote for him."

"Won't you?"

"Ah God, probably. Unlike his films, a good fuck is something I can understand."

"This private-eye business. Let's do this for me, then. So I can sleep nights."

"What does he look like?"

Pam sighed. "Big. Dark. Muscular. He's wearing cowboy boots."

"Ooh," said Anna.

"He's got a broken nose."

"Will I like him?"

"He doesn't strike me as the type who's going to let you climb into his lap," said Pam.

"Yes," said Anna, "but will I want to?"

"I wouldn't be surprised."

"Send him out here," said Anna.

"My vote is that we try this one fully clothed."

"I haven't finished my laps."

"Right," said Pam. "You've just climbed out of the water and dried off in order to catch your breath. Look, I'm sure he'd be thrilled at the sight of your delectable body, but this feels desperately close to pimping, if you don't mind."

"Since when," said Anna, "did you become a fucking Mormon?"

"Gee," said Pam, "I guess it was just about the time you started showing your ass to absolute strangers."

"Honey," said Anna, "it's the same shopped-around ass that furnishes your paycheck. Nobody has complained yet. Show him around first then bring him out here."

Spandau was staring through a pair of tall glass doors that opened onto a balcony and a view over the trees and the Sunset Strip and into the heart of L.A. nearly as far as the airport. If you were going to live in L.A., this was the way to do it, in a shining mansion on a hillside, closer to the angels and a distant inspiration to the poor bastards below. Status in Hollywood was about constantly reminding them you were there, but they'd never have a chance at getting to you. He turned round when he heard her come in.

"It's quite a view," he said.

"I suppose it is," Pam said. "If you'll follow me . . ."

She took him on a tour of the estate.

"To be honest, there's not much in the way of security arrangements these days. It hasn't been necessary, if you know what I mean. A few years back maybe. There just isn't the attention there used to be. In a way I think she's actually flattered by these letters. There used to be a lot more mail coming in."

She pointed at various spots.

"The fence goes all the way around the property, and there are the cameras. A security service that comes round at night to check on things. We operate the gate from the house, and of course there's a camera there."

"It's not much."

"It hasn't been needed. You think there's a danger now?"

"We'll see," said Spandau.

"She's going through a bad time. The roles are drying up, and the ones she's being offered embarrass her, though she knows she'll have to start taking them sooner or later. She could retire— she's been smart about the money and it's invested well—but she wouldn't know what to do with herself. Either way it's humiliating to her. I don't suppose there's ever any dignified way to become a has-been."

"That's pretty harsh. It doesn't sound like you have much sympathy."

"It's a harsh profession. She could retire and live a quiet life, work on her charities. Go back to the stage, for God's sake. In spite of all the crap, she really is a fine and professional actress. But it's not about acting anymore, it's about being a star. The roles are there, she just thinks they're beneath her now. I know it's painful for her, and I understand. But you're right, I don't have much sympathy. I hate to see her in pain, but it's not the end of the world. She's forty-three years old, for god's sake. She could act for another forty years. Look at Kate Hepburn and Laurence Olivier, I told her."

"What did she say?"

"She said Hepburn ended up doing *Rooster Cogburn,* and that Olivier did *The Betsy.* She said you could either wander off into the woods like a whipped dog or hang around to become a caricature of yourself. She said Bobby Dye had the right idea, though he could have milked it awhile longer."

She watched his face for a reaction. There was none.

"You knew him, didn't you?"

"A little. I wouldn't exactly offer him as a role model."

"But he was good, wasn't he? I've heard actors talk about him. They said he was the one they watched, the one they could feel about to overtake them. It's funny, they were all kind of afraid of him."

"It worked both ways."

"The question is, where was there to go? Would he have gotten better? He won the Oscar for *Wildfire* and was one of the few that everybody thought deserved it."

"Would he have gotten better? I don't know. It's a silly question, isn't it? I mean, when did acting become a competitive sport? Your sister is talking like she's a ballplayer past her prime. At what point did it all become about money and fear?"

"You are a romantic, aren't you? You and Anna are a lot alike."

"She has to make the decision."

"She'll bitch about it and play hard to get, but if nothing else, you're a pleasant distraction. She needs a bit of drama right now—other than this scarf business."

"I'm not exactly boy-toy material, I'm afraid. And I don't get into relationships with my clients."

"For God's sake, don't tell her that. She needs you to protect her. What the hell do you care what her reasons are, as long as you keep her safe? That's what you get paid to do, isn't it? If you can avoid her clutches, more power to you. It'll be fun to watch."

"You make her sound like Foghorn Leghorn stalking a hen across the barnyard."

"Don't laugh, that's pretty much the way it is. Men like Anna and Anna likes men. It's a sight to behold."

Anna was swimming laps again when they got out to the pool. She did three or four very graceful passes, putting on a good show. She climbed up out of the water, looking like an actress pretending to be an Olympic swimmer. The black one-piece suit left very little to the imagination. She tilted back her head and squeezed water from the famous honey-blond hair, arching her body slightly and raising her arms. It was all very artfully done and Spandau was appreciative. He didn't think he was meant to swoon but you could tell she liked getting the upper hand any way she could.

"Would you hand me that towel?" she said to Spandau. Pam groaned almost imperceptibly and rolled her eyes. Spandau gave Anna the towel and she went about letting him imagine she'd just stepped from the shower. Spandau watched and waited. Anna finished, picked up a pair of sunglasses from a table, and put them on. She lay down on a lounge chair and pretended to stare at the sky.

"Pammy, would you have Bettina bring out some coffee and sandwiches?"

"Of course," said Pam. "Right away. And should I lay out your summer undergarments or would you prefer the flannel?"

Pam left without waiting for an answer. Anna acted as if she'd never heard her. She lay there. Long seconds passed. Spandau looked up at the hills and trees in back of the house. He knew he was supposed to say something but he didn't feel like it.

Finally she said: "Pam is my sister."

"I can see the resemblance."

"Much of the time," said Anna, "I would like to strangle her."

"Yes," said Spandau. "Relatives can be nearly as bad as the servant problem."

"Why, Mr. Spandau. You have a dry sense of humor."

"Yes, ma'am. A dry sense of humor and exquisite table manners are a boon in my profession."

She tipped down her glasses and looked at him. "Are you making fun of me, Mr. Spandau?"

"Oh, no, ma'am. That would be displaying an unprofessional lack of humility."

"You and Pam would get along like a house afire. No wonder she wants to hire you. The question is, do I?"

"You're the only one who can answer that."

"The last goddamn thing I need is somebody trailing behind me every step. There's little enough privacy as it is."

"We try to maintain a low profile," he said.

She looked him up and down. "Honey, you're about as low profile as a water buffalo. I hate to break this to you, but unless you intend on sticking shrubbery in your ears and pretending to be a tree, you're going to stand out."

Pam came out carrying a scarf and a bundle of letters. She handed them to Spandau, who went over and sat beneath an umbrella and examined them.

"I think this is all a lot of hoopdedoodle for nothing," said Anna. "I probably just snagged it."

"No," said Spandau. "It was cut."

"And there's nothing unusual about the letters except the red ink. I'm not worried about the letters."

Spandau looked through the letters. The maid brought out sandwiches and a pot of coffee and sat them on the table. Pam poured cups of coffee.

Anna continued to lie on her back and said: "This is ridiculous. Look, if they'd wanted to hurt me, they were close enough. Why just the scarf?"

"It's not about hurting you. It's about seeing how close they can get." He said to Pam: "You think the letters are from the same person?"

"We've been getting them for a while. They picked up in frequency just before the incident at the restaurant. Nothing violent, nothing threatening, but obsessive. How beautiful she is, how he thinks about her, how he feels he understands her.

That sort of thing. You get the feeling he's working up to something."

"How do we even know it's a he?"

"This may sound like a chauvinist statement, but women generally aren't whacked enough to do this sort of thing. Take your sister, for instance. She'd be far more likely to poison you than cut your throat."

"Ha!" said Anna.

"So you mean there's a sexual element in all this?" asked Pam.

"Jesus," said Anna from her chaise longue. "Sigmund Freud rides again. People have been getting crushes on actors for a thousand years. It's what we want them to do, isn't it, for Pete's sake?"

Spandau scraped at the red ink on one of the letters. It flaked and fell away from the page. It looked like blood but he didn't mention it. "Most people realize that their fantasies are just fantasies," he said. "Some don't."

"Why don't you want to admit there's a problem?" Pam said to her sister. "A crazy person walked up to you on the street and sliced through your clothing. It could have been you, not the scarf. I can't understand why you're sticking your head in the sand on this."

Anna sat up. "Because I fucking well don't want my life upset because some fucking lovesick space cadet got a little too close. I'll have Chandler stay nearer or something."

"This isn't Chandler's job. Mr. Spandau is trained for this."

"No thank you," said Anna. "No." She stood up, began gathering up her things.

"I don't get you," said Pam. "I swear to God."

"I'm an actor, that's all," said Anna. "Just a fucking actor. What they fucking do in their heads out there isn't my responsibility.

I'm entitled to a life. I'm not going to let some little pervert dictate how I live it."

"Fifteen years ago," said Spandau, "you posed nude for a magazine spread, then changed your mind and spent half the national budget trying to buy the pictures back from the guy who took them. Your boyfriend at the time, as I recall. I haven't seen the photos, but I'm sure they were tasteful. All the same, it's a little hard to pretend you're not contributing to the fantasy."

Anna glared at him.

Pam said, "Mr. Spandau, I really don't think—"

"No, Pammy," said Anna. "Let's hear Mr. Spandau. Well, you get right to the point, don't you?"

"Yes, ma'am, that's why people like you hire me. I don't like wasting your time, or mine either."

"I don't have to explain shit to you, Mr. Spandau. Not a goddamn thing."

"Yes, ma'am."

"I can show you the photos. I'm sure they would give you a thrill. Lots of people were willing to pay for the honor."

"Yes, ma'am. I'm just surprised you still have them."

"Oh, I still have them. I take them out every so often, when I need to be reminded what utter shits men can be. And to make sure nobody ever again talks me into doing something I don't want to do. This isn't breaking your heart, is it? Does it morally offend you, me exploiting my body? Is that it?"

"No, ma'am. You're beautiful, you want to use it. Then somebody else decides to exploit it instead. This doesn't make you an innocent, it just makes you lousy at business. On the other hand, nobody died and made me moral arbiter of the universe."

"You've never made any mistakes? Done anything you're ashamed of?"

"Sure. You plan on something going one way and it goes another. That's not the same thing as claiming I didn't know what I was doing. I knew what I was doing, I just didn't get the results I wanted."

"You're not a Jesuit, are you, Mr. Spandau?"

"No, ma'am. But I've been in Hollywood long enough to know better."

"Just like me, you mean?"

"Oh, children," said Pam anxiously, "we are not playing well together."

"Fuck you, Mr. Spandau, and your fucking ten-cent ethics. I left Texas to escape this sort of crap and I'm not likely to take it from you, you narrow-minded, judgmental peckerwood."

"Maybe Mr. Spandau would like to apologize . . ."

"No," said Spandau, "I don't think he would. Mr. Spandau is trying to make a point. You spend your life trying to create a fantasy so real that people cross the line into a world you've created. Sadly, some of them never make it back again."

"What are you saying? That every goddamned film we make, we have to worry about what one fucking loon out of a million is going to do with it? I didn't make this guy crazy. He's crazy because he can't tell the difference between make-believe and real life. I didn't do this to him. He walked into the fucking movie theater crazy, Mr. Spandau. It didn't happen while he was there."

"It doesn't end there, though, does it? How many people have you got who help you carry that fantasy right on out the door? It doesn't end on the screen, does it? There's you on the talk shows, there's you making personal appearances, walking down the aisle at the Oscars, the Foreign Press awards, the magazine interviews. You're telling me that's not all part of the fantasy? You're saying the illusion is supposed to end on the screen, and you pay how much to your PR consultant to see that it doesn't? You make a mistake, you buy it back, hush it up. You're the one who brings the fantasy down off the screen. Suddenly the guidelines are blurred for everybody."

"Mr. Spandau," said Anna, "kiss my ass. Pam, have somebody throw this son of a bitch *over* the fence."

And stormed away.

"Are you crazy?" Pam asked him.

"I often wonder," said Spandau.

"Brilliant," she said. "I was trying to help keep my sister safe and now you've made it impossible."

"She's in denial," said Spandau.

"All actors are in denial, Mr. Spandau. It is what they do. Thank you for making my life so much easier."

They had just walked in the door when Anna came rushing up in a terrycloth robe. She threw a hairbrush, which hit Spandau in the forehead.

"You son of a bitch. How dare you, you son of a bitch."

She came at him. Pam stepped between them and pushed her away. "Calm down. He's leaving."

"I ought to gouge your stinking eyes out," said Anna to him.

"Anna, calm down," said Pam.

"Calm down, my ass. The son of a bitch."

Spandau touched his head and brought back blood.

"Anna, sit down. I mean it. Sit."

Anna sat down on a sofa.

"Are you okay?" Pam asked.

"I'm fine."

"Sue me, you bastard," said Anna. "I dare you."

"Anna, shut up, for God's sake."

"It's fine," said Spandau. "Nobody is going to sue anybody."

"Don't do me any favors," said Anna.

"Shut it, Anna. I mean it." Pam looked at the wound. "She got you pretty good. We could call a doctor."

"No," said Spandau. "Christ, I'll sign something if it makes it any easier."

"Let's calm down and talk about this," said Pam. "We need to end this amicably."

"Look, I'm fine. I'm sorry I upset her. It was my fault."

"Fucking-A it was," said Anna.

"Just sit here," Pam said to Spandau, "and we'll put something on this."

Pam left the room. Spandau knew damned well she'd make a call to a lawyer long before she ever reached the medicine chest. He thought about leaving, but in truth he'd fucked up and he did need to work it out somehow.

"I'm sorry," he said to Anna.

"What the fuck is wrong with you, anyway?"

"I was trying to make a point. Believe it or not, it was for your own good. Regardless, it was unprofessional. I did it badly. I truly am sorry."

"It hurt, you know," she said.

"Yeah, I gather it did."

"You think I don't worry about shit like that? Yeah, you're right. We fuck up all the boundaries, we exploit it. But we don't make these people crazy. Look at all the people who are just fine. We can't be responsible for the rare ones who are fucking nuts anyway. You see my point?"

"Yes."

"Ah shit," said Anna. "I don't even know the fucking difference sometimes."

"Me either," he said, and meant it.

She started laughing. "Are you just not very good at this or what?"

"It's the 'or what' I've been having trouble with lately," he said.

"You've got a real knot coming up on your head."

"I'm okay."

"You're not going to sue me, are you?"

"No."

"An attorney named Michael Stivich is going to ask to speak to you in the next few minutes."

"I figured."

"You could make a good buck off this. I'd hold out for at least twenty grand. That's what we paid the last one. He'll offer five but tell him you're feeling dizzy."

"You and I both know I could get a whole lot more."

"Yeah," she said. "Well, it wouldn't be the first time."

"You need the protection," Spandau said. "The guy has a knife or a razor and he got close enough to touch you. You can't just wish him away."

"So what are you saying? You won't sue me if I hire you?"

"No," said Spandau. "You do need somebody, but not me. I'll have my boss recommend somebody else."

"Now I'm really confused," she said. "Exactly what are you saying?"

"In my own special way," said Spandau, "I'm telling you that you need someone to help you out, just not me."

"You're mad at me now, right? I really am sorry about the hairbrush."

"It has nothing to do with the hairbrush. It has nothing to do with you, honestly."

He dabbed at the wound with a plain cotton handkerchief. With the mussed dark hair and the big dark eyes and the trickle of blood trying to find its way around his right eyebrow, he sat there looking like some kid waiting outside the principal's office. Anna had this overwhelming desire to comfort him, then thought of where this very desire had landed her before. It wasn't so much that she liked flawed men, it was just such a relief and somehow touching when the arrogant shits finally owned up to an imperfection.

"Oh, honey," she said, "I know that look."

Pam came back in, without a first-aid kit. "Mr. Spandau, if you wouldn't mind—"

"Tell your attorney I'm feeling too dizzy to come to the phone," Spandau said to her. He stood up.

"We need to talk about this," Pam said. Panic was starting to creep across her face. "I'm sure we can work something out . . ."

"Let him go," said Anna.

"Anna, for God's sake."

"Just let the poor man go."

She looked at Spandau and gave him a soft and knowing smile. He left. Anna sat on the couch and stared at her bare toes.

"You need to talk to Michael," Pam said.

"Fuck Michael," said Anna.

"Michael says you were provoked. If the guy tries to sue, Michael says we could countersue and ruin him."

"He's not going to sue."

"You can't be sure."

"Honey, he won't sue. Sweet Jesus, have you forgotten everything about the place we come from? We grew up around guys like him. Hell's bells, Daddy was a guy like him. He won't sue. It never even entered his mind."

"I'm sorry," said Pam. "They told me he was good. I was only trying to help."

"You see those eyes?" asked Anna.

"We'll find somebody else."

"No," said Anna. "I want him."

"Are you crazy? He spent ten minutes insulting the hell out of you and you half killed him with a hairbrush."

"It's an interesting start," said Anna. "But I got this feeling."

"Are you sure?"

"Oh, honey," she said, "I'm never sure about a goddamned thing. But that's half the fun."

Anna got up and went upstairs humming to herself, leaving her sister to deal with lawyers, lawsuits, and the contrary wisdom of the human heart.

6

IT WAS A SHORT HOP DOWN SUNSET TO THE OFFICES OF Coren and Associates. Spandau was an associate, which meant he got a rental BMW, no office, no personal assistant, and all the social status of a Russian serf. When Spandau got back to the office, Pookie was sitting at the desk in a new guise.

"Is he in?" Spandau asked her.

"Nope," she said. She was angry. "What happened to you?"

"They've lowered the traffic light at Sunset and Sweetzer."

Pookie took the "all the world's a stage" maxim about as far as it could go. She viewed each day as a new performance with a fresh identity that allowed her to dress accordingly. Today she wore a red dress with white polka dots, a blond wig, red lipstick, stiletto heels, and vintage silk stockings that ran a seductive line up the backs of her legs. Marilyn Monroe. *The Misfits?* The cleavage was cut low enough that male eyes struggled to avoid its gravitational tug. All last week she'd been Audrey Hepburn in *Funny Face,* looking boyish in a black turtleneck. Spandau tried not to imagine the hydraulics that went into such a transformation.

In any event, Pookie was both pretty enough and smart enough to get away with it nearly all the time. The only time Walter ever sent her home was the day she showed up as Yum-Yum from *The Mikado*. Even then it wasn't really the clothing but the fact she'd sing "Behold the Lord High Executioner" every time he stepped into the room. Gilbert and Sullivan can pall when you have a whopping hangover.

"You know where he is?"

"I can't say I know where he is, but wherever it happens to be, he's about three martinis down by now."

"Jesus, Pook, what happened to the AA meetings and all? I thought he was off the sauce."

"He went to two, and said AA meetings were the best argument in favor of alcoholism he'd ever seen."

"What sort of mood was he in?"

"Deep into the Mean Reds, as Miss Golightly would say. He mentioned something about biting the heads off small dogs, if that's any indication. And he blew off a client, which is not a good thing. She waited for him for nearly an hour and he never showed."

"I'll see if I can find him. Call me if he turns up, will you?"

"It's worse than before, I think. He's in bad shape."

"Did that redhead crap all over him?"

"Oh yes, and from a considerable height. She cheated on him in Reno, and confessed that she boinked one of the croupiers while Walter was downstairs at the blackjack table."

Spandau picked up the phone and made a call. A man's voice said, "Pancho's."

"Frank, this is David Spandau. I'm looking for the old man."

"Oh yeah, he's here all right. You want to talk to him?"

"Nah. What kind of shape is he in?"

"Let me put it this way: you want to talk to him you better do it now. It's a toss up whether he'll just drink himself unconscious or somebody'll do it forcibly. He's insulted everybody in the place. He even tried to pick a fight with me."

"Great."

"You might want to get over here. I offered to put him in a taxi but he won't go. You know him."

"I'm on my way."

He hung up.

"I have to go get him."

"That's like the blind leading the blind, isn't it?"

"What's that supposed to mean?"

"It means that all I've got to worry about now is two of you getting shitfaced and disorderly. You're getting to be as bad as he is. Frankly I'm getting tired of covering for him and I don't want to take crap for you too."

"Just mind your telephone."

"Fine. Thank you. I appreciate the depth of your understanding about what I do around here all day long."

"I'm sorry, Pook . . ."

"Excuse me, but take your goddamned sorrys and shove them up your ass. You two need to get your act together. I'm sorry your love lives are a mess, I really am. And I don't mind acting as temporary guidance counselor slash whipping boy provided I thought either of you was actually trying. But you're not."

"Thanks for the sympathy."

"Oh, come on. Sympathy for what? In a town full of eligible women, he goes out and homes in on the ones who'll do him the most damage, and he knows it. You, you don't do anything. You slump around hangdog and pining because your wife left you. Well, hey, she left you because this is the way you run your life, you never fucking confront anything, you duck behind whatever available cover. In the end people just get tired of living for you. Fucking wake up, will you. Both of you."

"Pook . . ."

"I don't want anything to do with either one of you right now," she said. "I mean it."

Spandau left. She managed to let him clear the room before she began to cry.

7

Walter's own cream BMW was parked outside of Pancho's. Spandau pulled up next to it and parked and went into the bar. Frank was behind the counter and shook his head when Spandau came in. There were three tough-looking guys at a table. Walter sat in a booth, drunk, talking to the tough guys.

". . . And that's not to say there's anything homophilic about guys walking around with their pants halfway down their cracks," Walter was saying. "No, sir, but let's keep in mind that the whole fashion statement originated in prison to show you were somebody's bitch. Any of you guys been in prison? I ask just out of scientific curiosity . . ."

Spandau and Frank exchanged looks. Frank shrugged and shook his head again. Spandau went over and sat down across from Walter.

"What the fuck do you want?" Walter asked him.

"I have come, like the old family retainer, to escort you home."

"You're wasting your time, sport. I'm happy here."

"Yeah, I can see you're making yourself a valuable part of the community."

"I'm making friends. I was just talking to my pals over there, about grown men showing their cracks in public. I'm not sure they understand the implications."

"Look, you want to shut your buddy the fuck up?" said one of the tough guys.

Spandau said to Walter, "I believe it's about time to go."

"No, I don't think so. Jesus, what the hell is wrong with you? Don't tell me you're worried about some asshole punk with his drawers down and his hat on backward?"

The tough guy stood up. "I don't care if he is drunk. I'm going to beat the shit out of your friend."

"No," said Spandau, "I don't think so."

"Then take him out of here."

"What?" said Walter. "Tell him to go fuck himself, David. Deal with the riffraff in a summary fashion. Manhandle the cocksuckers, I say."

The tough guy started at Walter. Spandau stood in front of him.

"This would be a mistake," said Spandau.

"Get out of my way or you'll get it first."

"Thrash him, David!" cried Walter, cackling with delight. "Pull his pants down! Spank the bitch!"

"Jesus, Walter, will you shut the hell up?"

"I'm going to kill the fucker," said the tough guy.

"Would it help if I did it for you?" asked Spandau.

"Ask him if he wants to dance," said Walter.

The tough guy came at Walter again and Spandau pushed him back. When Spandau's hand touched his chest, the guy took a right cross. It was wide and Spandau blocked it, but the guy was quicker than he looked and followed fast with a left jab that clipped Spandau's chin. Spandau took a step back and bent to come in again, but there was a deafening crack behind them and everybody froze. Frank had slammed a baseball bat on the bar.

"Next one of you assholes throws a punch, I'm going to split his head. That don't work I got a Colt .44 back here."

"You telling me you'd pull a gun?" Tough Guy said.

"Son, I used to be a Los Angles cop and I can shoot anybody I damn well please. I'd like you and your friends to leave my bar."

"We didn't do shit! That drunk motherfucker over there was causing all the trouble!"

"Yeah, but unfortunately that drunk motherfucker is a friend of mine."

"You tell 'em, Pancho," said Walter

"Shut the fuck up, Walter," said Frank. "Jesus . . ." To the tough guys he said, "Don't worry about your drinks. The drunk motherfucker will pay for it." Then he said to Walter, "You say another goddamn word, Walter, and I'm gonna club you to death like a fucking harp seal."

The tough guys had run up a hefty bill and seemed pleased with the arrangement. They left and Spandau sat back down across from Walter. Frank shook his head and put the baseball bat away.

"Goddamn surly bunch, aren't you?" said Walter.

Frank brought over some napkins and some ice in a baggie for Spandau's chin.

"Talk to him, David," said Frank, as if Walter wasn't there, which, in a very real sense, he wasn't. "Tell him he can't insult my customers. Tell him this is how I make my living and if he can't behave he can't come in here."

"There are other fucking bars, Pancho," said Walter.

"Look," said Frank, "you got my ass out of a jam once. I owe you for that, but I don't owe you my business. I got responsibilities, same as everybody else. Talk some sense into him, David."

"Me? He almost got me stomped."

"I was willing to put up good money on you," said Walter.

"You were willing to watch me get my ass kicked for your own amusement."

"A man," said Walter, "needs to take his pleasure wherever he can find it. Besides, you should have seen that left coming. He practically mailed it in."

"Who the hell are you now? Howard fucking Cossell?"

"All I'm saying is that, when I hired you, you'd have never let a bozo like that clip you. That's all I'm saying."

"I can't keep doing this."

"Nobody asked you to, sport," said Walter.

"I ought to leave your ass here."

"You ought to," Walter said to him. To Frank he said, "Maestro, give this man a medicinal drink."

Frank looked at Spandau and Spandau nodded. Frank went to the bar for the drink.

"She dumped you, did she?" Spandau said to Walter.

"You bet."

"I tried to tell you. She was randy as an alley cat, that one."

"I'll have you know you're speaking of my former fiancée. But indeed she was friendly. And often."

"You're better off."

"That's what the casino manager said after I tried to strangle his croupier. They threw me out, but they were very gentlemanly about it. Francine got to keep the room."

Frank brought over the drink.

"We should have a toast," said Walter. "Have a toast with us, Pancho."

"You know I don't drink. I'll do an apple juice. What are we toasting?"

"Women."

"What the hell you want to do that for?" Frank said. "With your track record?"

"Bear with me, friends. I'm swearing off. I'm taking the pledge. Enough is enough."

"Women or booze?" Frank asked.

"Women, of course," said Walter. "Alcoholism is at least something I do well."

Frank poured himself an apple juice and they raised their glasses.

"To women," said Walter. "Goddamn them."

They drank. Walter said, "Another round, please, maestro."

"You've had enough," Frank told him.

"Now, Frank, you know goddamned good and well I'm going to get plastered tonight. If I have to get up and go somewhere else, I'm liable to kill somebody. Much safer to let me get drunk here among friends. David can drive me home. That's reasonable, isn't it?"

"The way you think gives me a headache." Frank looked at Spandau. "You going to be responsible for him?"

"It's probably the only way we're going to get him home."

"What the hell," said Frank. "Give me your keys. Both of you."

"Why me?"

"Because I know where this is going. I seen it all before."

Frank held out his hand and both men dropped their car keys into his palm.

Frank was right, of course. In a short while both men were drunk. Though they were drinking at the same pace, Walter seemed to have hit a plateau which Spandau soon reached. Walter's drinking was like this. He drank until he reached a level of inebriation just short of unconsciousness and, though he kept drinking, rarely went beyond it. Walter often said there was no point getting shitfaced if you were going to sleep away the best part of it.

Spandau drank himself into and through a brief jolly period. Now the bottom began to drop out of the world and he could see what life would be like in the morning.

"Are we finished?" Spandau finally said to him.

"Am I still breathing?" Walter asked him.

"I believe so," said Spandau.

"Then we're not finished."

"Then I have to take a piss," said Spandau. He stood up uneasily. He started for the men's room but stopped and turned to Walter. "You miss her?"

"Which one?" said Walter.

"Francine. The bimbo that just dumped your ass."

"Oh yeah. Sure. Hell, I miss all of them. That's the problem."

Spandau nodded seriously, as if this answer concluded some philosophical problem they'd been working on all night. He staggered into the toilet and pissed while staring at a drawing of a woman's snatch, sketched above the urinal by someone with more enthusiasm than a genuine knowledge of anatomy. The artist had written *Rebecca the Bitch* next to the drawing and Spandau found himself consumed by the poignancy. Spandau zipped up and washed and dried his hands while battling a wave of sadness that threatened to wash him over the edge and into a loneliness that would be inescapable. He fumbled for his cell phone, and, as he knew he would, dialed her number.

"Hello?" said Dee. "David?"

He wanted to speak but there was nothing to say. Or, rather, there was everything to say and it tumbled around in him like cats fighting to get out a door. He knew what he was doing was utterly useless and even harmful to his cause, but he needed to establish now, this instant, some connection with her, however tenuous, before he felt himself lost. He stood there mute, unable to speak, the telephone connection to her a frail lifeline that would be cut at any second. If he could just hold on, if he could just hold on until something happened, some sort of magic, and she would come back.

"David?" she said.

"I wanted to call," he said at last.

"Have you been drinking?"

"I wanted to talk to you."

"What is it you want to say, David?"

Nothing. Nothing to be said. I love you but I can't say that.

"You've got to stop this," Dee said quietly. "You can't keep calling me, David. Can you make it home?"

"Fine. Just fine." Lie.

"I can't do this now, David. I'll talk to you later."

"You with him? He there?" And there it came. How pathetic it sounded. Say it and just let it kill me and get it over with.

"I'm not going to do this, David. Just go home now. Be careful. Don't drink any more."

And it ended. He waited for the drop into oblivion but it didn't come. Instead there was the self-hatred at his weakness and his need. He wanted to hate her, but he couldn't. All this was his fault and he didn't blame her for leaving him. He simply hated being who he was. He began punching the toilet stall, making dents in the metal with his knuckles, as if trying to kill some ghost of himself that kept fucking up his life. Frank and Walter came in. Frank pulled him away from the stall, and Spandau turned on him, ready to strike. Frank took a step back and held up his hands.

"What the hell are you doing?" Frank asked him.

Walter said, "It's just the Black Dog out dancing, Pancho. Go tend your bar."

"You guys are killing me, you know that?" said Frank, and went back into the bar.

"Well, go ahead," Walter told Spandau. "Kick the shit out of it. I'll pay for the damned thing."

Spandau leaned against the wall and slid to the floor. He sat there with his head in his hands. Walter sat down next to him.

"We are sitting in the middle of a piss-stained floor," said Walter. "I just want you to know that."

Spandau said nothing, just sat there holding his head.

"You call her?" Walter asked.

Spandau nodded.

"Stupid goddamn thing to do," said Walter. "I ought to know, often as I've done it. Didn't help, did it?"

"No."

"Probably made things worse."

"I have no fucking idea what I'm doing anymore."

"Well, shit, sport, I can't think of anybody who does. Why should you be so fucking special? You want to talk?"

"No."

"Good," said Walter. "It's fucking useless anyway."

After a couple of attempts and some swearing, Walter got to his feet. He held out his hand and Spandau stared at it for a second then took it and Walter tugged him to his feet. They both nearly fell over.

"Come on," said Walter. "You can watch Frank's face while I puke in his ice machine."

They wove their way back into the bar.

8

SPANDAU WOKE LATE THE NEXT MORNING, HAVING TURNED off the alarm when it rang at the regular time. The hangover was just as bad as he knew it would be. He drank water and then puked and drank some more water. He managed to make a pot of coffee. Food seemed to be indicated, but he had no idea where it was going to come from, since there wasn't a chance in hell of him fixing it. The sense of dread he felt was nearly as bad as the hangover itself. One more seam in his life had just come loose and he awaited the consequences. He flung himself into the arms of fate and called the office.

"Are you proud of yourself?" Pookie asked him.

"Please, God, don't start. Please."

"He's not here either. He did manage to call, though, in between retches. And Pam Mayhew phoned. You're hired. Once again charm somehow triumphs over substance."

"I've got a couple of things to check out. I'll file a report later."

"I'll have the *Times* hold the front page," Pookie said.

* * *

Spandau's car was still at Pancho's. Frank had put them into a
cab and given the driver instructions, on fear of eternal persecu-
tion by the LAPD, to get them both home safely. Spandau had to
take another cab—he told himself the humiliation was good for
his soul—back to the bar. Pancho was setting up for the day and
gave him a sideways look.

"You got my keys?" Spandau asked him.

"In the drawer under the register."

Spandau got the keys.

"I'm sorry about last night," he said to Frank.

"It used to be just Walter I had to worry about. Now there's
you and Walter's got worse. What the hell is going on with you
two?"

"Just a bad time all around, Pancho."

"I don't want to have to ban him."

"I know. Look, I'll see what I can do." He held up the keys.
"Thanks."

"Sure, sure . . ."

Spandau pulled up outside the restaurant. A bored-looking valet,
apparently the only one on duty, handed him a ticket and took
the BMW keys. The valet climbed into the car and shot off in his
own little Formula One fantasy around the corner. Spandau felt
a twinge of possessive anger until he remembered that the car
was leased by his company and had nothing to do with Spandau,
so Spandau wasn't obliged to browbeat the little shit. Spandau
hung around on the sidewalk outside the restaurant, looking for

the cameras he knew were there. He found only one, watching the front entrance and that part of the street. It wasn't much of a setup.

The valet came back and saw him still there. He figured Spandau was waiting to chew his ass about roaring off in the car, and he put on a defensive scowl. He was Spandau's height but Spandau had maybe twenty pounds on him. He thought Spandau looked like a cop, but cops didn't wear Italian suits.

"Who was working the shift here on Monday lunchtime?" Spandau asked him.

"Why?" said the valet. Shit, maybe he was a cop.

"You're not in any kind of trouble. I just need some information."

The valet studied him. "You're no cop. Cops don't wear suits like that."

"Your point being . . ."

"So maybe I need to be coaxed," said the valet, smiling just the way he'd seen the wiseguys do it in the movies.

"Coaxed," repeated Spandau.

The valet stood there smirking like an Elvis impersonator. Spandau had dearly hoped this was going to be uncomplicated. His head hurt and when he walked there was a peculiar tendency to veer left. He didn't even want to hear his own voice, much less argue with this asshole. He didn't say anything for a moment, sighed deeply, then took off his sunglasses. Excruciating pain filled his head and there was a short cry of agony he'd hoped he'd been able to stifle. He moved close to the valet and widely opened his eyes.

"Kid," said Spandau, "I want you to look carefully at these eyes. These eyes look like they've been attacked by some pissed-off graffiti artist with blood on his mind, some poor son of a bitch who despised the entire goddamned planet but could only afford one can of paint. You can see that, can't you? Right?"

The valet looked into Spandau's eyes. They did indeed look like one of Jack the Ripper's more eventful evenings. There was also, behind the blood and gore, the distant vision of a parking valet being strangled to death.

"Now," continued Spandau, "I want you to imagine how you appear right now through these eyes and tell me again how you want to be coaxed."

The valet's smile crumbled away and he said, "Me. I was working that shift. Me and a guy named Peter."

"Thank you," said Spandau. He put his sunglasses back on. His head still throbbed but his eyeballs no longer threatened to explode. "You know who Anna Mayhew is? She left just after lunch on Monday."

"Yeah, I remember. But I didn't park her car. She had a driver."

"Did you see her when she came out?"

"Yeah, she came out and stood around for a couple of minutes, talking to some women. Then the driver picked her up."

"She was standing there, talking, and somebody walked by her, close. Maybe bumped her, brushed up against her. A guy, probably. You see that?" Spandau asked him.

"Like I said, I was busy, and those old biddies were pouring out and I was jacking cars all the time. I just remember she was here, is all."

Spandau reached into his jacket. The kid had a fleeting vision of being either arrested or shot. Instead Spandau handed him a card and a twenty-dollar bill.

"You happen to have any clouds get swept away, call that number and there might be a lot more."

The valet felt a renewed sense of life. "I thought you didn't feel like coaxing anybody," he said to Spandau.

"Bipolar," Spandau said, spinning his finger near his temple. "Last time I just picked up a tire iron and beat a guy half to death. Who knows?"

The restaurant manager was a fresh-faced young man in his early thirties with a zit on his chin inexpertly covered by his girlfriend's makeup. He was too young and inexperienced to be managing a restaurant of this size in Beverly Hills, and he knew it. He hated and feared the owner, a cheapskate Lebanese thug, but if he could endure it another year he'd have a shot at one of the hipper places, maybe something involving Gordon Ramsay. This place catered to Crones Who Lunched and geriatric Hollywood has-beens who kept chewing and chewing their meat loaf because they couldn't remember to swallow. Of course the owner would have pitched a bitch about it, but talking to Spandau was a huge relief in a day otherwise spent trying to find a replacement for the illegal Mexican waiter he'd fired last week. They sat in his office and he pointed to a bank of video screens on the wall behind him.

"It's a good thing you asked now. We usually only keep the tapes for a couple of weeks, then we use them again. Owner's a cheap bastard. Let's see, camera four . . ."

The manager pulled out a DVD and slid it into a player.

"You say lunchtime?"

"She went in around noon, came out around one-thirty," Spandau said. "So let's start at eleven-thirty until she goes in, then when she comes out."

The manager sped through the disc, watching the time code. He stopped it at 11:30 a.m.

"There you go. Mind if I ask what you're looking for?"

"I don't know yet," Spandau said truthfully.

The frames jumped by, one taken every half second. People moved like in a Chaplin movie, hobbling in, hobbling out, waddling past on the sidewalk. Finally: "That's her," said Spandau. "There she is. Eleven fifty-five. Okay, speed it up until she comes back out."

The manager loped through. At 1:33 p.m. she came out.

"Right there," said Spandau.

Anna came out of the restaurant. She was stopped by some women on the sidewalk and briefly spoke to them. The black Lincoln Navigator pulled up and waited. Just before Anna turned away from the women, a small male figure in a dark jacket entered the frame from the right. He walked past her, brushing her lightly, and disappeared. Anna barely noticed it, moved slightly to let him pass, went on talking for a moment, then turned and climbed into the SUV.

"Can I see that again?"

They replayed it.

"Can you zoom in?" Spandau asked him.

"Yeah, but it won't be worth a damn. Like I say, it's a lousy system."

The manager backed it up, zoomed it. The image pixelated into a blur. Spandau stared at it, thinking.

"Let's go back to eleven-thirty."

"You finding what you need?" asked the manager.

"I'm getting there."

They rewound to eleven-thirty. Watched again.

Suddenly: "Freeze it right there," said Spandau.

The screen froze and Spandau moved closer to the monitor, squinting at the enlarged but blurred image of Anna and the small man about to touch her.

"Can you make me a copy of this?"

"Sure," said the manager. "You don't tell the owner, I won't even charge you for the disc. You want to tell me what it is you found?"

"A man," said Spandau, "with a very peculiar hobby."

Spandau took the DVD to a video lab in Santa Monica the agency often used. Irv, the guy who owned the place, looked like Jerry Garcia and Spandau had never seen him without a Dr Pepper in his hand. Irv was one of the few video surveillance people in L.A. who could actually be trusted, since most of them did a thriving sideline of selling copies to multiple sources. Industrial espionage, movie stars cheating on their spouses, Colombian drug dealers making a trade-off. You sold them to the people who'd commissioned them, then you sold them to the people you'd shot, then you sold them whole to CNN or frame by frame to the tabloids. Oh, it was a thriving business okay. Trouble was, Irv often worked for the government and couldn't afford to be that enterprising, lest one day he suddenly found himself dead from a rare can of toxic Dr Pepper.

They sat in the lab, Irv sipping his soda and emitting a series of small, elegant prune-smelling belches.

"The guy was right," said Irv. "It's a shitty system. Cheap-ass camera, cheap-ass lens. With a good outfit you could count the hairs in the guy's nose." He noodled with the image a bit. A little better but not much. "Best I can do. Sorry. Better than nothing, though, right?"

"If you say so."

Irv was hurt. "There's no need to pick on me. Garbage in, garbage out. Remember the old hacker saying? Same for video. You shoot with shit, you get to see shit. This is one of the few places money actually means something. Tell these fuckers to get a better system and quit giving me tsuris. I'm no magician."

"Can you give me some stills? Maybe eleven-by-fourteen?"

Irv sighed. "I can give you stills. But the stills will still look like the goddamn picture. The stills will still be shit. Shit will still be shit equals shit, right?"

"Thank you, Gertrude Stein," said Spandau.

Irv looked at Spandau, opened his mouth like a lion, and belched loudly. Then he said, "And thank you, Alice Toklas, and kiss my fat yiddish ass." Irv turned and went into the back to make the prints. In a previous incarnation, Irv had done English at NYU and wasn't fixing to be outliteratured by a guy who wore cowboy boots.

9

ANNA, PAM, AND SPANDAU WERE SITTING IN ANNA'S LIVING room. Spandau gave the DVD to Pam and she put it in the player and handed the remote control to him. He leaped through the action then slowed it to normal.

"This is eleven thirty-seven. Here he is. Dark jacket, baseball cap. He's walking by, he peeks in, looking around. Very casual. Looking for you."

He sped up the disk, stopped it again.

"Here's one-forty. You come out, stand around on the side-walk, talk to the ladies. Then Lincoln pulls up. And then—"

He moved frame by frame.

"He here comes . . . Up to you . . . Leans slightly . . . There! You see it? A glint in the sunlight, about waist-high, a thin knife or a straight razor . . ."

He backed it up and they watched it again.

"Look at the way he's hiding it. He's wearing gloves and the blade is between his fingers. He makes a fist, see, and the blade stands out. Opens his hand again and you can't see it. He's rigged up some kind of special glove for it. Very clever, in a sick kind of way. Anyway, it's clear this is not something he did on the spur of the moment."

He looked at Anna. She was pale and very quiet.

"You going to be okay?" he asked her.

"I need a drink," she said to Pam.

"I think we all do," said Pam. "Mr. Spandau?"

Oh yes, a drink. Yes, give me a drink please. Please.

"No, thank you," said Spandau.

Pam left to get the drinks and Spandau pulled out the set of blurry stills.

"This is the best we could do. You recognize him? The hat or the jacket?"

"No."

"Maybe somebody you worked with on a set? A production assistant? A technician?"

"You know how many films I've made?" she said to him. "This may sound snobbish, but I can't remember their faces from one film to the next. Anyway you can't even see his face."

He laid the still on the coffee table and showed them to Pam when she returned. "How about you?"

She examined the pictures and shook her head.

"It's a start, anyway," said Spandau. "He's probably late twenties, early thirties. Small. You're around what, five eight? That makes him maybe five five or six. Hard to tell with that jacket, but he looks kind of slight. Like a jockey. Probably not more than one-thirty, one thirty-five. I can't make out what's on the cap, but it's a NASCAR jacket. Problem is, they sell them at Target."

"I don't get it," said Anna. "If he wanted to hurt me, why didn't he? What's the point?"

"It's like counting coup. The Sioux Indians used to see how

close they could get to the enemy. Rather than kill them, they'd strike them with a stick. The whole point was to let them know they could have killed them but didn't. He could have hurt you but he didn't, because he chose not to. It's a power issue. He's showing that he's in control. Maybe not even to you. Maybe just to himself."

"Cowboys and Indians," Anna said. "Fucking hell. What now?"

"We catch him. And keep you safe in the meantime. The big question is, do we let the police in on this?"

"If I'd wanted the police I'd have called the police," Anna said.

"You're the pro," Pam said to him. "What do you recommend?"

"It's a matter of your comfort level. Frankly, there's not much the police could do. They won't have any more to go on than we do, and they're not going to put anybody on it full-time. Maybe the guy has a record and an MO, and I'll check that. We don't even have a positive link to the letters, which aren't outright threatening, just creepy. The police would recommend a body-guard, which you already have."

Anna knocked back her drink and stood up.

"I don't want to think any more about this. I have a lot of work to do. Protecting my ass, Mr. Spandau, is your problem now. Pammy, I need you to help me work on that speech for the theater dedication tomorrow."

"It's a lousy idea to go out in public right now, especially in a crowd," Spandau said to her.

"I have complete faith in you. Anyway, you said he was harm-less."

"You're not listening to me. I never said he was harmless, I said he simply chose not to harm you this time. He's capable of it, and you can bet he's thought about it. This guy is a psychopath, Ms. Mayhew."

"I'm not letting some asshole basket case dictate my life. This work is important to me and I'm going to be there. The rest, like I say, is what you get paid for."

"And there's the other thing," added Pam.

"What other thing?" asked Spandau, looking from one to the other.

"I'm going to the Cannes Film Festival next week," said Anna. "I'm a judge on one of the committees. You'll be going with me."

"You're kidding, right?"

"We had a long talk with your boss and he's worked everything out," Pam said.

"Maybe he's forgotten we're not licensed to work outside of California."

"He doesn't seem to feel that's an issue," said Pam. "You need to discuss that with him."

"Oh, I will."

"So you see, Mr. Spandau," said Anna Mayhew, "everything is going just swimmingly."

It was nearly 7 p.m. when he got home to his house in Woodland Hills. He'd got caught in the Sunset traffic, then the 405 traffic, then the Ventura Freeway traffic. He'd closed the windows and cranked up the a/c, but the glare still beat him in the face and the stop-go, stop-go and the kamikaze lane shifts ate at his nerves. These were the days when a guy got out of his car, walked calmly back to the gentleman who was honking at him, and politely blew his brains out through the window.

Somewhere out in the world were the paintings of Monet, the music of Shostakovich, and the poems of Pablo Neruda. But this is what humanity in Southern California had been reduced to, angry rats trapped in isolated glass-and-metal cages, making twisted faces and obscene gestures at each other as they inched forward along the hot asphalt, vulnerable and afraid. Even if you managed to get to where you were going, even if you somehow managed to be on time and arrived cool and crisp and prepared, you were still angry. You had that rage still pumping in your blood, still had that fight-or-flight heartbeat, and when you nodded your polite hellos and sat down at the table for that meeting with your colleagues—who'd all just been through exactly what you'd just been through—it was like suspicious animals gathering around a water hole. You couldn't turn off that feeling you had to be ready to attack or defend yourself, that everyone and everything was the enemy.

It had nothing to do with the brain. That's what made it so hard, confused so many people. It wasn't a logical thing at all. It was all chemical, animal, basic. You couldn't reason it away. It had to do with blood. Your blood, their blood, blood waiting to be preserved or spilled. Blood that was inevitable. This was the world you had made.

The house was quiet and dark and cool when he got in—he'd had sense enough this time to leave the a/c running. He said, "Lucy, I'm home," and carried the bags of deli food he'd bought into the kitchen. A gourmet meal tonight, sir, of hot pastrami on rye, German potato salad, kosher pickle, and can of cream soda. Will Sir be eating in the blue dining room or the red one, or perhaps Sir will hang his head over the kitchen sink as usual and watch the crumbs get washed away with the pastrami drippings? I shall alert the staff.

There was beer and whiskey, but he'd put it away. Hadn't gotten rid of it, no, the total absence of it would have made him want it still more. It was there, and if he didn't drink it, it was because it was an act of choice, not lack of opportunity. The difference was important. He was still in control, not some poor wasted bastard who had to hide things from himself.

He went into the office—the Gene Autry Room, Dee had called it, filled with his cowboy memorabilia—and looked at the answering machine. Blinking. Whatever it was, he knew he couldn't deal with it. He went back to the kitchen and unwrapped a sandwich and put it on a paper plate, upended the container of potato salad next to it. Popped open the can of cream soda, slid open the patio door, and went out into his garden, the small patch of brown grass and plants he forgot to water and a pond with a handful of large goldfish who sometimes stared up at him like an abusive father they still loved.

Spandau's own father had beaten him and his sister and his mother like Chinese gongs until Spandau had left. Dee had wanted children but Spandau kept making excuses. That hadn't helped the marriage, Spandau afraid he was going to be like his old man, petrified one day he'd look down at his own child with his fist raised and the look of fear and helplessness and confusion on the kid's face, and for Spandau the transformation would be complete, he'd have become the very monster he always despised. Even now when he thought about the old man it made him sick. Where does the rage come from, how do we dare to pass it on to our children? Sometimes he felt like going back to Arizona and digging up the old bastard's corpse, doubtless still fresh from being pickled in schnapps, then sitting it up against the gravestone and firing shots into it. That would be useless as well. You couldn't do shit about things like this. Americans were so sure you could fix anything. But some things couldn't be fixed. Sometimes things just limped around broken.

He sat at the plastic table in the plastic chair. He took a bite

of the sandwich. He took a bite of the pickle. He took a bite
of the potato salad and a sip of the cream soda. He looked around
the yard, surveying his domain. He took a deep breath. Everything in the garden needed to be watered and fed. Yes, there was
a metaphor skulking in this. Things were bad but there was hope.
A little water, a little time, a little care. He was banged up but
still alive. There was hope. Not dead yet. Philosophy and rational
thought may triumph. "Cultivate your garden," said Voltaire. He
also said, "I've decided to be happy because it's better for my
health." Spandau strolled over to the small pond and looked in.
The half-eaten corpse of a goldfish floated on the surface. The
others, still alive, bobbed in the water around it, looking up ac-
cusingly at Spandau, the god that failed.

"Son of a bitch!" said Spandau. "Goddamn son of a bitch!"

He got the net, fished out the nibbled body. The raccoons had
done it again. The bastards sometimes raided the pond, pulled
out a fish and just tasted it, took a few bites, and flung it back
in. They weren't even hungry. They did it for spite. They did it
for the fun of it, the sheer malicious joy. The nasty little fuckers
with their opposable thumbs, vile little pseudo humans who've
inherited our evils through living too close. They were up in the
trees, somewhere, laughing about it.

"You fuckers!" said Spandau into the leaves. He looked down
at the remaining goldfish, gathered in a clump and staring at him.
"It's not my goddamn fault, okay?" he said to them. They didn't
believe a word of it.

"You're ranting at fish now?" said a woman's voice behind
him. Spandau turned. It was Dee. She'd come round the house
through the side gate.

"I'm sure they can hear you on the next block. No wonder they
love you around here."

"The goddamn raccoons. They killed another one. They don't even eat them, they just take a bite and throw them back in. They just do it for the sake of doing it."

"You convince yourself that raccoons are out to get you, David, and you really do have a problem."

Spandau tossed the dead fish into the bushes.

"I left a message. A couple, actually. You've conveniently turned off your cell phone. And I came by earlier. But you didn't listen to the messages, did you?"

"I just got in."

"I talked to Pookie. Going through one of your more responsible periods, are you?"

"Just trying to maintain any way I can, sweetheart. You want a beer?"

"Sure."

Spandau went out to the garage refrigerator, where he'd exiled the alcohol. He got two beers. There was a bottle of vodka in the icebox. Spandau opened it and took a long long hit, then another. He went back out to Dee.

"Charlie know you're here?" he said, handing her the beer.

"You want me to say no, don't you?" she said. "Yes, he knows I'm here. I want this marriage to work, David."

"You want me to go into all the reasons it shouldn't? Talk to your mom."

"Yes, I know Mom is your biggest fan. But she didn't have to live with you, I did."

"He can't make you happy, Dee."

"And you can, right? Mr. Sunshine. This has got to stop, David. Charlie wants me to get a restraining order but I said I'd talk to you. No more phone calls, no more hanging around outside the school. I want you to let me alone, David. Let it go. If you love me—in whatever way you do in that twisted little heart of yours—you'll let it go and get on with your own life."

"What you see in that pencil-necked dweeb—"

"He's my husband, David. I'm not going to let you talk about him."

"He's a goddamned space filler."

She sat the beer down on the table.

"I can see this was a waste of time. You call me again, sober or drunk, and I'm taking out a restraining order. Don't call, don't come anywhere near me. I mean it. I'm sorry you're in pain, but this isn't the way to handle it."

She turned her back on him. Suddenly she was walking away. She was there and she was standing in front of him and there was hope and now she was walking away. Unfair, unfair. She came because she wanted to see me. She came because she feels the same way I do, she can't say it, she needed an excuse, she's hoping for the same bit of magic to appear and fix things. But it's unfair, unfair, to show me what I want most and then take it away again. I never knew she could be this cruel.

And then it was all about the blood again, our history of rage waiting in a duct somewhere to be squeezed into our veins and make us become what we fear. He went after her, grabbed her arm, spun her around savagely. She was tall, but thin and elegant and rattled like a doll in his hands. He grabbed her shoulders, nearly lifting her off the ground, then saw his hand go to her neck, envelope her throat below that lovely chin. For the first time he saw in her eyes a fear he'd created himself. She had never been afraid of him before, but she was now. They looked at each other and suddenly it passed. What was left was that sick feeling when you know your life has irrevocably rounded some tragic corner.

He let her go. Stepped back. She turned and continued walking toward the gate. No words exchanged, no drama to milk. It was beyond that.

Then she was gone.

10

THERE WAS A CHITTERING IN THE BUSHES, MOVEMENT. Spandau awoke in the darkness, sat quietly, still very drunk. Stared through the dark toward the pond. He was outside on the patio, in a sleeping bag in the lounge chair. He waited. There were the emptied vodka bottle and the half-drunk bottle of Jack Daniel's on the table beside him. In the sleeping bag, next to his chest, were the flashlight and the pistol.

More movement coming down through the trees and through the bushes toward the pond. Spandau eased the sleeping bag away from his body. Readies the flashlight but doesn't turn it on yet, wants to catch the little fuckers in the act. Raises the gun, a huge Navy Colt .44 he'd taken off the Gene Autry Room wall and loaded precariously while leaning to and fro from the drink. He didn't even know if the thing would shoot. Symbolic act. This is the gun that won the Civil War. Show those little fuckers who's boss. This is America. Scare the shit out of them. Rid yourself of the raccoon jihad.

More movement.

He leaps from the chair, snaps on the light. Runs headlong toward the pond, light beam waving.

Yaaaaaaahhhh . . . !

Fires the hog leg. *Ka-whoom!* A sound like the end of time, water erupts from the pond. *Whoosh!* Skittering through the bushes, scratching of nasty little claws up tree trunk. Spandau raises the gun and fires again up into the trees. *Ka-whow!* Screeching (birds? them fucking raccoons?). The leaves come alive, life scattering everywhere. Ha!

Spandau stands in the middle of the backyard like Yosemite Sam, weaving back and forth, side to side, the giant pistol's barrel making circles in the air at the end of his outstretched arm. Consarned furbearing varmints. Spandau is enormously overjoyed. Take that, you little shits. He aims again and pulls the trigger but it doesn't go off. Around him windows are opening, lights come on, neighbors are shouting, and in a moment the distant but growing whine of a police siren.

Well, shit.

Spandau staggers into the house, closes the door, pulls the curtains. Falls across his bed with the gun still in his hand. Goes immediately into a thankfully dreamless sleep.

11

SPANDAU WENT INTO THE OFFICE. POOKIE IGNORED HIM, still nursing her righteous anger. He tried to ignore her right back.

Walter was at his desk, drinking coffee. He looked fresh as a daisy—a clear moral affront, since Spandau knew damned well he'd been snockered himself the night before. Meanwhile Spandau felt, in the words of his old mentor Beau Macaulay, like he'd been pissed at and missed, shit at and hit.

"I'm not going to France," said Spandau. "Are we clear on this?"

"I thought you liked France," said Walter. "You're always spewing off about that indigestible frog pig fodder."

Walter hated French food, but this had nothing to do with France. Walter ate only American food, which meant red meat, which meant beef, which meant he laid out a fortune every month to Gelson's for steaks that had wiled away their lives nibbling Omaha grass instead of chewing up half of Argentina and farting their way through the ozone layer. Walter was a complex man.

"Walter, I am not going to France. Get somebody else."

"Sure, sure, if that's how you feel. Jesus, you look like Mother Teresa's tits. Have some coffee."

"I don't want any coffee. I want to know this is settled."

"You don't want to go, don't go, for God's sake. Jesus, what the hell have you been doing?"

Spandau paused, then said: "At three o'clock this morning I tried to murder a pair of raccoons with an antique .44 Colt Dragoon."

"Where'd they get the gun?"

"This isn't funny, Walter. I don't even know if there *were* any raccoons. I can't even function here, and you want to turn me loose in a foreign country."

"Fine," said Walter. "Don't go."

"Good," said Spandau. He stood there.

"Sit down, for Christ's sake." Spandau sat down. Walter yelled out the door, "Pook!"

Pookie came and stood in the doorway, scowling. "What are you mad about?" Walter asked her. "Whatever it is, stop it. Get him some coffee."

"This isn't part of my job description."

"You know what your job description is going to be? Unemployed, that's what it's going to be. Get the man some coffee."

"I went to Swarthmore," she said, and went away to get the coffee.

"I'm falling apart," Spandau said. "Dee came by last night. She wanted to talk. Said she might get a restraining order." He stopped. Then: "I blew up. I went at her. Jesus, Walter, I grabbed her by the throat. Ah God. It's all fucked up now. Really fucked up. I can't stand the thought of it. What I did. I've never laid a hand on her, never even came close. Now this."

"The labyrinths of the human heart," said Walter. "I once shot at one of mine."

"And that's the other thing. Shooting at goddamn raccoons in the middle of the night. I could have killed somebody. I'm lucky not to be in jail. Thank Christ the pistol stopped working before they found out who did it."

Pookie came in with the coffee, set it rattling on the desk in front of Spandau. She'd planned to give him another scowl, set his ass to rights, but she saw his face. He looked up at her with those brown eyes and that beat-up face and she knew he was about as close to losing it as he was likely to get. Instead she smiled, put her hand briefly on his shoulder, and went to the door. She turned in the doorway and gave Walter an angry look that said, *Do something! Fix it!* Walter frowned at her.

"What do you want me to do?" Walter said to Pookie as much as to Spandau. "You want some time off?"

"No, God, I got any time on my hands and I'll kill myself."

"Then what?"

"I don't know."

Walter leaned back in his chair and put his hands behind his head. "You got me in a kind of bind here, sport. You don't want to work but you don't want not to work. I'm at a loss to see how this can be resolved."

"I didn't say I didn't want to work."

"Yes you did. You said you didn't want to go to France. That's work. That's the job I've got for you. Not much else going on. I thought you'd be happy to have it. You know, get you out of the country. Wine, women, and the grand debauchery of the south of France. I was thinking it'd be a goddamn vacation."

"I can't do it."

"Okay," said Walter. "Then you tell me what you can do. How about that?"

"You're not helping."

"Help, my ass. I got a business to run. You can work or you can not work. It's up to you. You've got a job. You don't want to do it, fine, I'll get somebody else if they'll let me. But I can't solve your existential angst for you."

"You know, I forget what a shit you can be most of the time."

"It's a hard life, sport. You can't get up enough steam, then pull over and let everybody pass. That's the way it goes. Oh, look at that face! You want to quit, quit. You think that's going to help? You don't want to go, fine. Don't. But you don't go and we lose this account and you sit around the house sucking on Jack Daniel's tit and blasting away at Disney cartoons until you kill somebody. That's fucking proactive as all hell."

Spandau stared at the floor. "Let me think about it."

"Sure. Let me know by the end of the day. Now go get something to eat. And coffee. Lots of coffee."

Spandau left. Pookie came to the doorway.

"You were listening," said Walter.

"I was listening," said Pookie.

"I'm a goddamn businessman," said Walter. "I don't have time for this shit."

Pookie came over, put her arms around Walter's neck, and kissed him on the cheek.

"What the hell was that for?"

"Pam Mayhew just phoned and said his tickets and accommodations are all set. He's traveling on a private jet with them, and he'll be staying with them in the villa they've rented. She said to thank you for setting it all up. You knew he was going, you sweet bastard. You waltzed him right into it."

"Don't you have something to do?" said Walter. "Jesus, people stand around this office like it's a goddamned prayer meeting."

Pookie smiled, blew him a kiss, and left. She was young and sexy as hell and sometimes Walter thought he was a little in love with her. Trouble was, he liked her far too much. Walter knew himself to be one of those people who were good at business precisely because their personal lives were so fucked up. You at least required business to make some kind of sense, and it did much of the time.

Whenever a woman left him, and they always left him, Walter threw himself into manic days of aggressive commerce and dark nights of equally aggressive boozing. He paid for one with the other, and so a balance was reached. He was killing himself but he didn't much care. You simply had to find a way to get through the hours and then the days and let the years, if there were to be years, take care of themselves.

Pookie was all right. She was a good kid and Walter was no good for her. He was no good for Spandau either. Maybe at one point in the past, maybe at some point again in the future, but not now. He could see Spandau wanting to follow him like the Mad Hatter down into Walter's own hellish little rabbit hole. Sometimes you had to protect people from yourself.

Spandau would be fine. He would go to France and do his job even if he didn't believe he could do it. That's just who Spandau was. He'd eat well, get some sun, he wouldn't booze, and if Walter knew anything about women, that Mayhew broad was looking to hump his brains out. Best of all, he'd be far away from Dee. He'd never be able to sort that out here.

Walter thought about the Mayhew woman, then got out his address book and phoned a big blond dental technician he knew in Oxnard. That was tonight. Now there were the seconds, minutes, hours to get through until then. He got out the list of calls to return to potential clients that Pookie had given him earlier, and he began dialing. Already, Walter thought, see how the moments fly past.

12

THE HAPPY HAIR BEAUTY BOUTIQUE WAS ON WESTERN Avenue at the southern edge of Koreatown. It was a sunny day and the street outside was busy, a bright and continuous parade of ethnic mixes—black, white, Latino, Asian—but Perec never once looked at them. Perec didn't care. Perec didn't like them, whoever they were, whatever they looked like. It wasn't racial— Perec simply had no use for people. People were an inconvenience. Had Perec been able to push a button to eliminate the whole of Los Angeles, he would have done so without a moment's hesitation. (Well, except for Anna.) Perec's mother despised people because she thought they were evil and lived in defiance of a pissed-off God. Perec didn't despise them, but he wished they'd go away and leave him alone. He didn't care how it happened, extreme violence or natural causes. He'd see on TV the human casualties of bombings in the Middle East or tsunamis in Asia or gang assassinations a few blocks away in South Central and he'd think, Okay, how many more to go? It wasn't that Perec was angry at them. Perec didn't feel anything for them, nothing at all. He just wished they'd keep out of his way and let him get on with his own life.

He was cutting the hair of a rotund little Korean woman. She had nice hair but it was thinning and had a tendency to fly away, like light black straw. He held strands of her hair in his fingers, cutting it gently and at a careful angle with the straight razor. She'd probably never used a conditioner in her life. Perec thought about recommending something, but it was expensive and he knew she'd never use it. One day soon there'd be these bald spots appearing. It served her right. Imelda, one of the two Filipino stylists who worked in the shop, was working on a black woman and chatting happily away. Perec sometimes wished he could talk to people like that, just to make the day go faster. But he had nothing to say.

"You not cutting it too short, right?" said the Korean woman.

"It's not too short," said Perec.

"You cut it too short and I look like a man."

"It's not too short. Here, look."

Perec turned her to the mirror.

"Ha!" exclaimed the Korean woman. "It's too short! You ruin me!"

Perec shrugged. She did this all the time. He wanted to boot her out of the shop, ban her, but they were all like this. Always looking for an edge, a way to chisel, save a couple of cents. The entire world was like this. They were all so predictable.

"I'll fix it, okay?"

"You better, or I don't pay."

He finished with the Korean woman. She got up, looked in the mirror, shook her head in disgust. They went to the register.

"I look like a man! You give me discount!"

"I'm not giving you a discount."

"I talk to owner!"

"I am the owner."

The Korean woman made a sour face and paid reluctantly. She left the shop, muttering to herself in Korean. Imelda looked at Perec and smiled sympathetically. Perec ignored this. Imelda was small and very pretty and sometimes Perec thought she was flirting with him. He didn't like it.

A pretty Thai girl in her early twenties came into the shop. Long beautiful black hair. She too smiled at Perec. He turned red and averted his eyes. Began to get that sick feeling he got.

"Can I get a trim?" the girl asked him.

Perec nodded. She got into the chair. She tossed her hair and it flowed like a stream over the back of the seat.

"Like an inch?" said the girl. "Just the ends? Okay?"

Perec nodded. He stared at the back of her head. He had a hard time starting.

"Okay?" said the girl over her shoulder.

"Sure," said Perec, "just the ends."

He touched her hair reluctantly. Stroked it. Like silk.

"You want me to use the scissors or the razor?"

"What's the difference?"

"The scissors, they blunt the ends of the hair. A razor, it cuts it at an angle, it lays smoother."

"Yeah, sure," said the girl. "Whatever."

He made the first cut. The small strands of hair gave way into his hand. He was reluctant to let them go, to drop them on the floor. He finally released them, took a few more strands in his fingers. It was so long, so beautiful. Beneath the hair he could just see her neck. He raised the cascade of dark hair and there it was. So pale, so delicate. The long gentle curve of it to her shoulder. He thought of the straight razor sliding softly down the back of her neck, freeing the hundreds of near-invisible tiny hairs that clung to her skin, leaving in its path an ultimate smoothness. He imagined a tiny nick, almost painless, that would blossom at the base of that clean path at the bottom of her neck. There was always an imperfection. Flesh was never pure, never without flaw. The small crimson drop on that skin, so small it wouldn't run, it would remain there like a dab of paint on a canvas.

He began to get sick. He said quickly to Imelda, who was working on another woman, "Finish here."

"Sure, but—"

Perec, bent as if his stomach ached him, ran toward the bathroom. He hurriedly locked the door, unzipped his fly, and came after a few strokes. He leaned back on the toilet. Then he began to cry, and beat himself angrily with his fists.

"*Sale cochon, sale cochon . . .*" he cursed himself in his mother's French. Dirty pig, dirty pig . . .

He sat crying enclosed in his own arms. Somewhere in his mind they were the arms of someone else, he wasn't sure who. When he was pretty sure the girl had gone, he went back out into the shop. She was just leaving. Perec saw the girl give Imelda a look. They'd been talking about him. Strange Perec, they'd say. Perec the weirdo. Perec knew people thought he was different. But they were wrong. Perec was just like everyone else. He thought, felt, needed, cried. Just like they did. It's just that you couldn't tell them anything. Everyone was busy, everyone was running, they wouldn't hold still long enough for Perec to get out the words or to somehow find a way to show them how he felt. So in the end you had to stop it. You could never convince them that you were actually good, better than they were, really. You had to stop feeling. There was nothing else you could do about it. You had to be strong.

"You okay?" Imelda asked him. "You got a stomach thing?"

"Yeah."

"You eat at that sushi place down on the corner? They nearly killed me the other day. I swear it was them, I was in the toilet the whole day. You shouldn't never eat sushi in hot weather, I'm telling you . . ."

She talked. Perec let her, but turned off his mind.

13

PEREC AND HIS MOTHER LIVED NEAR THE ANGELUS CEM-
etery half a mile from the shop. Perec always walked. They didn't
own a car and he hated buses, hated the smell of the people,
the twisted faces. Today he stopped at the grocery as always and
picked up the things for dinner. His feet hurt. He grimaced with
every step and he was limping and the inside of his shoes made
tiny squishing noises. There were black and Latino kids playing in his street. They watched Perec but said nothing. It was
only the teenagers who did that. They said things but never approached him. It was as if they knew how he felt, knew that Perec
was unafraid of them because he didn't care, had nothing to lose.
Perec had never feared death. The thought of infinite loneliness
and quiet only relaxed him.

The Perec house was an old two-bedroom single-story cot-
tage. It must have been beautiful once, perhaps when his father
had been around, but Perec couldn't remember it. The grass grew
in dry clumps and the concrete walkway was cracked and wobbly.
The windows were shut and the curtains drawn. He hobbled up

the steps and opened the door and entered the darkness and the dry, dusty smell of his mother and her old age.

"I'm home, Maman!" Perec called in French.

No reply, but he hadn't expected one. From another room came the sound of the TV. An evangelist calling to God.

He went into the kitchen and put the groceries away, then into the living room, where his mother sat in a ratty overstuffed chair in the middle of the room, her eyes glued to the flickering screen. She said nothing. She lit a cigarette and never once took her eyes off the man in the expensive suit and bad hair who reminded her of what a sinner she was.

"Do you want the chicken tonight?" Perec asked her, again in French. She refused to speak English to him.

"No," said Maman.

"You told me you wanted the chicken."

"Well, I don't want it."

"There's the lasagna."

Maman grunted contemptuously.

"It's the chicken or the lasagna, Maman."

"I don't care. It all tastes the same."

Perec went back into the kitchen to get out the microwave dinner he bought for her. He cooked it in the machine, then put it on a tray and poured a glass of cheap red wine and put that on the tray next to it. He folded a paper towel, put knife and fork on it. He checked to see that everything was there so she wouldn't complain. He'd forgotten her roll. He took a small round bread roll out of the bag and added it to the edge of the plate. A pathetic elegance. Perec opened a drawer near the sink and reached back into it and took out a small vial of pills. He mashed several of the pills into powder with a spoon and stirred the powder into her wine.

"You should learn to cook," she said when he put the tray in front of her.

"I don't have time to cook."

"We eat this slop."

"You could cook."

"I'm a cripple!" she said, and raised her arthritic hands. "Raising you made me a cripple!"

Perec started to leave the room, but she said, "Where are you going?"

He went back to Maman and helped her slide from the chair to her knees in front of the TV. He got on his knees next to her. She closed her eyes and mumbled a long and passionate prayer in French. Perec watched her carefully. When she finished, Perec helped her back into the chair.

"Do you need to go to the bathroom?"

She nodded. He walked toward the bathroom to prepare it but first stopped by his room and tore a few pages out of his Bible and put them in his pocket. In the bathroom he raised the toilet lid and set out the bowl of water she would use to wash herself at the end. He went back to the living room and half carried her into the bathroom, removed her diaper, and balanced her on the toilet. He turned away and waited until her loud and watery bowel movement was finished, then he turned back to her and helped her rise, bend over, and Perec carefully wiped her ass with the pages of the Bible, throwing them in the toilet and flushing before she could see them. She'd pissed small amounts into the diaper, so he put on a fresh one. She was capable of going to the bathroom by herself but chose not to. Perec took her back into the living room and redeposited her in the chair.

"Where are you going?"

"To my room."

"What do you do there? Do you do something filthy?"

"No, Maman."

"Are you lying to me? You're a man. All men touch themselves, like beasts. It's disgusting."

"No, Maman. I just read."

"Filth, probably. Keep the Bible where you can see it. If you keep it where you can see it, it will remind you."

"Yes, Maman," he said.

Perec's room was as sterile as a monk's cell. There was a single bed with a blanket and a small pillow. A desk and chair. A nightstand with a lamp on it next to the bed. Above the bed was a crucifix. There were no photos, posters, or reminders of his past or his identity. Maman would have been offended and Perec didn't care anyway. This was just a place he slept. Real life was elsewhere. Perec lay on the bed, staring at the ceiling, waiting.

Half an hour later he went into the living room and Maman was asleep. He went over and grabbed her by the hair and shook her head. She murmured but didn't wake. Perec went back to his room and shut and locked the door, just in case. He opened the closet door, pushed aside some hanging clothes, then took the desk chair and set it in the closet. He stood on the chair and reached up, pushed open the small trapdoor, and climbed up into the only place where he truly existed.

AnnaWorld.

The floored attic wasn't tall enough to stand up in, but Perec had kitted it out. Cushions, an old computer, and a printer. A video player with headphones. Stacks of videos—mostly Anna's. All around the place he'd pinned up computer-printed photos of Anna Mayhew at different points in her career, posters of A.M., printed articles about her.

Perec sat on a cushion in front of the computer. He turned it on, connected to the Internet, then did one of his Google searches on Anna Mayhew. Today turned up a new article about her making an appearance to reopen a classic movie theater downtown. Perec noted this.

You could find anything on Google. Google was wonderful.

Then he did an image search. The screen filled with thumbnail images of her. Perec sat back. He opened a box and took out the nude photos of Anna daubed with blood. His hands shook as he held them. He undressed. His thin naked body was covered with small scars. He lay back on the floor, holding the pictures to his chest, and masturbated. Afterward he beat himself again with his fists. If you do these things you must pay. Perec didn't believe in God but you didn't need God to be impure. A balance had to be struck. He took out his father's straight razor, the only thing he had left of the old man. There were already slash marks across the soles of his feet, which had bled all day and now painted the bottoms of his feet the color of ocher. He made another painful cut on each foot. He would spend tomorrow again in misery but it was worth it.

14

THE HALCYON THEATRE IN DOWNTOWN LOS ANGELES HAD
been closed for more than thirty years, sitting like an old pen-
sioner on the side of Broadway and watching over the decades
as the neighborhood went from flush to bad to mixed and now,
in an attempt at urban revitalization, on its way to flush again.
Everything came around if you waited long enough. The drug
dealers—as well as the small ethnic businesses and homes—
were mainly pushed out as the gays and successful artsy types
moved in, following the smell of fresh real estate and landing, as
always, on a good deal well before the market knew what hit it.
The most useful function artists have always had for the rich is
acting as real-estate ferrets. Follow an up-and-coming painter to
his lair, for instance, then buy the building and price his bohe-
mian ass out of it. It's a sure thing, and of course in downtown
L.A. the rich came and the artists moved out, and the industrial
lofts became penthouses with half a dozen zeros attached. There
were still drug dealers but they drove Porsches now and let their

girlfriends dance with the stoned young movie execs in the hip clubs that had sprung up near the Staples Center.

In the early part of the last century, the Halcyon had begun life as a legitimate theater. Sarah Bernhardt had actually done one of her strange but alluring interpretations of Hamlet on the stage. As a legit theater, it went belly-up and became a successful music hall, then a burlesque house in the twenties and early thirties. When the Depression hit and it became obvious that Americans would happily spare a nickel to see a motion picture—with sound yet—in order to escape from the clutches of their bleak real life, the Halcyon became a cinema. The likes of Dick Powell and Myrna Loy flickered across its screen well into the fifties, when television hit. It limped into the sixties, the Age of Aquarius and free love, when it became a porn house. Linda Lovelace blew Johnny "Wad" Holmes on the very screen where Fred and Ginger once danced.

Anna thought: You don't have to look far for a metaphor, here.

The original owner died and left it to his son. Then the son died and left it to his three children. The son thought he was doing them a favor, but of course the children immediately turned on each other like famished stoats. The theater became the focus of a twenty-three-year legal battle that nearly bankrupted the entire family but put their attorneys' children through various Ivy League schools. Finally it dawned on the grandchildren that: (a) this old fossil of a building was gobbling up every cent they had, (b) every time one of them died and left it to an offspring, their share of it diminished, and (c) there was the possibility of a grand tax write-off for everybody if they could only find somebody stupid enough to buy it, since that movie bitch Anna Mayhew and her smarmy dilettante cohorts had persuaded the city council to list it as a historic landmark, making it impossible to tear down and therefore worthless in terms of resale. Who the fuck wanted a hundred-year-old movie theater? Built before goddamn movies even *had* sound?

Oh, Anna Mayhew had learned a few things in Hollywood . . .

A small temporary stage had been erected in the plaza at the front of the theater. Spandau, Anna, and Pam waited inside the front doors as the crowd gathered outside. The theater manager and staff scurried around with last-minute preparations for the film, a beautifully restored 35mm version of *The Lady Eve* with Barbara Stanwyck and Henry Fonda. It was one of Anna's favorites, a classic she'd grown up watching in Texas. She'd even tried getting the film remade, with her doing the Stanwyck role, something she'd dreamed about as long as she could remember. Everybody she'd pitched it to just stared at her. Nobody knew what the hell she was talking about, nobody had ever seen it. Didn't she want to do *Bonnie and Clyde*? Now there was a goddamn classic. Think of all the special effects whatshisname the director never had . . .

No, said Anna, fuck you very much.

One day, Anna always told herself. And now I'm too goddamn old. I'll never do it now. But they couldn't stop her from showing the film, shoving it down their goddamn throats. Here, you ignorant bastards. This is what a good film looks like. She'd been worried at first that it would be a washout, that nobody would show up. But they'd done a good job with the PR, and Anna had stumped for it on various L.A. chat shows with an enthusiasm she rarely if ever had given to one of her own films. Now it was paying off. The plaza was filling with people. Somebody said they were even spilling out onto the street. It was more than what she'd hoped for, and her heart pounded. For the first time in years she felt she'd actually accomplished something.

Spandau paced pack and forth in the lobby, talking to a micro-phone at his wrist. There was a tiny button receiver in his ear. He was keeping in touch with two guys he had in the crowd outside, milling around.

"You're making me nervous," Anna said to him.

Spandau, looking out the door, said, "That's supposed to be my line."

"Is it standard that we pretend to be joined at the hip?"

"It is until we get you out of here and back into a safe place."

"It's filling up out here," said Bruce, one of the operatives, into Spandau's ear. "They're pushed all the way into the gutter now. It keeps up like this, the cops are going to show up and start bitch-ing. What do you want me to do?"

"You and Mel just work the crowd," Spandau said to him. "Move around, but not too fast. Don't look obvious. You know what to look for. You see anything at all, you call me."

"Right," said Bruce.

"What movie did you say this was?" said Mel.

"*The Lady Eve,*" Spandau said to him.

"Never heard of it," said Mel. "It sounds like a feminine hy-giene spray."

Spandau could hear Mel and Bruce both laughing. Spandau had used them a few times before. They were both trustworthy but very young, in their early twenties.

"Guys, what are you doing right now?" Spandau asked them.

"I'm standing here talking to you," said Mel.

"Right," said Bruce.

"Very good," said Spandau. "Both of you are just standing there talking into your shirt cuffs and we are having this fine old conversation. Very discreet, very professional."

Silence on the other end. Spandau smiled. Somewhere in the

Pleistocene age he himself had been that young. Mel raced dirt bikes and Bruce had a three-month-old daughter. Both had day jobs and needed the extra money.

"Are we ready?" said the theater manager to Anna, then looked at Spandau. Anna nodded. The manager went out the door, then Spandau, followed by Anna. The manager climbed the step up to the stage platform. Anna ascended behind him, followed by Spandau, who stood midstairs, just high enough above the crowd to see down into it.

The manager began to speak.

"There's a shitload more people than we thought," Bruce said into the mike.

"Where do you want me?" asked Mel. "I'm at the edge of the crowd."

"Mel, just stay there. Anything happens, I'll call you forward," said Spandau. "Bruce, I want you working the middle, right?"

"Got it."

There were five or six hundred people, twice as many as anybody had thought. Anna had publicized the event well, then there were the people who'd stopped by out of curiosity. Spandau hoped there wouldn't be any more. He didn't have enough people working the crowd. Two guys weren't nearly enough for a group this size. Hell, they weren't enough even for the group anticipated. What the hell had he been thinking? The theater had hired its own security, seven or eight amateurs in dopey hats, who held on to a thin yellow nylon cord to keep back the crowd, which now pressed forward as the ones in back tried to keep out of the street. Spandau stood watching. It was fine that people saw him, and they'd know there were people working the crowd. He looked for his own men but couldn't see them. That at least was a good sign.

The manager introduced Anna, who walked up to the microphone.

About seventy feet away, a small figure in a black cap and NASCAR jacket pushed his way forward.

Shit.

Spandau buzzed Mel. "Small guy in a dark jacket, about sixty, seventy feet straight in front of the stage. I want you to check it. He's pushing forward."

"It him?"

"I dunno. It might be nothing. Just check it. Come forward, then work back. Cut him off. Bruce, be ready to move if I tell you."

"Roger that," said Bruce.

Spandau could see Mel shoving his way roughly through the crowd, leaving a wake of grumbling spectators. He lost the dark figure for a moment, felt his heart lurch, then found him again. The crowd was thicker the closer to the stage you got and Mel had slowed down. Still trying to inch forward, but slower. Spandau kept his eyes locked on him, afraid to lose him again. The figure pushed forward, edged determinedly sideways toward the foot of the stage. Then the figure stopped—who knows why—and looked up at Spandau. Their eyes locked for a moment, just a moment, before the figure pulled off the dark cap and turned and disappeared into the crowd.

"I think it's him," said Spandau. "He's up close to the stage. Mel, come in quickly, to my left. Bruce, I want you outside the crowd, now, ready to move any direction and catch him if he makes it out."

"Got it," said Bruce. "Moving now."

"I'm coming down. Mel, I want you next to him, but don't make contact. I'm coming down there. Be careful. If it's our guy, figure he's got a knife or razor."

"Roger."

Spandau jumped from the steps and went round behind the stage in the direction in which he'd last seen the figure. He came out into the crowd, pushing aside one of the rent-a-cops and dodging under the nylon cord. Spandau plunged through into the mass of bodies. He was a big man and moved quickly—more imposing and faster, he hoped, than the smaller man. Spandau was also six two, and that helped. He caught sight of the black jacket ten yards away, making for the edge of the crowd.

"He's moving left, away from me, parallel to the stage. Mel, you see him?"

"Not yet."

"Bruce, come around my left, outside, outside now!"

Suddenly Mel appeared in front of him.

"Shit," said Mel, and made an apologetic face. They both pushed forward toward the perimeter. They could see the top of his head, nearly clear now.

"I see him!" said Bruce. "He's coming out!"

"Don't make contact," Spandau said. "You hear me? Just keep up with him until he's clear. We're nearly out. Once he's clear, just stay with him. Don't try to stop him. You got that? Bruce? You copy that? Bruce, goddamn it . . ."

They were both shoving now, two big men shouldering regardless through the wall of innocent flesh. Then, one big push, and they were through, stepping out onto the street. Bruce was kneeling at the curb, his hands to his face, blood pouring through his fingers. A glimpse of the figure moving back into a corner of crowd.

"Stay with him," Spandau told Mel, and leaped back into throng. The figure darted back and forth, changing direction a few times, trying to lose his pursuer. Spandau, taller, kept following the head, never taking his eyes off it. Finally it changed direction once more at the far end and darted out of the crowd. Spandau cleared too and loped off after the small figure running down the sidewalk. Spandau was nearly on him, when he veered suddenly and cut into a Mexican restaurant. Spandau burst in and followed the surprised looks toward the kitchen.

He shoved open the metal kitchen door and the small man in the black NASCAR jacket had a straight razor to the throat of a teenage busboy. An older Mexican cook stood watching, frozen. Spandau stopped, watching the panicked face peering over the busboy's shoulder. The figure danced the busboy slowly toward the screen door to the alley. In a moment the figure was going to be out the door and away. Human instinct dictates we protect out own asses first, and if Spandau moved forward, the initial reaction wouldn't be to cut the busboy but to let him go and break for the open door. Spandau took a step forward.

It was at that moment that the cook swung a greasy black three-pound Dodge cast-iron skillet and connected with the back of Spandau's head. Spandau pitched forward into a volley of fireworks. He came to a few seconds later at the feet of the busboy, his cheek stuck to the oily tile floor and his nose inhaling the rancid smell of a recently mopped floor. Spandau looked up into the face of the cook bending over him.

"He's my son," the cook said apologetically. Spandau smiled and thought, He means the busboy, then felt very dizzy and just decided to go ahead and pass out.

15

Y OU'RE CONCUSSED," SAID LIEUTENANT LOUIS RAMIREZ OF
the LAPD. He looked sympathetic but made no move toward
calling a doctor or even handing Spandau a paper towel as Spandau puked repeatedly into the toilet of the Mexican restaurant.
"No doubt about it."

Spandau was big but Ramirez was bigger. Ramirez was like
a goddman wall, six four of muscle and urban weltschmerz. His
dark hair was cropped short enough to see the four-inch scar some
PCP-inspired cholo had made with a broken muscatel bottle.

"Is this your professional opinion," said Spandau between
retches, "or are you just guessing?"

"I used to box," said Ramirez, "but I got a head like an egg-
shell. I remember the symptoms. You want to flush that thing?"
he said, making a face.

Spandau reached up and flushed the toilet. He'd known
Ramirez for a couple of years. Spandau wasn't bothered by many
people, but Ramirez made him uncomfortable. He was smarter
and better educated than he let on, but he had a reputation for

violence and Spandau always felt like he was trying to balance a seesaw when he was around him. It took very little to tip it one way or the other.

"If you're going to have an aneurysm," said Ramirez, "I'd appreciate if you'd wait until we've finished talking and somebody else gets to drag your ass to the station. Then you can just die any old way."

"Why would I go to the station?" said Spandau, rising his mouth in the sink and spitting.

"Gee, I dunno," said Ramirez. "Public endangerment? Failing to notify a police officer during the perpetuation of a crime? Is that a law? Is that even a word? I think it is. It must be. Sounds good, anyway. Speeding, then. Jaywalking. I don't care. How many people did you nearly get killed? Let me count the ways."

"I'm as innocent as . . ." Suddenly Spandau's mind just quit. His head hurt.

" . . . A lamb in spring?" Ramirez finished for him. "You want to tell me why you were chasing this guy through the middle of a Mexican restaurant in downtown Los Angeles in broad daylight?"

"We saw him in the crowd. He had a razor. We went after him."

"You think he was going after your client?"

"I figure it was a possibility, yeah. What do you think?"

"Gosh," said Ramirez. "I think you were looking for him, and you found him, that's what I think. I also think it's a really swell idea to let the police know when nutcases with razor blades are running around loose. We'd've had cops all over the place. We do that sort of thing."

"He didn't write to tell us he was coming."

"But you thought he might. That would have been enough. Now you got your partner cut and you endangered, oh, I don't

know how many innocent lives. A good day's work. You know who
he is?"

"No."

"You're fibbing to me, Dave, and I'm going to fry your balls on
that griddle over there."

"We don't know who he is. How's Bruce?"

"The young man who now looks like Boris Karloff thanks to
you? We sent him to the hospital. He'll have a nice memento and
I'm sure will hold you forever in high regard, bub. Give your statement to Sanchez here. It'll be a lie, but make it as convincing as
possible. I don't want to have to chase you down and do it again."

"What about Anna?"

"We followed her home. Maybe her statement will read a little
more satisfying than yours. I think she likes you."

"How can you tell?"

"I kept kicking you until you woke up and she told me to
stop," said Ramirez.

Spandau drove uneasily to the hospital. He asked after Bruce at
the desk and was told he was still in the emergency room. Bruce
had lost some blood but his condition wasn't serious. Still, they
told Spandau, he'd have to wait until they took Mr. Hamill up
to his room. Spandau nodded, and when the nurse's back was
turned he went through the doors back into the emergency room,
and walked past the cubicles until he saw Babe, Bruce's wife,
standing outside a cubicle holding their daughter. She glared at
Spandau as he came up.

"You've got some goddamn balls," she said to him, "showing
up here."

Bruce was lying in bed, his face swathed in bandages. The

cut had gone from between the eyes nearly to the left earlobe, slicing into his sinus cavity and laying open the entire left side of his face. He was doped on painkillers but as friendly as ever, making Spandau feel even worse. There were times when you really hoped people would behave like shits, which is the one time they never did.

"How you holding up?" Spandau said to him.

"Pretty good. They tell me I'll never play the piano again, though." It was hard for Bruce to talk. The bandages kept his jaw from moving much and there was the small matter of half his face lopped off.

"Look . . ."

"It was my fault, man," said Bruce. "You told me not to make contact and I got buck fever and did. It's my fault. It was stupid."

"You okay otherwise? You need anything?"

"This is like a vacation, man. I'm still getting paid for this, right?"

"Hell yeah."

As Spandau was leaving, Babe said to him, "That's it. He's not coming back."

Spandau just nodded.

"And that business about it being his fault, well, I don't think you get let off the hook that easy."

"What do you want me to do?"

"I want you to back up the goddamn clock about twenty-four hours and give my husband his face back. A couple of inches lower and it would have been his jugular. Thank God for small favors."

"You need anything, call me or the office, we'll take care of it."

"Walter was here earlier. Mr. Slick himself. You're two of a kind. Users, the both of you. You turn my stomach. No wonder your wife ditched your ass."

Spandau just kept nodding. He didn't feel there was much point in arguing, since he was convinced she was right.

16

He pulled up at Anna's gate, buzzed. They let him in. The two ex-marines Spandau had hired that day met him when he pulled into the courtyard. He went over their instructions again until Anna came out of the house.

"How's your friend?"

"They've got him stitched up and medicated. He'll need a good plastic surgeon."

"I'll see to it. That's the one thing you can find in Hollywood."

They went into the kitchen and sat at the table and she poured two mugs of coffee. Suddenly, for both Anna and Spandau, the room felt like the hundred ranch kitchens they'd grown up in.

"It's my fault," said Anna. "I should have listened to you. I shouldn't have gone."

"No, it's mine. It was my operation."

Anna shook her head. "You ever get tired of wearing a hair shirt?"

"I get tired of being stupid," Spandau said.

"You want to be cuddled? I'm sorry, I don't have a motherly

bone in me. Look, we fucked up. Both of us. You mind if we share that? I figure fifty percent of being a fuckup is only half as lousy and almost bearable. I'll see that your friend gets the best."

"That's not the point."

"What is the point?" she asked him. "You looking for an excuse to beat up on yourself? You know, the whole time I've known you I've watched you set yourself up for one fall or another. You did it with me that first day. I never saw anybody try to fuck something up so badly. What the hell have you done to make Spandau hate Spandau so badly? It's fascinating to watch."

"That why you hired me? Entertainment value?"

"Fucking-A. I'm a washed-up old movie star. I got nothing better to do these days. Besides, you've got a crush on me."

"Do I?"

"Oh, hell yeah," she said. "You want me bad, you're just going about it in the wrong way. Negative attention only works when you're in grade school. You know, pigtails in the ink bottle. That crap."

"There's a better way?"

"Oh sure. Maybe I'll let you in on it at some point. Meanwhile you look beat. There's an extra room if you want it. I think I can curb my lustful ways for one night, so you'll be safe."

Spandau drained his coffee and stood up. The last of the sand had run out of him. Anna saw it in his face, and even his large frame seemed to sink a few inches. She didn't want him to go, had clearly lied about the motherly thing, which surprised her. She couldn't remember the last time she wanted to care for a man rather than fuck him. All she wanted now was to lead Spandau upstairs, put him to bed, maybe climb in with him, and listen to the rise and fall of his breath as he slept in her arms, nothing more.

"I think I'll head on out," said Spandau.

"Spoken like a real cowboy. Jesus, you remind me of my dad. He looked like Randolph Scott. Even rolled his own cigarettes. We had a tiny ranch outside of Waco. That man was tough as nails. He cut off his little finger milling wood and worked the entire goddamn day with it hanging there in his glove."

"I grew up with guys like that. Still know a few of them. What happened to him?"

"One Sunday morning after breakfast he went out behind the stables and cut his throat. No particular reason, or if there was he never told anybody. No note, none of that dramatic crap. I was ten. It wasn't until I was well grown that I realized he'd just turned to stone and couldn't live with it. The toughness just finally reached all the way to the center and that was that."

"This a true story?" Spandau asked her.

Anna smiled. "Well, my father actually did cut off his finger, except he slammed it in a car door. And he owned a Toyota dealership in Waco until he had a heart attack in his sleep. Too many T-bones."

"Did he at least look like Randolph Scott?"

"Oh yeah. Right down to the little cleft in his chin."

"Good story anyway."

"It was meant to be inspiring."

"I'm afraid it pretty much sucks in the inspirational department."

"Really? Well, shit."

They looked at each other for a moment. She wanted to kiss him. She wanted him to *want* her to kiss him. She wanted to reach up and put her arms around his neck, but she'd have to move forward two feet and stand on her toes and find some excuse to explain why the hell her hands were moving in that direction. It would have been much simpler if the big bastard just kissed her instead, but he showed no inclination and she couldn't read his face. That big dark broken-nosed hangdog face. She'd spent all her life pushing men away and now she couldn't get this one to advance a lousy couple of inches. She watched him go out the door and all the lonely nights for the rest of her days opened up before her.

He was climbing into the car when Pam came out and said, "I just phoned the hospital. Your friend is doing fine. We've got one of the best cosmetic surgeons in the country having a look at him tomorrow."

"Thanks," he said. "They've got a baby . . ." as if somehow that explained everything. Then he asked: "Your dad really have a Toyota dealership in Waco?"

"And died in his sleep from too many steaks? That's Anna's PR version, anyway. No, Dad killed himself when I was eight. Anna was always ashamed of it, as if it marked her somehow. She been weaving you tales?"

"Yeah, sort of."

"That's what she's good at. Anna's greatest talent has always been to create her own world and then suck everybody else into it."

Spandau got into the car. He waved at the marines and the gate opened and he drove home.

17

PEREC FOUND A WIG SHOP IN BEVERLY HILLS, THEN SPENT half an hour walking up and down in front of the shop before he worked up the courage to go in. All kinds of wigs lined the walls. The clerk was a small man of indeterminate age, and in spite of working in a wig shop, his own black-died backswept hair was thin and flecked with dandruff. He had dried spittle in the corners of his mouth.

"Can I help you?" the clerk asked him. He fixed a distasteful stare across the counter at Perec, who struck him as a vile little pervert. The clerk himself was a vile little pervert, so it was a safe call.

"I'd like a wig?"

"For yourself?"

"No. For . . . for my friend. A girl."

"It's best to bring her in and have her fitted."

"It's a surprise."

"Do you know her head size?"

"What?"

"How big is her head? What size?"

"I don't know." Perec felt himself go red and his stomach churn.

"Perhaps," said the clerk, doing his best Clifton Webb imitation, "you'd be happier in some other shop."

"No," said Perec, and pointed to a wig. "I want that one."

"The Anna Mayhew?"

"Yeah."

"Again, what size are we—"

"My size. The same size as my head."

"Would you like to try it on?"

"Yes," said Perec, smiling.

The clerk took out a tape measure and measured Perec's head.
He went into the back and in a few minutes came out with a box.
He pulled the honey-blond wig out of the box and came round
behind Perec and fitted the wig onto his head.

"There," said the clerk. "Would you like to see a mirror?"

"No. I'll take it."

"This one is eight hundred dollars . . ."

"I'll take it. This is the one I want."

That night Perec endured a bus ride downtown, carrying a small
duffel bag under his arm. He walked up and down past the strip
clubs and bars. Every so often a woman approached him and
asked if he wanted a date. Perec recoiled in horror. Finally Perec
saw the girl he wanted, a slim white girl a few inches taller than
himself. She had dark hair but she looked close enough. He had
trouble working up the nerve to go up to her. He'd never done

this before. The girl noticed him watching her. She stood there looking at him and Perec realized she was waiting for him. He went over to her.

"You shopping, honey, or just browsing? You looking to party?"

"I think so. Yes."

She looked him up and down. "You ever done this before?"

"No."

"You mean not with a girl, is that what you mean?"

"No, it's not—"

"Honey, it don't make any difference to me. What you got in the bag?"

"Some clothes."

"You want to dress up, I don't care, the price is the same. You want to dress me up, the price is higher. You want us both to put on a production of fucking *Romeo and Juliet,* then it gets even more. Which is it?"

"Just you," said Perec.

"Okay, fine. Come with me. It's a hundred dollars, plus thirty for the room. You give me the money and I pay the hotel."

"That's a lot. I didn't think—"

"High prices and spiraling inflation, honey. Don't you watch the news? It'll be worth it. I'll ride you like a bronco, baby. I'll rock your world. If you ain't got the money . . ."

"No, I've got it . . ."

Perec reached for his money. The girl stopped him.

"No, shit, goddamn, don't go waving it around out here. Pay me inside. Come on."

"What's you name?" Perec asked her.

"Chantarelle."

"Like the mushroom?" Perec asked.

"Like the what?" said Chantarelle. "It's French," she said.

They walked toward the girl's hotel past the open door of a bar. Chantarelle slowed down a bit as they went by and looked inside and gave the high sign to a black man sitting at the bar talking to a white guy.

"Fucking Kiri Te Kanawa, baby," Special said to Vito. He watched Chantarelle lead the scrawny little john past the door and toward the hotel down the street. "Now that woman got a voice."

Vito made a face of mock horror. "What's some fucking kiwi fucking may-ori goddamn jungle bunny pardon me know about opera. Fucking Maria Callas, motherfucker. That bitch could sing."

"Yeah, yeah," said Special, "she's good, you know, she got the emotions all down and shit, but she ain't got the range. She fucking sound downright flat some of the time. But she got the soul, I give you that."

"Now, fucking Caruso—" said Vito.

"Don't, don't," said Special. "I don't want to hear that Italian shit again."

"Us fucking guineas invented opera," Vito said defensively.

"Well, you know, the goddamn French got an opinion on that, and maybe the fucking Greeks, you know, singing through them fucking masks at Plato and shit."

Vito took a swig of his beer. "What the fuck do you know. My ancestors conquered the entire known world and yours were fucking running around dressed up like fucking lions and chucking spears at each other and shrinking each other's heads."

"There you go. You always got to go racial on me. You paint your white ass in a corner you can't get out of, and then you got to go racial. I know how this works. It don't win the argument."

"Fuck you," said Vito. "You finished with that José Carreras CD I lent you?"

"I got it in the car. I'll give it to you tomorrow."

"Fucking Kiri Te Kanawa," said Vito. "You'll be giving me black motherfuckers next."

"Paul Robeson," said Special. "Leontyne Price. Kathleen Battle."

" 'Old Man River' don't fucking count."

"The fuck it don't."

"You're a fucking savage. I don't even know why I talk to you."

"So you can fucking learn something about opera," said Special.

A door opened at the back of the room. A man in a leather jacket stepped out and motioned for Vito to come in. Vito drained his beer, gave Special a friendly slap on the back, and disappeared into the back room. Special fitted a Bluetooth phone set into one ear and put an iPod plug in the other. He tickled the iPod until he found the music he wanted, then motioned to the bartender for another beer.

Perec followed Chantarelle upstairs to the room. The hallway smelled of Lysol over puke. She unlocked the door and went in and tossed her purse onto a chair. Perec stood just inside the doorway.

"Close the door," she said to him, "unless you fixing to run away."

Perec stepped in and closed the door, still clutching the duffel tightly under his arm.

"What you got in the bag?"

Perec opened the bag, held it out for her to see. She looked inside. It contained a green dress and a blond wig.

"What you want me to do?"

"I want you to wear them," said Perec.

"Well, I figured one of us was," she said. "Then what?"

Perec didn't know what to say.

"You going to jack off, you got to do it in the toilet paper. You want me to jack you off, I charge the same thing. Pussy, hand, it's all the same to me. You want me to suck you?"

"No!" said a shocked Perec.

"You want to dress me?"

Perec nodded.

Chantarelle smiled and said, "Oh yeah. You going to like this, ain't you. You got that look. Oh, I bet you come long before I got to do anything."

Chantarelle began to undress as Perec stood there with the bag under his arm and watched her. She undressed slowly, doing a little swaying dance. She had a good body and she ran her hands up and down her torso, wiggling her fingers slowly like she was playing something quiet on a flute. She unhooked her bra and snaked down her panties, looking at Perec and smiling and licking her lips. Sometimes she closed her eyes and moaned a little as she touched a breast or between her legs. She watched Perec's face and laughed.

"Oh, you liking this, I can tell. You are liking what you see. You looking at these hard little titties and this pussy, oh man, you want to feel this pussy it's so good . . ."

She touched herself, smiled.

"Let me see it," she said to him. "I bet it's hard. I bet its throbbing right now like it got a mind of its own."

Perec shook his head, though he was clearly excited. His face was flushed and his lips were dry. There was that sick feeling in his gut and That Thing was happening Down There, but he was too excited now to feel ashamed, he did nothing to hide it or stop it.

"Well, come on then," she said. "Let's do it."

Perec took the dress and wig out of the bag and laid them out carefully on the bed. Chantarelle stood naked in the middle of the room, a hand on one hip. Perec picked up the dress and went over and carefully put the dress over Chantarelle's head, let it slide down to cover her arrogant nakedness. She reached out and touched his Down There and Perec leaped backward and she laughed. Perec took the wig and slowly put it on her head, as if it were the crown of Britain. He stood back and looked at her then tucked some loose strands of her dark hair away.

"I look like her now?" she said.

"Yes," said Perec. His throat was very tight and dry.

"What's her name? You want to call me her name while we do it?"

Perec shook his head.

"What now?"

"I want to cut your hair," he said to her.

"Shit you do."

"Not your hair. Not really. Just the wig."

"You got me up here to haircut a fucking wig?"

Perec just looked at her.

"What the fuck," she said, shrugging.

There was a small desk and chair. Chantarelle sat in the chair facing the stained wall. Perec stood for a long time behind her, just looking at the back of her head. Finally he reached out and stroked the blond hair. It made him dizzy and his breathing quickened.

"You going to jack off, you do it on the dress, okay? I don't want to be cleaning your jiz off the back of my neck."

Perec reached into his pocket and took out the straight razor. He opened it and after a few moments picked up a strand of the wig and began to cut. Chantarelle felt the small tugs, but she'd been waiting for the snip of scissors or the burr of electric clippers.

"What the fuck you doing? That ain't no scissors. What the fuck you using?"

She spun around, saw the razor in his hand, and jumped out of the chair.

"You didn't say nothing about no fucking razor. You got to put that thing away now."

"That's how I want to do it."

Chantarelle said quickly, "Okay, baby, but I got to think about this. You done scared the piss right out of me with that thing. I got to go pee, I'll be right back, okay?" and went into the bathroom with her purse. She locked the door and got out her cell phone and called Special.

Special had moved to a booth in a corner of the bar, where he sat eating a plate of fried calamari, listening to Frederica von Stadt sing one of Canteloube's *Songs of the Auvergne* and leafing through the *Opera Times*. Domingo was talking about a massive staging of the complete *Ring Cycle* in L.A. Special had only seen them performed on DVD—he had the German TV set—and wondered if he could actually sit through something like sixteen hours of Kraut opera. He thought it was something he probably ought to do, as a sign of serious dedication, and then he'd never have to do it again. The back door opened and the guy in the leather jacket peered out again and then Vito came walking out with a large Ralph's bag full of something and rolled and stapled shut at the top. Vito had a serious look on his face, which Special would have thought about if he hadn't been so excited about the Wagner article.

As Vito walked past, Special said, "It says here that—"

"Yeah, yeah, later," said Vito, and walked out the front door. Special went back to his *Opera Times* and there was a squeal of brakes outside and the sound of a crash. Special jumped up and went to the door and Vito was lying in the middle of the street. A car was up on the sidewalk half buried in garbage from the trash containers it had plowed into. Special ran out to Vito, who was clearly in agony but still clasping the paper bag.

"Oh man," said Special, "oh fuck . . ."

Vito was shaking and barely able to talk, but he motioned for Special to bend down and said, "You got to take this!"

"What?"

"You got to take this fucking bag!" said Vito. "The cops are going to be here in a minute. You got to take the bag to Jimmy Costanza. You got it? Now take the fucking bag!"

Special took it.

"Now get the fuck out of here," said Vito, and put his head down and started crying. An Orthodox rabbi was now walking up and down in front of the car, shouting loudly in Hebrew to nobody in particular and frantically trying to dial something on his cell phone.

Already there was the sound of sirens and Special slowly walked away with the bag. He walked around the corner toward his car then gave in to curiosity and peeked into a small hole that had been made in the bag. A very large amount of money. Special swallowed hard and tried to remember where the hell it was that

Jimmy Costanza hung out so he could unload this as soon as humanly possible. He thought about turning around and going back into the bar he'd just left, just handing it back to them, but there'd be cops all over the place and he didn't think the boys in the back room would appreciate that. Then his cell phone rang and he answered it without thinking. It was Chantarelle.

"Where the fuck you been?" she said to him in a hoarse whisper.

"I got a thing happening," Special said. "Can you speak louder? We got a bad connection or something."

"You got to get your ass up here. This fucker's got a razor."

"A razor? What kind of razor?"

"Well, pardon my fucking ass while I go out there and ask him what brand it is. It's a fucking razor, and he's a fucking wackadoo. You got to get up here."

"Where are you now?"

"I'm in the bathroom, taking the longest goddamn piss known to man. You fucking get up here, now!"

"Baby, I got to—"

"Now!"

"Okay, okay . . ."

Special thought about putting the bag in the car. Then he remembered the neighborhood. Carrying the bag, he headed toward the hotel. He trudged up the stairs to Chantarelle's room and knocked on the door.

"That you?" Chantarelle yelled from somewhere inside.

"Yeah, its me. Open the goddamn door."

"I can't get to it."

"Shit," said Special. Through the door he said, "Motherfucker, whoever you are, I advise you to open this door."

No reply.

"Break it down!" said Chantarelle.

"I ain't wanting to break down the goddamn door," said Special. "Just open the door, motherfucker, and everything will be fine."

"Break it down!" cried Chantarelle. "Break it down!"

"Okay," Special called to her, "I'm going to break down this goddamn door, but it's coming out of your wages. You better be in some serious fucking danger, is all I got to say."

Still holding the bag, he started kicking at the door. It was a cheap-ass door but it still took half a dozen good stomps. Special was out of breath when it finally splintered at the lock and opened. Perec stood in the middle of the room with the razor in his hand.

"First thing you got to do, motherfucker," Special said to him, "is put that razor away. Then we got to talk."

Perec just gave him a frozen, wide-eyed stare.

"Now I've done broke down the goddamn door and you've got my whore in the bathroom scared shitless. You throw that fucking razor on the bed or I am fixing to get angry."

Perec's eyes kept darting to the open door.

"You want to go," Special said to him, "I got no problem with that. Chantarelle, he pay you?"

"No," said Chantarelle.

"What the fuck?" said Special. "What about Basic Whoring 101? What about always collect the fucking money before you start? What about that?"

"I was about to collect. Then the fucker pulled out that razor."

"You see what happens when you don't follow the program? Now we got a goddamn situation. How much he owe you?"

"A hundred and thirty."

"Okay," Special said to Perec, "you put a hundred and thirty on the bed and you can go."

Perec fished around for the money with one hand, threw it on the bed. Special thought for a second, then said, "And there's the goddamn door. That's at least seventy-five."

"Fuck the door," said Chantarelle from the bathroom.

"I told you I ain't paying for the goddamn door," he said to her. "I ain't going to leave here looking like no fool." To Perec he said, "Now, you put down another seventy-five and I'll slide right out of the way."

"Let him go!" said Chantarelle.

Special was getting irritated now. He was about to tell her to shut her goddamned piehole and let him handle this when Perec made a break past him for the door. Still holding the bag of money, Special reached out with his free hand and grabbed Perec by the collar as he went by. He tugged and swung Perec back into the room. Perec sprang forward again and cut Special across the chest.

"Shit," said Special, truly surprised, because the little bastard didn't look at all like the sort of guy who'd do that.

"Special?" cried Chantarelle. "Honey? You okay? Special? Baby?"

Special watched the front of his shirt blossom into red and felt warm liquid pour down into his belt. He put his hand to it and his finger sank into a narrow opening across his belly. He looked at the blood pouring now down over his trousers and onto his good Ferragamo shoes and felt tired. He stepped back and thankfully found the wall and slid to a sitting position on the floor. He remembered the bag and saw it over next to Perec. The small hole in the bag had opened and several large bills had fallen out. Perec stared at it.

"Motherfucker," said Special, "don't even think about it . . ."

Perec picked up the bag. Special tried to rise but he could feel the cut in his belly yawn. He started to crawl toward the bag but Perec slashed at him again and opened a three-inch gash in his shoulder. Special lay on his face and grabbed Perec's pant leg and Perec cut his hand and stepped over him.

"Special, honey? You okay?" Chantarelle said from the bathroom. She opened the door a crack and the room looked empty, but then she saw Special on the floor. She stepped out and saw the blood and him just lying there on his face. She started screaming.

Special thought: This is a really stupid way to die but at least I don't have to worry about the goddamn money.

He was wrong.

18

THAT NIGHT PEREC SAT IN ANNAWORLD, GOOGLING ANNA, as always. The money sat in a nice neat pile in the middle of the floor. He'd counted it—over a hundred thousand dollars. Perec knew it was probably drug money and that they'd be looking for it. Maybe if they looked long enough they could find him, but he didn't care. There was something he'd been thinking about that made all that pointless. He'd discovered Anna was going to Cannes, that she'd been invited as a judge for the film festival. Perec had actually been born near Nice and gone back there once as a child, when his father was still around, before his mother had become crazed by God. He remembered the place as being airy and full of light. He could imagine Anna there. It would be a good place for her, though he didn't know about all those people around her. Anna was going to the place of his birth. Perec thought this was some kind of sign, though he didn't know from whom or what, since he didn't believe in God. Perec didn't know what he believed in. Probably nothing, it seemed. Anyway Perec would go to Nice. He would find Anna, and he would do it there. Perec looked at the money. He wasn't quite sure why he took it, except that he was angry at the Negro who kept trying to get money from him. He supposed it was a good thing he'd done it, taken the money, because now he certainly had enough to do whatever he wanted. More than enough to go to Nice. More than enough to find Anna.

He went to work the next morning and thought about it all day. The thought of going away made him happy, and he took his time going home because he knew his mother would spoil it for him, that his happiness would stop the moment he walked in the door. And it was true. When he finally went home he opened the door and smelled her smell and her sharp, piercing voice cut him worse than his own razor.

"Where have you been?"

"I stopped at the grocery. For some coffee."

"You're lying. It doesn't take that long."

"I took a longer way home . . ."

"You see, I've caught you lying. You're a liar, you're like your father, you lie about everything. I know where you go, the things you do. I know where all of you go."

"All of who?"

"Men. Filthy men. How many whores have you touched? How many whores have you touched today?"

"Stop it."

"I should have cut it off when you were born. I thought about it. I thought about taking scissors and cutting it off, to free you, so that you could be a decent man. And now you're filthy and a liar like all the rest. Come here. Come here and pray."

"Maman, no, please."

"Come here, I said! Come here or you'll be in the street! Come here or I'll cut you off without a dime, I'll change my will. I'll leave it all to the church, every cent of it! I swear!"

Perec went over and knelt with her. They prayed. Or rather Maman prayed as Perec watched her. When she was done he helped her back into her chair.

"I have to go," she said.

"I'll get it ready."

Perec went into the bathroom. The undergarments he'd washed for her were hanging on a line over the bathtub. They sickened him. He tore them down, pulled the line from the wall, and carried it into the living room, where he went up quickly behind Maman and, crossing his arms, put the line over her head and around her neck. He pulled and the line tightened and he pulled harder still. He put his knee against the back of Maman's chair and pulled until his body shook.

Maman made no vocal noises because none could escape. She grabbed at the line and twitched and kicked her legs. She clawed and clawed with those horrible hands at the line, then tried to reach for Perec over the back of the chair. She kicked and farted loudly and Perec smelled shit and urine but she still kept struggling. It seemed to take forever, far longer than he could have imagined. She finally stopped struggling and went limp, but Perec did not trust her and kept pulling on the line.

Two, three minutes went by. Perec had lost the idea of time. He stopped simply because his own arms were shaking and weak. When he loosed the line she didn't move. Perec went in front of her and slapped her hard several times. He'd wanted to hit her as far back as he could remember, and now he was surprised to feel nothing, nothing at all. He turned off the television.

Perec went out and walked to a hardware store a few blocks

away. He bought a sheet of heavy plastic, a roll of duct tape, fifty yards of rope, and a nonslip block-and-tackle pulley. The girl at the cash register smiled and talked to him about the weather. She was young and petty and had small even teeth. Perec for once did not hate her. Perec said, Yes, it's a beautiful day, I wish it were always like this.

He went home and wrapped Maman in the plastic and taped it securely and dragged her into his room. He stood on his chair in the closet and pushed open the trapdoor and climbed up into AnnaWorld. Using some of the rope, he fixed the pulley to a beam and fed the rope down through the pulley with the ends resting like confused snakes at Maman's feet. He climbed down and moved the chair and wrapped the rope again and again around Maman's ankles.

Then he pulled and Maman slowly rose into the air, as if, at last, heaven had accepted her. As he hoisted her, Maman stared at Perec. She looked surprised and stupid and her false teeth had slipped and lay askew in her mouth. Perec pulled and Maman disappeared through the trapdoor. He checked to see that the pulley would not slip and then he climbed up after her, pushing her plastic cocoon aside so he could enter.

He was tired and he sat there for a while watching her sway back and forth. Her clothing and her weight had shifted down and the bottom of the cocoon bulged, making her look very much like a smoked ham. Perec thought this was quite funny. Maman liked ham but always thought it too expensive.

He pulled up the other end of the rope and then sat in front of the computer and did a Google to see how much a ticket to France would cost.

19

Greed," said Chantarelle. "Greed is what got your ass cut."

"What got my ass cut," said Special, "is me having to get money out of a crazy motherfucker who should have paid you first. That's what got my ass cut."

They were leaving the hospital and walking toward Chantarelle's car in the parking lot. Special was in pain and hobbled along. Every step hurt. Breathing hurt. He didn't feel like talking. He thought about taking a swipe at her, but they'd warned him about fast movements. Like he needed to be reminded.

"How are the girls?" he asked her.

"Eddie been coming around."

"I see one of you bitches talking to Eddie and you going to wind up in the hospital like that cocksucker Eddie when I find him."

"You know he was going to come around when he heard you was out of business."

"I look out of business to you? I could have my fucking liver hanging out down around my ankles and I could still take that fucking Eddie. Goddamn stupid bitches, I ought to just give your ass to him, you ain't doing my ass any good, forgetting to get paid. Yeah, you go on with Eddie. Eddie'll treat you right."

"Ain't nobody going off with Eddie. Everybody knows about him."

"That's right. A woman got it good with Special, everybody knows that. You think you can do better, you go right off. You go on to Eddie. He'll fix you right up. He'll be pushing that shit through your veins and everything you make'll feed that. You be looking like fucking Grandma Moses in a year."

"I ain't going nowhere. I got it good with you."

"Goddamn right you do. Stupid goddamned bitch, ain't got sense enough to collect her goddamn money."

"I get you home, I'll take care of you. Put you in bed and feed you soup."

"Fuck a bunch of soup," said Special. "You still got that bag that motherfucker left?"

"It's at the hotel."

"Take me there."

"Doctor said you got to rest. Them stitches . . ."

"Fuck the doctor, the doctor ain't let some crazy little motherfucker run off with a shitload of the Mob's dough. I got to get that money back."

They drove by the hotel. Special sat in the car while Chantarelle went up and got the bag. She brought it back and Special looked at the wig and the dress. The dress was from some off-the-rack collection he'd never heard of, but he figured it wouldn't be traceable. On the other hand, the wig looked expensive and had a Beverly Hills label in it. Well, that was a start. Now he had to go find Jimmy Costanza and explain to him why he didn't have the money, because Jimmy was right about now trying to explain the same thing to his boss, Salvatore Locatelli, whose money it actually was. Nobody was going to be happy.

Chantarelle pulled up in front of Special's apartment building. She parked and started to get out of the car.

"Where the hell you going?"

"I'm going to come up, fix you some soup, like I said."

"Fuck that. You ain't making me no money playing goddamn Florence Nightingale. Get your ass to work and see if you can make me enough this evening to replace that Ralph's bag you cost me."

She drove away and Special, carrying Perec's bag and his own little bag of medicines the hospital gave him, started toward the front door of his apartment building. He was nearly inside when he saw the two guys walking quickly toward him. He didn't recognize them personally but he knew the look. He barely got through the security door before they did. They watched him through the glass and he cursed the elevator and it opened and he cursed it all the way up to his floor. He got out and walked down the hall fishing for his keys and had just unlocked the door when they came bounding out of the stairwell and pushed him into the apartment.

"Now, guys," said Special.

"My name is Sam," said the bigger one. "That's Donnie."

"Nice to meet you," said Donnie.

Sam walked Special over to a chair in the dining room and sat him down.

"You okay?" Sam asked him. "I heard you got cut pretty bad."

"I been better," said Special.

"How many stitches?"

"Seventy-two on the stomach. Twelve on the shoulder. Six on the hand."

Sam winced.

"Ooh, shit," said Donnie.

"But you're okay now?" said Sam. "I mean, they fixed you right up and everything?"

"Yeah, they sewed me right up."

"Thank God for modern medicine, right?" said Sam.

"Fucking-A, man," said Donnie.

"Good," said Sam. "You know who we are?"

"I got a pretty good idea."

"Great," said Sam. "Now where is it?"

"I don't have it."

"You don't have it," repeated Sam. "Uh-huh."

"Oops," said Donnie.

"That crazy freak who cut me run off with it."

"And where would he be?" asked Sam.

"I dunno," said Special. "I told you, he cut me and run off."

"Uh-huh," said Sam.

"Not good, not good," said Donnie.

Sam and Donnie looked at each other. Sam shook his head wearily and sighed at the floor.

"Let me have the tape," he said to Donnie.

"I didn't bring the tape," said Donnie.

"Didn't I fucking tell you we might need the tape," said Sam.

"I thought you said you already had the tape, all you needed was the other thing," said Donnie.

"Jesus. Okay, gimme your fucking belt."

"Why my belt?"

"Because you forgot the fucking tape, that's why."

Donnie took off his belt and gave it to Sam.

"You move," Sam said to Special, "and I am going to hit you really hard."

He began to strap Special's ankles to the chair.

"Guys, I think this might be something we should talk about, guys."

"Put your hands behind you," Sam told him.

"Guys, I think we really ought to—"

Sam hit him, really hard.

They moved his hands behind him. Donnie held them.

"You see how much easier this would be," Sam said to Donnie, "with the fucking tape?"

"Man, you got to be clearer about your requests," said Donnie. "I ain't taking all the blame. We're out of belts."

Sam looked at him and then took off his own belt and gave it to Donnie. Donnie smiled and bound Special's hands behind the chair.

"I'm going to ask you one more time," Sam said to Special.

"Look, give me a couple of days and I'll find the fucker, I swear I will."

"You said you didn't know where he is."

"I got connections all over the place. I'm like a fucking bulldog. I'll find the motherfucker. I swear to God."

"You believe him?" Sam asked Donnie.

"I think he means well," said Donnie.

"Yeah, sure, what the hell," said Sam, and shrugged.

"You letting me go?" Special asked.

"Nah," said Sam. "We're just fucking with you."

"It relieves the tension," said Donnie. "Ours, anyway."

Sam tore open Special's shirt. He grabbed one corner of the large bandage covering Special's chest and pulled hard. Special screamed.

"You didn't cover his mouth," Sam said to Donnie.

"You didn't say anything about it," said Donnie.

"Find something and cover his fucking mouth, will you. Jesus."

Donnie went and looked around the apartment and came back with a small sofa pillow. Sam looked at him quizzically and Donnie just shrugged. Sam reached into his pocket and took out a pair of needle-nose pliers.

"Where is it?" Sam asked Special.

"Guys," said Special, "there's got to be some way we can—

Sam nodded to Donnie and Donnie covered Special's face with the sofa pillow. Sam reached over and grabbed one of the stitches and yanked it loose. Special's scream filled the pillow and Donnie had to hold it tightly to keep it over Special's face as Special's head thrashed back and forth. When Special stopped screaming and thrashing Donnie lowered the pillow.

"Ouch," said Donnie.

"I bet that hurt like a motherfucker," Sam said to Special. "I figure we got about twenty or so of these bastards before you start bleeding to death or tell us the truth."

"Goddamn, I told you—"

The pillow again. Another stitch. Scream.

"Talk to me," said Sam.

"I swear to God, I swear on my mother's grave, I'm telling the truth . . ."

"You think he's telling the truth?" Sam asked Donnie.

"I believe him," said Donnie.

"Well," said Sam, "I figure we'll know for sure in about"—he looked closely at the stitches—"three inches."

Another stitch, another scream.

Then another.

It was, for Special, a very long night.

20

THEY WERE IN THE HOSPITAL AGAIN. THE DOCTORS HAD resewn the ten stitches Sam had less than artfully removed. Special told the doctors he'd caught them on something. The doctors knew he was lying, but they also knew he was a pimp and they didn't care. This time Chantarelle and one of his other girls, Micki, a small slim girl with short boyish blond hair, pushed him out to the car in a wheelchair. Special was very tired.

"I got two weeks," Special said to them, "to come up with one hundred and forty-seven thousand dollars and fifty-three cents. How much you got on you?"

"That's a joke, right?" said Micki. She actually wasn't sure.

"Yes, baby," said Special. "It's a joke."

"What you going to do?" Chantarelle asked him.

"I am going to find that little motherfucker," said Special, "and I am going to cut off his balls and shove them inside his goddamn mouth and then I am going to see how far I can shove that head up his own rectum. Then," continued Special, "I am going to find some way of seriously hurting him. But not before the little

fucker gives me that money. Tell me again," he said to Chantarelle, "how he cut your hair."

"Wasn't my hair," said Chantarelle. "It was the wig."

"I know that," said Special. "You say he cut it like a pro, like
maybe he did this for a living. Like a barber or something."

"Just like a hairdresser," said Chantarelle. "He knew what he
was doing."

"Uh-huh," said Special.

It was nearly lunchtime when Special went into the wig shop in
Beverly Hills. The clerk, a man of indeterminate age with thin
hair and spittle in the corners of his mouth, looked Special up
and down with as much condescension as he could muster. Special pulled the wig out of a paper bag and showed it to him.

"And?" said the clerk.

"You sold this."

"Yes, probably," said the clerk. "It's an Anna Mayhew. Very
popular."

"Your tag is in it."

"Then I guess we sold it," said the clerk.

"You know who you sold it to?"

"No," said the clerk.

"There's a serial number on the label," said Special. "You record the serial numbers?"

"Not necessarily," lied the clerk.

"I see," said Special.

The clerk smiled. "We're getting ready to close for lunch," he
said.

"Is that a fact. You the only guy who works here?"

"During days I'm the one," said the clerk. "It's not horribly labor-intensive."

"I don't reckon it is," said Special. He studied the clerk. Mid-forties. Not married, but not queer—leastways he doesn't know it yet. Lives with his fucking auntie. I could offer him money but money ain't his real problem, thought Special. Hmm.

Special went out onto the sidewalk and called Micki. "Get your ass down here," he said to her, "and come dressed for school."

Micki showed up fifteen minutes later, just as the clerk was closing up for lunch. She was dressed like an English public-school boy—short flannel pants, white shirt, blazer with a little school crest on it. (If you looked closely it said *Fellashi U.*) A cute little cap. Special took her inside.

"This is my friend Micki," Special said to the clerk. The clerk looked at Micki. Then he looked at Special. Then he looked at Micki, for a long time. Then he looked at Special and raised his eyebrows.

"Micki is just fascinated by wigs," said Special. "Aren't you, Micki?"

"I am," said Micki. "I really am." She looked at the clerk with her large blue eyes and began sucking the small finger of her right hand.

"Micki likes to dress up. Likes to play games and all that sort of thing. Micki is really special. She's also an artist. Micki, draw the nice man a picture."

Micki, who studied art on her days off, took out a small notebook and skillfully but quickly produced a small sketch. She smiled impishly and handed it to the clerk.

"Jesus," said the clerk, looking at it and turning pale.

"Micki," said Special, "would like to have lunch with you."

"I really would," said Micki.

"What's it going to cost me?" asked the clerk.

"Half an hour with Micki here for that address."

"I could lose my job."

"There are other jobs," said Special, "but there is only one Micki."

"Oh God," said Micki, and began rubbing her crotch.

"What is it?" asked the clerk.

"I'm about to peak," said Micki.

"Pee?" said the clerk. "You need the bathroom?"

"Peak," said Special. "I told you she was unique."

"You mean . . . ?" said the clerk.

"I figure you got about a minute and a half," Special told him, "or the party starts without you."

"I don't know the guy's home address," the clerk said quickly as he watched Micki wriggle. "It was a business account, a credit card, some beauty shop over on Western."

"Give it to me," said Special.

"Oh God," said Micki, rubbing her legs together. "Oh God."

The clerk glanced at his watch, then ran into the back office. He came out exactly thirty seconds later with an address scribbled on a piece of paper. He handed it to Special, then glanced at his watch.

"You got a minute left," said Special. As he walked out he said to Micki, "Don't hurt him."

"Not too much I won't," said Micki.

The clerk was frantically locking the door behind him. Special saw Micki grab his hand and drag him into the back. Special looked at the address and chuckled to himself. There were many

games Micki liked to play, some of them involving the introduction of unorthodox objects into snug places, not necessarily hers.
Half an hour with Micki was like taking a Disney gondola through
Teddy Bear Land and winding up in the kitchen of the Marquis
de Sade. Special genuinely hoped the poor bastard hadn't packed
his own lunch, otherwise he'd spend the rest of the day pulling
bits of a bacon-and-tomato sandwich out of his wazoo. Not, Special thought, that he'd probably mind it.

21

SPECIAL FOUND THE BEAUTY SHOP ON WESTERN. PEREC wasn't there, which was a relief in a way because Special didn't want to half kill him in front of witnesses. Much better to find the little fucker at home and surprise him on the shitter or something.

There were a couple of Filipino girls cutting hair in the shop. One of them wasn't bad-looking and Special wished he had a couple like her working for him. This was a trade hazard, every good-looking woman you met you wondered automatically how much she could turn on the street, and you wondered what it would take to turn her. There were pimps who were convinced every woman could be turned, that there was a part of every woman that wanted to whore, all you had to do was create the right circumstances. Special was willing to believe there was some part of every woman that was a whore, but there was a big difference between getting her to fuck someone for you once and getting her to do it five or six times a night month after month. You could put a bitch on the street and tell her you were going to whip her ass if she didn't make you some money. Or you could give her a habit that would keep her there. Neither way made any sense to Special. Beating a whore was like kicking around a goddamn melon and then trying to sell it. Besides, it took too much effort.

They say, Special, you ain't nothing but a goddamn pimp, where you get off coming on so uppity?

And I say, I ain't doing nothing that the big boys don't do. Politicians, CEOs, popes, movie producers, fucking generals in the field. I form a company, I got my employees, I find out what the customer needs, and I sell them that product and I make me a little money.

GM sells cars and I sell pussy.

I'm willing to bet the quality of my pussy is better than the quality of them cars.

What's your fucking argument again?

Special said, "That little guy that works here, he around?"

"You mean Vincent?"

"About so tall? Popped-out sort of eyes, like that guy in the Bogart movies?"

"You mean Peter Lorre," said Imelda. "Yeah, that'd be Vincent. No, he's not here. He ain't been in for a couple of days. Said he wanted to take some time off."

"Sounds like you got a pretty obliging boss."

"Vincent is the boss. Or at least his mother is. She owns the place and Vincent runs it."

The shop was quiet. Special was leaning against the counter at the register. Imelda sat on the stool across from him. She had dark eyes and perfect white teeth and skin like very pale chocolate. A tight little body with that pink smock unbuttoned a few extra holes and them very fine titties on display. Oh, we could make some money okay. But you doing just fine on your own, ain't you. You got a job and big boyfriend at home and guys like me coming up and hitting on you all the time. You need the attention. You need men looking at you, wanting you. I got you figured now, honey. It ain't like rocket science.

"He's about an odd little squint, ain't he?" said Special.

"He's my boss, you know, I can't be talking about him."

"Oh sure, sure, I understand that. It's just that I met the little guy, you know, and we started talking and he was into some strange shit, if you know what I mean."

"He told you?"

"Well, you know, me and him had a couple."

"I didn't know he drank," said Imelda. "His mama half kill him, I guess. Poor little . . ."

"Vincent, yeah, all that stuff about dressing up . . ."

"Dressing up? You mean . . ."

"Wig and everything," said Special. "Right down to the thong panties."

"Oh my Lord."

"And scared to death of his mama, old Mrs. . . ."

"Perec."

"Yeah, she sounds like a holy terror, that one. No wonder little Vinnie as squirrelly as a nutshell."

"She keeps him on a tight leash, all right. Everything's hers— the shop, the money, the house, everything. She don't turn loose of nothing, that one, and cheap as the day is long. Can't keep nobody here on what she's willing to pay. You know she takes half of everything we make?"

"Bet she's loaded. Them are the ones that are. Got a big house somewhere, probably."

"Nah, they got a dumpy little place over near the cemetery. I drove him home once. Looks like the Addams Family except smaller."

"Well, you see him, tell him old Bob dropped by to see him."

"You sure you don't want a haircut?"

"Maybe next time."

"I do a real good head-and-neck massage," she said.

"Oh baby, I just bet you do. But I got to be running now. I'll come back."

"You do that," said Imelda.

Special went out to the car and pulled out the *Thomas Guide*. He found the Angelus Cemetery and started calling information, looking for a Perec on the streets nearby. He hit it after four tries.

Imelda was right, the place looked like a cut-rate haunted house, even in broad daylight. Special drove by a couple of times. Didn't appear to be anybody moving around inside. It was a mixed neighborhood and Special figured it was safe for a black man to get out of the car, nobody going to call the cops to report a roving nigger. He parked and went up to the house, nearly breaking his ankle on a loose piece of sidewalk.

He knocked on the door. Waited. No sound. He stood on the porch and looked around. Nobody watching that he could see, and even if there were, this wasn't the sort of place where they got together for Neighborhood Watch. You get south of Wilshire and it's every asshole for himself. He went around to the back. No dog, no cat, nobody. He took a pair of gloves out of his pocket and pulled them on. He tried the back door and when it didn't open he put his fist in the pocket of his jacket and rammed it through one of the small glass panes. It didn't break but popped

right out of the ancient caulking. He reached in and opened the
door.

It reminded him of his grandma's house when he was a kid.
No proper cabinets but open shelves and a curtain across the
bottom of the sink. A Formica table with a couple of ass-split
plastic-and-metal chairs. Everything neat but ready to fall apart,
a badly preserved museum to the 1950s. It even smelled like old
lady, like talc and tired sweat. He went into the living room. An
overstuffed chair and a thousand-year-old TV. Pictures of Jesus
on the wall. Checked the bathroom: denture cleaner and laxa-
tives. A half-empty box of Depends. Damn, that's an ugly fucking image. Checked a bedroom: thankfully no fucking old broad
asleep on the dark narrow bed under the painting of Christ and
the map of France. Next bedroom: this is his, the little bastard,
like a goddamn monk's cell. Where is the money, you miserable
little cocksucker? Not that many places to look. Special looks
anyway. Under the bed, in the bureau, in the closet. And there's
this smell, like shit or something . . .

Special looks up. There a small brown stain on the plywood
trapdoor. Special stands on the chair, pushes it open. A drop
falls on his face. Goddamn! Wipes it off, smells his shirtsleeve:
shit, piss, and just a little something extra. Looks up again and
there's Maman, hanging like a shrink-wrapped bat, staring at him
through the small brown pool that has formed in the bottom of
her plastic cocoon.

Special gags, nearly falls off the chair. Stands on the far side of
the room, trying to get back his breath and stop his heart wanting
to jump out of his chest. It now occurs to him what a truly strange
little fucker this Vincent Perec might actually be.

There was no way around it. He stood on the chair and tried
to slither up past the body. The liquid dripped onto his back and

legs. He gagged. He elbowed the carcass aside so he could climb up, it began swaying back and forth over the door. It was dark and hot and Special pulled a string and a light came on.

AnnaWorld stretched the length of the attic, a madman's jack-off palace. Pillows, a small mattress. Tissues and paper towels, the used ones filling a wicker wastebasket. Guess what Vinnie has been doing. Pictures of this actress Anna Mayhew everywhere. An old PC with a monitor and printer, plugged into a jerry-rigged phone jack coming out of the floor. Special searched. No money, but he found the empty bag. Shit.

In a drawer he found the nude pictures stained in blood. Oh my, what is this boy into. He turned on the PC. It came alive, no password needed. Special opened the files on the desktop. More downloaded photos of the Mayhew woman, articles. There was some sort of diary, pages of it. Special clicked on Google, and when it came up he looked at the search history. What you'd expect. He clicked on one of the last sites and it was a story about Anna Mayhew going to Cannes as a judge. A few articles like this. He clicked on one that contained *airfrance* and up popped ticket information and online registry. Hmm.

Special went back to the desktop and clicked a file that said *AFT* and opened up the documents for a one-way first-class ticket for Vincent Perec on Air France to Nice, France, leaving yesterday afternoon.

Special then opened up the diary and read twenty-some pages of lunatic drivel that told him more than anything anybody ever wanted to know about Vincent Perec, boy psychopath. It told, among other things, why Vincent Perec had murdered his mother. It told what he intended to do with Salvatore Locatelli's money. It told how much poor Vinnie loved Anna Mayhew and why. It told what he intended to do to Anna Mayhew.

But most of all, it made it very clear that Vincent Perec was not coming back, and why Special needed to get to Cannes as fast as the laws of physics would permit. Special carefully erased it all and turned off the computer. No reason to make it easy for the cops when they discovered all this, and he didn't want them to find Perec before he did. Needless to say, Maman had to hang there and ripen awhile longer. Special slid past her again, re-placed the trapdoor, wiped his footprints off the chair, and drove home to get his passport.

PART TWO

CANNES

1

SERGE VIGNON WOKE.

He pushed the cat off his face and sat up in bed, thanking God, as he always did first thing in the morning, that he was no longer married. The cat, Jane, a slim and elegant little tabby, climbed up into his lap and purred seductively. Sometimes Vignon woke up and was afraid to turn over lest he find his wife, Adèle, still there, puffing sourly on her side of the bed. He'd been doing this for three years. So far it appeared not to be a dream. Instead he woke with Jane sitting on his face, suffocating him, a not unpleasant state of affairs after a decade with Adèle.

He'd married her at thirty-seven, late for a Frenchman, after a lifetime of unsuccessful relationships with women. Lots of affairs, lots of broken hearts. He hated leaving them, so he'd connive ways of making them miserable until they left him. It seemed more diplomatic that way and he didn't mind being hated. At least until someone shot him. Also every morning he touched the tiny, puckered scar at his side where the bullet had entered and nearly lodged in his spleen, which reminded him of how close to dying he'd come. He'd done a lot of thinking in the hospital. He'd also had sex with his nurse, who came into his room without panties and performed happy but clinical blow jobs while he groped around beneath her starched white skirt.

He did not, of course, marry her for this. Vignon was an attractive man and oral sex is not exactly unheard of in France. It was later, when he was out of the hospital, and they began dating, then living together. Vignon marveled at her cool detachment, her efficiency, her cleanliness. There was something Zen-like about her that captivated him. She did not love him. He did not love her. It was wonderful, it was pure, it was untainted by all those stupid emotions that had gummed up his life before. They married and sailed toward a clean and open horizon.

For all of six months he relaxed in a kind of antiseptic conjugal bliss. Then slowly, insidiously, he began to understand the fallacy of his situation. He'd assumed that if two people didn't love each other in the first place, then it was impossible to fall out of love and into disappointment. And this was true, as far as it went. What he hadn't counted on, however, was that not loving each other in the first place didn't rule out the growth of mutual hatred, which happened blazingly fast.

Vignon and Adèle thought of murdering each other daily for ten years, a loathing that burned quietly like the flame of a pilot light. One day Adèle said to him, "I despise you, you know," and they embraced and Vignon went to help her pack. They'd not seen or spoken a word to each other since. Not long after, Jane showed up on his patio, small, sick, and scrawny. He fed her, gave her medicines, let her sleep in a box next to his bed. One day he woke up and she was sitting on his face, true love at last.

Vignon got up, naked, and pulled on a pair of jeans. He went into the kitchen and fed and watered Jane, then pulled a Gitane from the pack on the counter and went outside on the patio to smoke. Smoking was a vile dirty habit he allowed himself—he was virtually perfect in every other way—but never in the house.

His house was in Grasse on a mountainside above Nice, and the patio had a sweeping view above the city all the way to the sea. His parents had left him the property, it was where he'd vacationed as a child, and he knew it was valuable because Americans tried to buy it from him regularly. One of his great pleasures in life was turning them down. Today was a sunny day in May. A gentle breeze blew and he could spy sailboats and yachts in the Bay of Angels.

It was a perfect day to go up into the hill and climb, but he had to meet an American actress and her entourage at the airport. It was a bit after 7 a.m. and he still had three hours. He finished the cigarette and then went inside to the room he'd converted into a climbing gym. Plywood walls sloped at odd angles, covered with ceramic holds that mimicked bits of crag. They screwed loose and Vignon changed them every so often, creating routes for himself that would challenge his skills. The latest one had him climbing on the ceiling across the room. He'd not yet managed to get halfway across.

He pulled on a pair of cramped Italian climbing shoes and dipped his hands into a canvas bucket of chalk. He started climbing. He got halfway and dropped like a shotgunned mallard onto the mat. He needed to keep at it. After this business with the pain-in-the-ass Americans (they were always a pain in the ass, it was a foregone conclusion), he'd have enough money to make the climbing trip to the Dolomites. He'd hire a guide, spend two weeks climbing in fresh air, no cities, no cars, no goddamned Americans.

Bliss.

*   *   *

He was at the airport when the plane arrived. A small Goldstar, undoubtedly stuffed to bursting with every material possession they owned. Ah, Americans! The bedouin of Western civilization! Fortunately it was a movie star and nobody was actually going to check her baggage in case they actually found something. A representative from the festival was there to see that everything went smoothly.

Vignon was there because he'd been hired to be in charge of security, though now he'd been told the actress was bringing along her own personal bodyguard. Yeah, sure. Some lanky boy toy more likely, given the title in order to squeeze him somehow into the festival's budget. Instead she got off the plane with a smaller and more nervous version of herself and a big man with a face like a boxer.

The woman from the festival, Eva Schmidt, introduced herself and took the passports from the flight attendant. Then she introduced Vignon. Everyone shook hands, and when he got to the big American and looked into his face, he was pretty sure the man was what he claimed to be. The nest question was, why the hell was he here?

"Vignon is in charge of your security while you're here," said Mademoiselle Schmidt. "This has been explained?"

"Yes," said Pam. "It's all clear from the e-mails."

"I want Mr. Spandau to have full privileges," announced Anna. "He'll be coordinating everything."

They all stared at her. Then Vignon and Mademoiselle Schmidt looked at each other.

"I'm afraid that's not possible," said Mademoiselle Schmidt.

"This is why we have Monsieur Vignon. Monsieur Vignon is an ex-policeman and very experienced. He knows the city well."

"I don't care," said Anna, "if he's goddamn General Douglas MacArthur in a tutu. Mr. Spandau is in charge."

"I'm afraid what Mademoiselle Schmidt is trying to say," said Vignon, "is that there's the small matter of a license. French law requires that Mr. Spandau be properly vetted and registered, and under no circumstances would Mr. Spandau be allowed to carry arms."

"Does he look to you like he needs a gun?" Anna asked him.

"Then," said Vignon, playing his trump card, "there is the question of language. *Vous parlez français, non?*" he said to Spandau. Spandau shook his head and turned red. Vignon smiled. "You begin to see the problem."

"Where's the goddamn car?" Anna said, and pushed everyone forward.

The villa had once been a winery specializing in a very light and crisp rosé. Nobody knew why the winery had closed, since the rosé was said to have been pretty good. It was sold in the fifties to an English lord, who tried to live in it but couldn't stand the damp or the scorpions. It changed hands again three times after that, until a wealthy American couple bought it in the eighties and had it renovated. They hired a famous Italian architect who kept the outside shell of the place intact but created what was essentially an entirely new dwelling inside, a two-story structure that filled the cavernous space within two feet of the stone walls all around. This surrounding zone served to protect and circulate air around the place—sort of like double-glazing a window—

fixing the dampness problem and allowing all the ultramodern air-conditioning and plumbing Americans seemed to genetically require. It was a brilliant solution, and it was a pleasant surprise to open the old, heavy doors of the stone winery and step into a world of bright light and all the latest mod-cons.

Mrs. May, the English real-estate woman, met them outside. Anna marched past her like Mary Queen of Scots. Mrs. May jogged to keep up. She introduced Anna to the staff, a cook who looked like David Niven and a small middle-aged woman who did everything else. The cook spoke a little English and the woman spoke a little more. Anna chatted pleasantly to them, ignoring Mrs. May, who was twitching nervously behind her, desperate to show Anna the rest of the house in order to be able to rendezvous with her Spanish lover during the lunch break.

"Would you like to see the rest of the house?" said Mrs. May.

"What sort of cuisine do you prefer to cook?" Anna asked Franz the chef. She hated people standing behind her, trying to goad her on, and whenever somebody did it she stubbornly re-fused to move. She'd had people pushing at her all her life, and never once in that time had it turned out to be for her own good. The harder people pushed, the slower Anna advanced.

"Provençal," answered Franz. "Seafood, of course, and many Italian dishes."

"Sounds wonderful," said Anna. She turned to catch Mrs. May looking at her watch. This irritated the hell out of Anna. "Well, aren't you going to show me the house?" Anna said to her.

Mrs. May looked stricken but recovered quickly and began to lead her through the rooms. There was a huge vase of flowers on the dining-room table.

"These came for you this morning," said Elena, the housekeeper. "There are more in your room. There's also the fruit," motioning to a large basket on the sideboard.

The fruit would be from the festival committee. The French love fruit, thought Anna, maybe there is some sort of language of fruit here the way there is with flowers. An apple means love. An artichoke says, "I'm defensive." "I'm aroused," says a ripe peach, and a banana is pretty damned obvious.

Anna checked the card on the flowers, but she knew already who they were from. Andrei. He loved to send flowers, he thought it made him look like some sort of gentleman lothario. You couldn't read anything into the flowers, though, because he'd always have an assistant deal with them. Andrei never had the slightest idea what the hell they'd sent. Andrei wanted to live up to this image of himself as the Pushkin of cinema, but he hadn't a poetic bone in his body and substituted obscurity for profundity instead. It worked with most people. It had even worked for a couple of years with Anna. *It will be wonderful to see you again. Andrei,* said the card. No it won't, thought Anna. I won't let it.

Her room was a large self-contained suite upstairs. Bedroom, sitting room, bathroom like something out of *Caligula*. The sunken marble tub cried out for soapy orgies. No patio on the second floor (why the hell do the French call it the first?), that was downstairs, but the windows opened onto a large pool below and a spectacular view of the gardens and the hills. Maybe a couple of acres of land with a stone wall around it. She could see some grape trellises still in the garden. The vineyards had been sold off long ago, but she could imagine where they were, the look of them as they sloped gently down the hillside.

The sun struck her face and she believed she could smell lavender. It was heaven, this place, and she wondered for a fleeting moment why she'd never bought her own house here. She fell in love with the area every time she came. But she knew why. The thing is, she'd seen other actors do it and knew how it eventually played out. You talked about how great it was, how relaxed it made you, but in the end you never spent any time there. L.A. was where the work was, where the deals were made, where your people were, and where you were expected to be.

Everybody in Hollywood talked about the joys of Europe, but you spent too much time there and they started looking at you like you were a foreigner yourself, like you'd switched loyalties somehow—which, in effect, you had. They needed you to be as obsessed and frightened as they were, or else they couldn't trust you. Somebody happily farting about in their vineyards wasn't likely to accept the compromises and anxiety required to be a star. Shit, they didn't actually want you to be happy at all, and any genuine attempt at it was perceived as a big Fuck You to the entire system. They needed you hungry—for love, for fame, for drugs, for money, they didn't care, as long as they knew you remained desperate for something they could dangle like a carrot over your head. No, it never paid to get too far away from the place.

Spandau was unpacking when Anna knocked on the door and popped her head in.

"What do you think?"

"A few more servants and I could probably make do," he said.

She came in, walked over to the window, and looked out.

"Not bad. My view's better."

"You're the star."

"That's right," she said. "I'm the star."

He continued to unpack. She picked up one of his books. *Blood and Thunder* by Hampton Sides.

"Cowboy stuff?"

"Yep."

"Somebody told me you did rodeo."

"It's a way of making up for the shyness."

She laughed. "Right, I can see that . . . God, I haven't seen a rodeo since I was a kid. My father used to take us. What event?"

"Tie-down roping. Bronc riding, when something isn't already broken."

"You any good at it?"

"Nope."

She looked at him.

"Look, you fucking want to go home, go home. You've got the ticket. You're not being held hostage. I just had this stupid idea you might enjoy yourself."

"I'm about as useful here as tits on a boar," he said to her. "You heard Vignon. I don't even speak the language. It's a joke."

"You're here because I want you here. You're here because it makes me feel better."

"That's right. You're the star."

"Kiss my ass," she said. "What do you want me to say? That I feel safer with you here? That I like you being here because I'm scared and sick and fucking tired of being surrounded by people I can't trust, people I don't respect and don't want to see? Okay, yes, I like it that you're here. I want you to be here."

"So you just write a check and here I am."

"Okay, great. If it's a money issue, I'll take you off the payroll and you can pony up your share of the rent on this place. That make your masculine ego feel better? Look, I can afford it. I have

to do this shit, the least I can allow myself is doing it with somebody I like."

"There's nothing for me to do, Anna," he said.

"Your job is to keep me safe, right? Well, I feel safe with you.
Mission accomplished. What are you bitching about?"

"Do you ever *not* get your way?" he asked her.

"No," she said. "Does this mean you're staying?"

"I don't know," he said. "Yeah, maybe."

"I told you you were stuck on me."

"That's it, you think?"

"Like a pissant on molasses. Only a matter of time before you
make love to me."

"This comes under the heading of sexual harassment, I think."

"It's only sexual harassment if you ain't got the same idea.
Otherwise it's just nature taking its course."

"It's not going to happen, Anna. I don't get involved with clients."

"Right. You coldhearted machine, you."

She blew him a kiss and sailed out of the room. Spandau
couldn't help smiling, she had that effect on him. He went back
to his unpacking.

2

THE COMMITTEE HAD ITS FIRST MEETING THE NEXT MORN-
ing at the Carleton. Franz had made a light breakfast but it was
impossible for Anna to eat. She drank a cup of coffee and sat and
watched Spandau and Pam scarf down eggs and bacon and she
hated them. She had no idea what to expect and she tried not
to think about it. How bad could it be? Then she thought again
about the number of people who'd be watching her every move,
and the idea of having to defend her views to a bunch of Euro-
pean intellectuals. Watching movies was one thing, talking about
them was another. The whole idea was ridiculous and she should
never have come. She was going to look like an idiot and there
was nothing she could do about it now.

At least Spandau was coming with her, she'd insisted on that.
He couldn't sit in on the meetings, but she'd gotten the okay to
take him along for the screenings, provided she didn't discuss the
films with him.

The meeting was at nine. Thierry, the driver, picked them up
at eight o'clock. They drove leisurely down the hill and into the

city, which was just coming alive. They were followed by a car
containing two of Vignon's men, making Spandau feel even more
ludicrous. Traffic wasn't too bad, but it would quickly get worse.
The population of Cannes nearly doubled during the festival and
driving became a nightmare. Thierry was good, and by 8:40 they
were in the elevator of the Carleton, on their way up to the suite
rented for the chairman of the jury.

"I'm a goddamn wreck," Anna said to Spandau as they stood
outside the door. "I should never have let myself get talked into
this."

"You'll be fine," he said.

"What are you going to do?"

"I'll be downstairs. Maybe I'll sit around the pool and ogle
naked woman like a true American. And I brought a book. You
need me, just call."

"Wish me luck."

Five of the seven panel judges were waiting when she walked in.

Albert Carrière, the chairman, was a leading French TV cul-
tural commentator. He looked like Baron Philippe Rothschild
and dressed as the baron did in casual pale sweaters and expensive neckties. He wasn't the smartest person in the room, but he
was the only one who looked like nobility and therefore the only
one fit to lead.

Slumped on the sofa was Beppo Contini, the Italian novelist
and literary critic, who wore a constantly bemused look behind
a large dark mustache. While he was an easygoing pleasant man
in person, Contini's novels were heavily left-wing and his book
reviews were scathing. They called him "the Organ Grinder" be-

hind his back, though no one could remember if it came about because of the mustache or the reviews.

Also on the couch and talking at him was Tilda Frobe, the German director, a tiny woman with thick glasses in thick black frames. Tilda never laughed, never smiled. Neither did her films, though she referred to them as comedies, which of course they weren't. Tilda thought this in itself was pretty funny, and she was lionized in all the international circles where the noncomedic comedy was truly appreciated.

"The Organ Grinder and his monkey," Marc Pohl whispered into Anna's ear.

Pohl was a French journalist, but it was hard to believe he was touted as one of the country's greatest living philosophers. For one thing, he looked like Alain Delon, if Delon had let his hair grow to his shoulders and wore shirts open to the navel. He'd come up behind her and she felt his warm breath tickle the hair at her neck. He liked to do this sort of thing, sneak up behind a woman and come as close as possible to inserting a tongue in her ear. Given half a chance he'd do that as well. Anna had met him several times before. She'd never read his philosophy books but had a passing acquaintance with that tongue of his. She'd made the mistake of flirting with him at a party and later, when she was half in the bag, he'd done his little snaky-tongue thing and she'd shrieked and collapsed into a fit of giggles. He'd never really forgiven her for it.

And then there was Kat.

Katherine, Katie, Kitty-Kat.

Or just plain bitch to those who know her well.

Didn't Kat go to Cambridge? And didn't Kat do RADA? And didn't Kat know Hugh and Stephen and Emma and that sexy little bastard Kenny? And wasn't Kat just full of the cleverest stories about what Trevor said to her the other night in the Groucho?

And didn't Katherine Katie Kitty-Kat, dear old friend, just pounce on Andrei like a horny puma the minute Anna's back was turned?

You look like shit, thought Anna, and if there's one more facelift you'll be wearing a beard to shame George Bernard Shaw.

"My God, you look gorgeous!" Kat said to her. "You never age. Do you live on monkey glands in California? I'm so jealous."

Kissy kissy on the cheek.

"How are you, Kat?"

"Wonderful, dearie. I had my snatch done. Can't handle anything larger than a Japanese at the moment. I'm ever so popular again."

Poor dear. Twat like a horse collar and you never won an Oscar, did you, sweetie, just those dinky BAFTA things. And now the skin on your arms resembles a flying squirrel.

Anna suddenly felt much better.

They all introduced themselves. Everyone spoke English, which was one worry off Anna's shoulders.

"Everyone is here," said Carrière, "but Mr. Watanabe."

They chatted for several minutes until Hiroaki Watanabe, the Japanese director, burst into the room, accompanied by a large and beautiful blond woman. Watanabe beamed at everyone. He was tiny and energetic and never stopped smiling. Anna wondered if, as with a baby, it might simply be gas. The thought crossed her mind that she should inform him of Kat's operation.

"This is Mr. Watanabe," announced the blonde in French. "I am Pia Andersson, Mr. Watanabe's interpreter. Mr. Watanabe does not speak French."

"Does Mr. Watanabe speak English?" asked Carrière.

"Mr. Watanabe," said Ms. Andersson, "speaks only Japanese. I speak English, however."

"Then," said Carrière, "since English appears to be the common language, does anyone object if we conduct these meetings in English?"

Carrière nodded graciously toward Anna, who noticed a few of the others exchange snide looks. One more uncultured Yankee to patronize.

Other than making her feel like a monolinguistic rube, it was all far more relaxed than she'd imagined. They sat around drinking coffee and eating pastries while Carrière went over the rules. There were eighteen films in official competition and you were required to see all of them. You could not discuss the films with anyone other than a committee member, though you could listen to others discuss them. They would meet twice a week for the next two weeks of the festival to discuss the films, and there would be a long final meeting at the end where they would arrive at their selections.

"Any questions?" asked Carrière.

Anna noticed that everyone in the room seemed intent on playing to their national stereotype. The French looked bored, the Italian kept looking at his mobile phone and casting glances at Ms. Andersson's legs. The German took copious notes and looked suitably intense. Kat Lyons chain-smoked elegantly and gave Anna the occasional I-opened-a-Pinter-play smile. Mr. Watanabe kept grinning and Ms. Andersson patiently kept removing his hand from her knee while she translated for him in rapid Japanese.

The meeting lasted two hours, the last thirty minutes of it do-you-know-old-so-and-so chitchat. Anna was anxious to leave. She kept thinking of Spandau sitting around a pool full of topless sex kittens. She phoned him before she left and waited until he came to meet her outside the suite.

"How'd it go?" Spandau asked her in the elevator.

"It is not," she said, "going to be a yock-a-minute. The only person in that room who seemed to be enjoying himself was the Japanese guy, and he brought his own entertainment."

They drove back to the villa to pick up Pam, then had lunch at Le Moulin de Mougins in the hills. It was easily the best meal Spandau had ever had, and he calculated that the wine alone cost more than what he was earning in a week. He looked around and saw that if he tossed a nickel over his shoulder, a movie star would be picking it out of his soup. After the first bottle of wine, Anna began to relax. Spandau watched the relationship between Pam and Anna change as they became sisters again and Hollywood melted away for a while. They laughed and joked with each other, and Spandau imagined what it would have been like back in Texas, before all the fear and the inequality set in, and he realized how hard a situation it was for them both.

The three of them ate and drank away the early afternoon. At the end of the meal they were all jolly good pals, but Spandau knew it would tighten up again when the wine wore off. And indeed everything changed the moment they climbed back into the car. Anna became quiet and hardly said a word during the trip back to the villa, simply stared out the window. Pam fielded various e-mails on a mobile phone that allowed her to perform everything short of nuclear fusion. The meal had made Spandau sleepy and content. He wanted to lean back and close his eyes, but technically he was working, though at what was anybody's guess.

When they arrived back at the villa, Anna went up to her room without saying a word.

"Is she okay?" Spandau asked Pam.

"She gets like this," said Pam. "You'll get used to it. The trick is to realize it has nothing to do with you. You just go about your business and hope it doesn't escalate."

But it did escalate. An hour later, Spandau was sitting outside by the pool when he heard Anna yelling inside. He came rushing in and found her chewing out Pam, who stood there with her head down.

"I don't give a fuck," Anna was saying. "It's not up to you to filter my fucking calls, you got that?"

"I thought you were taking a nap. And anyway, filtering your calls is about sixty percent of my job."

Anna looked over at Spandau. "What the hell do you want?"

"I thought war had broken out. You okay?"

"No thanks to you. You sit out there lounging in the sun with a goddamn book and my ass could have been kidnapped half a dozen times already."

"I was sitting right below your window," Spandau said to her. "Unless they're ninjas coming in by helicopter, I think we're okay."

"Why don't you both do what you're paid to do, smart-ass. Gee, wouldn't that be refreshing?"

She turned and went back upstairs. Spandau looked at Pam.

"It happens," said Pam.

There was a reception at the Michelet Villa in Cap d'Antibes that evening. Michelet was one of the largest media companies in Europe and owned at least half the cinemas in five countries. Everyone wanted to be loved by Michelet and consequently their parties were one of the highlights of the Cannes festival. Anna, Pam, and Spandau arrived well into the party, which had moved into the rowdy and obnoxious stage. Pam drifted off on her own to schmooze, and Spandau followed Anna around like a pet terrier while she worked the room.

It had been an odd evening. Anna was still sullen but was no longer attacking anything that moved. She had dinner in her room while Spandau and Pam sat across the dining table and made small talk until it was time to dress. Spandau dusted off his tux and was thankful he hadn't lost the studs. When he came down Pam was talking on her mobile. She wore a clinging green gown that revealed a figure that, if not exactly outshining her movie-star sister, guaranteed she wasn't going to get lost in the shuffle. She gave Spandau an appreciative smile and the okay sign.

He stood around for half an hour with his hands in his pockets, waiting for Anna. Finally he sat at the dining table and played solitaire with a deck of cards they'd found. When she did come down, he had to admit it was worth the wait. She wore a simple black dress and little jewelry, but the neckline plunged and you recalled why adolescent boys still went to her movies. She'd done up her hair and her neck and the line of her shoulders seemed impossibly delicate. He'd forgotten she'd started out as a model in her teens. Now suddenly she was that younger, slimmer version of the woman he'd been with earlier, and it had nothing to do with the makeup or the dress. It was as if she'd simply willed herself into the luminous creature that appeared to float down the stairs. Spandau wanted to say something but was unsure of her mood.

Anna ignored him and said to Pam, "Well, let's do this," and went out the door. Pam and Spandau followed. Pam and Spandau made small talk, but Anna was quiet again, though every now and then he'd catch her watching him. He waited the entire journey for an outburst that never came.

Spandau hated these kinds of parties. He followed Anna around for a while, awkwardly introducing himself since she invariably failed to. If there was some sort of point to be made, Spandau couldn't figure out what it was. Finally he got tired of it and excused himself to go out onto the patio and smoke. He stood watching the lights of the yachts in the bay, wondering if any of them had forsaken all this foolishness and just ordered in pizza and a video. Anna came out with two glasses of champagne and sat one of them on the granite balustrade.

"You clean up nice," she said, "in case I didn't tell you."

"You didn't."

"Well, I was thinking it." She took a sip of champagne and leaned against the railing next to him. "God, I hate this shit," she said.

"Then why are you here?"

"To show the colors," she said. "It's like a gunboat cruising the Philippines. To instill fear in the hearts of the natives and keep them in their place. You're pissed off at me, aren't you?"

"I'm confused, is what I am."

"I'm not sure I could clear anything up for you."

"Treating people like shit is just the entitlement of nobility, is that it?" asked Spandau.

"You got me all figured out, do you?"

"Give me a little help, here."

She took one of his cigarettes and he lit it for her. She inhaled deeply then playfully blew the smoke into his face. "The fog of war, baby," she said. "You can't see a damn thing, you're scared shitless, and all you can do is just stumble toward the sound of the battle and hope for the best."

"You've gone all martial on me tonight. I'm sorry but it's wasted on me."

"You know what I was doing before we came here, why I kept you waiting? I was upstairs puking my guts out. Every time I come to one of these goddamn shindigs, that's what I do. That's one of the skills you learn as a model, how to vomit discreetly. I'm scared to death, and I get to dress up nice and walk into a room filled with a hundred other people who are just as scared but can't show it. We pretend we have the world by the balls and we try not to get too close in case we can smell the flop sweat on each other. We had such a great time at lunch, and then it was over. It hit me walking to the car that I was going to have to come here tonight and perform, pretend to be something I'm not for a bunch of assholes I can't stand."

"So stop."

"I can't," she said. "I know it's pathetic, but I'm a good actor. That still means something to me. And what the hell else would I do? This is who I am."

She crushed her cigarette out on the balustrade and tossed it onto the graveled path below. "And Andrei is here," she said. "He's been following me all over the goddamn room."

"And Andrei is?"

"Andrei Levin, the director. An old flame. He's got a film in competition here."

"You want me to beat him up for you?"

"Would you?" she said. "You were the only thing keeping him away from me. I can't go back in there without you."

He started to go inside but she stopped him.

"Okay," she said, "I've given you every opportunity possible to tell me how good I look. You've missed every one of them."

"I wanted to tell you earlier but I was afraid you'd chew my head off."

"You're safe now."

"You do look beautiful, Anna."

"Good," she said. "You may kiss me."

He bent forward and kissed her gently.

"You are very slow on the pickup," she said. "We'll work on it."

She took his arm and they went inside, where they shifted from spot to spot around the room in an attempt to avoid talking to anyone else. Andrei, a large man with a headful of unruly hair, finally came up to them. He'd been eyeing them for a while. He was carrying a glass of vodka, though it was hard to tell how drunk he was. He spoke clear and correct English with a Slavic accent.

"You're not mixing," he said to Anna. "This is bad."

"Why is it bad?" she asked him.

"Work," said Andrei. "We are all whoring for work. You look for parts, I look for money. I'm better at it than you are. I go—what is the word?—trolling. I troll around the room and look for fish. You stay in one place, which is wrong, unless you're a trout. Remember when I took you fishing in Scotland?"

"You're confusing me with one of the others."

"No, we went fishing, I'm sure of it. I remember watching you piss in the bushes. It was poetic," he said. "Who is this?" nodding toward Spandau.

"A friend of mine."

"What do you do?" he said to Spandau. "Do you have a job?"

"I breed cats," said Spandau.

"What sort of cats?"

"The hairless ones," said Spandau. "We ship them with interchangeable fur."

"I don't believe you sell cats," said Andrei, "but I'm certain you take care of pussies. Would that be right?" he asked Anna. "He is good at it?"

"Go fuck yourself, Andrei," she said. She took Spandau's arm to steer him away. Spandau was flushed and she could see the muscles in his neck tighten. As she turned to leave, Andrei grabbed her arm. Spandau put his own hand around Andrei's wrist and dug his thumb into the tendons at the bottom of his arm.

"Mister, you better remove that hand unless you want to carry it home with you in a plastic bag."

"David, come on," Anna said. "It's not worth it."

Spandau worked the thumb harder and Andrei let go. He pulled the hand back and massaged his wrist.

"You want to hit me," he said to Spandau.

"It's a thought."

"Tell him what will happen," Andrei said to Anna. "Does he know who I am? Who the fuck are you?" he said to Spandau. "You're a nothing. Why are you here? I snap my fingers and someone comes along and removes you like dogshit."

She moved quickly between the two men as Spandau came toward Andrei. Andrei stood there grinning and Anna pushed hard to keep Spandau back. "David, come away, goddamn it, I mean it!" She took Spandau's hand and led him to the other side of the room.

"That was stupid," she said. "I don't need you to defend my goddamned honor. You go around acting like goddamn Prince Valiant and it's all over the fucking newspapers in an hour. Where the fuck do you think you are? I thought your job was to keep me out of trouble, not ruin what's left of my career."

"I'm sorry," he said.

"Look, just go find Pam or something and stay the hell away from me for a while, will you? Just let me get through this."

She pushed him away. She watched him go back out onto

the patio, and when it was safe she went looking for Andrei. She found him talking to a young actress, showing her his wrist and relating the story.

"I want to talk to you," Anna said to him.

"You sent the kitty boy away. He's being punished?"

"I'm sorry, he was just being overprotective. How's your wrist?"

"It's not the first time you got me hurt," he said. "Remember when you pushed me out of the car and I went rolling down the highway?"

"You were cheating on me with Kat."

"Only a little bit," said Andrei. "Nothing serious. Nothing like the way we had."

"It was intense," agreed Anna.

"You miss it," Andrei said.

"Sometimes," Anna said.

"I think about you," said Andrei. "The sex was devastating."

"That part at least was good," she said.

"You stay with me tonight," he said.

"No," she said. "I can't."

He led her out of the room and down a hallway away from the crowd. He pushed her against the wall and kissed her, sliding his hand inside her dress. She pulled his hand away.

"Not here," she said. He'd refilled the glass of vodka and still had it with him. Anna pushed him a few inches away, giving him a wolfish smile. She took the vodka from him and drank a sip. She lowered the glass and looked at him. "You want it bad, don't you?" she said. "How bad do you want it?" Andrei pressed his body against hers and Anna spilled the vodka down the front of his pants. Andrei leaped back.

"Oh shit," she said, laughing. "Sorry . . ."

Andrei laughed as well and pressed his body against hers, kissing her. Anna put her arm around his neck and he felt her hand move between them and touch his damp crotch. He pushed his cock against her hand and barely noticed the tiny motion of her fingers and a barely audible scraping sound. Anna jumped away from him as the vodka on his pants burst into a large blue flame.

"You miserable piece of shit," she said to him as he danced and beat at the flames and made panicked noises. "I hope I've burned it off. I hope I've charred the goddamn thing. He's a real man, you Russian turd, and you can't treat him like that, do you hear me, or I swear to God I'll torch you like a Buddhist monk!"

She flicked the lighter menacingly a couple of times and then threw it at him. She walked away to look for Spandau as Andrei made repeated thrusts at the wall in a desperate attempt to snuff out his flaming genitalia.

3

IT IS PERHAPS FORTUNATE THAT MOST PEOPLE WHO ATTEND screenings at the Cannes Film Festival are film professionals and are already thoroughly sick of movies by the time they arrive. There are only so many grainy black-and-white Albanian films about a boy and his dying pet rooster that a normal person can sit through without losing faith in the idea of cinema altogether. Most people just want to be entertained, and the films at Cannes are the wrong place for that. Which explains why the focus has long since shifted from inside the theaters to outside on the beach. Here we get to see the rich, the beautiful, the famous, the crude, the stupid, the greedy, the needy, and often the just plain seedy. It's as good, really, as anything Fellini ever filmed. And all for free, no waiting in line, no cramming into smelly venues, no struggling with languages or misinterpretation of underlying themes.

There are young women with large breasts who frequently remove their tops, there are movie stars to be seen, and, most important, there is hardly an Albanian kid or rooster in sight.

*   *   *

Screenings began the following day. Each film was shown in the Palais three times a day and judges could turn up at whatever showing they felt like, though the evening screenings were more formal. And anyway, Anna was a morning person. She woke early and did her yoga then swam for half an hour. It was a private time for her and she didn't like anyone around, needed that brief morning buffer between her and the rest of the world, before the phone calls and the meetings and the battles began. There were always battles.

Spandau left her alone but liked to watch her in the pool from his window. The water seemed to welcome her, and she dived with hardly a splash and moved back and forth across the pool in an effortless crawl. He wondered if she knew how beautiful she was, not in the public way she was told constantly but in this private form where she played no role, where she surrendered for a while the horrible self-consciousness that was her stock-in-trade. Watching her body glide through the shimmering water, Spandau realized that she was far more beautiful than all but a very few would ever see. They glorified her public persona, which was only a weak shadow of who she was, a suit of armor, cleverly disguised to look like a woman, that she climbed into each morning and took off when she slept.

This was why Pam stayed, of course. Spandau wondered what Anna had been like in the days before it all started, the fame and the money and the fear. Pam knew and that was what kept her here. She must have been like this, passing through her young life as gracefully as she passed through the water. If she knew Spandau watched her, she gave no sign of it. He suspected she did and it felt to him like a gift.

Thierry drove them to the Palais for the 9 a.m. screening. There was no red carpet, no lights. Fans, of course, but nothing like the night screenings, which fulfilled the public's dream of what Cannes was supposed to be like. Spandau and Anna didn't take that long walk up the steps and into the front doors, but were driven to an entrance in the rear and followed an aide up into the cavernous theater and to their assigned seats.

It was a Japanese film today. French films were subtitled in English and English films were subtitled in French; otherwise the films were shown in their original languages. Spandau and Anna settled in, as the theater only partially filled. The Japanese director wasn't popular and few people could brave the Japanese language so early in the morning. The audience was mainly potential distributors, journalists, and a few die-hard fans.

It was a visually beautiful film about a young man during the Sino-Japanese War, and billed as an Asian version of *All Quiet on the Western Front*. The battle sequences were impressive, but the action would stop for long periods of time while the characters sat in Shinto temples or had tea in gardens. The lead actress was a beautiful young Japanese, but the director was determined that whatever sex she had was going to be violent, and the girl was raped repeatedly by Chinese soldiers and murdered in the end. Spandau wanted to discontinue his own life by the last reel. The final credits rolled and the lights came up.

As they left the theater, Spandau was dying to ask Anna her opinion of the film, but that was verboten. She couldn't talk about it. He searched her eyes for a hint, but it was clear that she was determined to maintain a poker face. It was frustrating, not being able to talk about it with her. He thought about the years of watching movies with Dee, when half the fun was going out after for pizza and picking the movie apart. He missed that, as he missed so many things about her. Now he was watching films with movie stars and he couldn't even talk about it.

Spandau was a movie buff and had spent years as a stuntman, which he'd enjoyed—at least up until he'd run out of fresh bones to break. But generally there seemed to be some unwritten rule that if you worked in the industry, the process wasn't allowed to be fun. Here they were at the most famous film gathering in the world, and unless they were at a party or peddling something in a meeting, people walked around like terminally ill patients. Even the parties had a kind of forced, manic feel to them—like the classic movie *On the Beach,* where people carouse and try to forget the fatal nuclear cloud that's drifting slowly toward them.

They left the theater and there was lunch across the Croisette on the terrace of the Majestic. A producer and director who were interested in casting Anna for a part. Anna's agent, Cheryl Silberman, was there as well. Spandau drank a beer and speared small shrimp with a diminutive fork and listened for an hour as they all talked about everything but the film they were making.

"Explain to me what just happened," Spandau said to Anna when they were in the car.

"What part?"

"The whole thing. What was the point of that meeting?"

"I told you. I was up for a part."

"Nobody mentioned the movie. Or any movie, come to think of it."

"Oh, you innocent. I thought you said you'd worked in the movie business."

"Sorry, I worked in the part where you actually did something."

"There, you see? To the untrained eye, you think nothing got accomplished. But to those of us in the club, it was actually a pretty good meeting. I shall explain, grasshopper."

She took one of Spandau's cigarettes. He lit it for her as she cupped his hand to steady it. The touch of her fingers on the back of his hand sent a small galvanized shock through him. This was starting to happen all too often. She sat back and started to talk. She was happy.

"First of all, nobody needs to talk about the goddamn film because everybody already knows everything there is to know about it. We've all read the script, it's not like somebody has to explain the goddamn story, and the director's won half the awards known to man, so it's not like he's got to defend his vision of it or something."

Spandau watched her face change as she warmed to her theme.

"In fact, the last thing you want to do is go in there and try to defend anything because then you look desperate and that's flailing around in shark-filled waters, it's like ringing a dinner bell for the piranha to gather. My job is to show up and be charming and pretend the director might actually want me for the part, which he doesn't. I'm too old and everybody knows it. Meanwhile everybody gets to see me meeting with the hotshot director and it is announced that, contrary to opinion in some circles, I am still in the game."

She puffed nervously at her cigarette, waved it around at the tip of her fingers like Bette Davis. She was playing for the cameras now and didn't know it.

"The director met with me because Cheryl can be like Kali, the goddess of destruction, and she's his only access to other actors he's going to need at some point, and, anyway, one of her other clients is going to get the part. The end result is that he and the producer and everybody else gets reminded that I'm still around and not aging as badly as *People* magazine says I am. Besides, talent never, ever talks business or money. Never. This is why God made agents and producers. They go off somewhere and close the doors and fight like pit bulls so that us sensitive artists don't have to be sullied by it. Strangely, I sort of like the idea. I like being in control, even if you do get a little blood on you now and then."

She still wanted it. In spite of what she said, how she tried to behave, she still wanted to be a star. She'd never be able to stop it any more than she could stop her heart from pumping. Spandau watched her talk, watched her come alive, and knew that whatever he felt for her, whatever he was growing to feel, was hopeless. There was no place for him in that world, there never had been. Best to pull back, not let everyone get hurt. Just do your job, keep your mouth shut, and go home alone when the time comes.

"Anyway, the whole thing's as formalized as one of those Japanese tea ceremonies we saw in the movie. We all know what we're supposed to do. I just smile and bow and hope there's no damp spot on my ass from sweating on the plastic seat cushions."

Cannes appeared to the outside world like an endless party, but in reality it was a marketplace where films—as well as careers—were bought and sold. Cannes was far less about the art of film than the art of the deal. How could it not be? It was the greatest single concentration of media powers in the world. Nothing else came near it.

Anna's agent had lined up meetings with as many important directors and producers as she could fit in. As Anna said, even if none of them panned out, she was still being seen. For now, anyway. It was only a matter of time before the meetings stopped, when you simply had to sit and wait for someone to call. Anna knew that Cheryl was already twisting arms. She wondered how much longer even Cheryl would bother. No one expected loyalty. It was business. Everybody understood that. So for the time being Anna allowed her days to be filled with an endless round of the cheek kissing and banal talk that hid her growing sense of desperation.

They continued to see films in the morning, if they were scheduled. This turned out to be a wise move, since if you'd had a decent night's sleep and enough coffee, there was less chance of dozing off. Granted, there were a few movies that kept you awake, but so many of the films took themselves too seriously (thought Spandau), their bleakness of spirit meant to be poignant but, after seeing so much of the same thing, becoming merely soporific. Even the violence became stylized, dull, and repetitive.

Spandau longed for a movie with a little laughter in it. You were meant to be impressed by the realism of these films, but in lacking humor, all they did was portray one more warped and dishonest view of the world. Spandau recalled his own childhood, haunted by a brutal father the whole family all feared, as hellish. But even he could remember it was the laughter, sometimes incredibly dark, that kept him and his sister and his mother sane in the face of the old man's booze-fueled violence.

So Spandau spent most of his days sitting in the dark theater, attempting to stay awake as one more young director tried to convey an experience he'd never actually experienced. Or at the edge of meetings where nothing was allowed to be said. Or sitting in a deck chair reading a book while Anna argued in a closed room upstairs the merits of films she'd watched through half-dozing eyes.

Spandau waited, and while waiting there was ample time for thought. Maybe this was what Walter had intended. He'd stopped drinking except for a little wine with dinner. He got a full night's sleep, ate well, got lots of sun. Sometimes he swam for a while in the evenings. There was nothing to be stressed about, unless it was coping with Anna herself. Vignon had hired two operatives to watch out for the place and they followed Spandau and Anna everywhere from a discreet distance. They were good at their jobs, which went even further toward making Spandau realize his own was ludicrous.

He had no business being there, but, shamefully, he was glad he was. He'd come because he was desperate, and even he could see the necessity of getting the hell out of L.A. before he hurt himself or somebody else. He felt as cheap as a paid escort, but however shoddy this felt, it was nothing like the self-loathing he felt after grabbing Dee. He felt like a boy toy, but an increasingly clearheaded one.

It was the night of the premiere of Andrei's new film, *White Square,* about the Constructivist artist Kazimir Malevich. For the first time Andrei had shot a film in French, so at least there would be English subtitles. It was one of the more talked about premieres at the festival. They'd originally planned to go to the big gala premiere screening, but since Anna had ignited Andrei's balls, and Andrei would be there, she debated going. On the other hand, she had to see the film, she was due for a splurge, and it would go a long way toward irritating the piss out of Andrei even more.

Spandau got out his tux again, and Anna turned out in a gold lamé number with the full panoply of jewelry. She was gorgeous and intended to make an entrance.

Spandau had been to premieres before, but he was prepared for nothing like this. This was Cannes and at the Palais and it didn't get any bigger or fancier. Andrei was a Cannes favorite anyway, and this time he'd made a French film starring well-known French actors. Thierry pulled onto the Croisette and within blocks of the Palais people lined the sides of the street, getting worse the closer they got to the theater. Thierry took his place in the line of cars disgorging celebrities onto the carpet.

As they waited their turn, faces loomed toward the car to peer inside. They fought and pushed, struggled to get close to the car, though the tinted windows gave no idea of who was inside. It wasn't any person they were attracted to, but the idea of celebrity itself. It felt to Spandau like a slow and extended drug hallucination.

"Jesus," he said as the car pulled up to the carpet.

"Just follow me," said Anna. "Do what I do and just take it easy. Nobody's in a hurry." She positioned herself at the edge of seat so that when the door opened she'd be able to simply extend her foot and gracefully emerge from the car. Anna had done this before.

Then the door opened and it began.

There's the noise first.

You've been hearing it for a while as the car approached, but you're so caught up in the faces that crane toward the windows you don't think about it. And anyway, it seems distant in the car, it doesn't quite register. Then the door is opened and it's the noise that hits you first, it suddenly fills the car and seems to blast you out of it like some kind of sonic boom. It's like no noise you've heard before, and that's what throws you. If you had time to think about it, you'd be able to pick out the clicking of cameras, the pop of flashes, the dull roar of the crowd, and the more specific bark of people around you, the questions being thrown from the press. The sounds of cars passing on the street behind you, a horn honking somewhere.

So it's the noise, yes, that hits you first, screws you up even before you set foot out of the car. You slide to the edge on the seat, and if you're a big man there's no graceful way to get out. You venture out with the foot and then try to get your head out next without knocking your brains out or messing up your hair. You have to try to slow down, slow down, because all you want is to get this over with, just let me get out of the goddamn car without falling on my face—even though it happens all the time.

Suddenly somehow you're standing on the red carpet and you know your troubles have just started. There's a mile and a few hundred people between you and the doors and the likelihood of you making it there without incident is slim. There are bright lights bearing down on you, and while your eyes struggle to adjust, everything beyond a few feet goes out of focus. As if this weren't bad enough, there's that incessant *chicachicachicachichic* of the cameras like insects attacking and the *popopopopopopop* of the flashguns, and even if you could focus, that alone would blind you.

You feel helpless. But there's a certain comfort in realizing they don't give a damn about you, it's the Beautiful People they're trying to capture for the waiting world, but unfortunately it's your sorry if unknown ass that gets captured as well. Thankfully, you feel her hand on your arm and a gentle and reassuring squeeze just before you decide to run amok. You stand there, waiting for the people in front of you to move forward.

Wait.

Step.

Wait.

Step.

Wait . . .

She says something to you but you can't make out what it is, just see the lips move. She smiles up at you and the eyes say, *I understand, it's awful, it will be over soon, trust me.*

Wait.

Step.

Step . . . Step . . . Step . . .

Now you come to the steps and you think, This is surely where I will fuck up.

Step up.

Stand.

Up.

Stand . . .

Most of it's in back of you now, the doors are a few feet away. All you have to do is not trip over your own feet and wipe out several yards of people behind you like bowling pins. Then . . .

It's over. You're through the doors, you're inside, you're safe.

And now there's the goddamn film to get through.

"You okay?" she asked him.

"Yeah, yeah, sure. Let's go back and do it again, want to?"

They went inside and took their seats, sitting in the row behind Andrei and the producers. Andrei came in to take his seat and glared at Anna before he sat down. Anna began to sing, "Chestnuts roasting on an open fire . . ." just loud enough for him to hear. To his credit Andrei ignored her. The lights went down and she reached for Spandau's hand in the darkness.

The worst part was that it was a good film.

In fact, it was the best film they'd seen so far.

Ah hell, let's face it, it was the best film he'd seen in a long time.

He'd expected it to be bad. He'd wanted it to be bad. From everything Anna had told him about Andrei's films, he'd expected one more plodding and pretentious waste of plastic, made more to be discussed at the Sorbonne than watched by real people. Andrei was the Euro-intellectuals' darling, so who expected the bastard to turn around and make a very simple and emotional and beautiful film about a subject as ripe for pretense as a Russian avant-garde artist? The film even had—yes, dare it be said?— humor.

It was a brilliant film and Spandau wanted to find a blunt object and beat the arrogant bastard to death with it. What right did he have to be such a foul, unmitigated shit and still get to make something so pure? It felt so grossly unfair. Spandau thought about Mozart and Salieri in the play *Amadeus*. What sort of god distributed such talent to the unworthy?

The whole thing upset Spandau's democratic sense of order, and he found himself in the weird position of resenting Andrei even more because he hated him less. He was faced with the untenable conclusion that there had to be at least something redeeming in a man who could make a picture like this, and he could now see why Anna might be attracted to him in the first place. He could also imagine why Anna might be attracted to him still.

Wait a minute, thought Spandau. Am I jealous? It was even worse when Andrei received cheers and a standing ovation. Spandau waited to see if Anna stood. She did. Spandau did as well. Andrei made an extravagant wave to the crowd, then turned and smiled at Anna and shrugged his shoulders before being swept out of the theater by his happy producers. Applause is fine, but this was money in the bank.

The lights were on now and Spandau looked at Anna. She

wouldn't look him in the eyes. Were her own eyes moist? They went to the car without a word. She sat quietly on her side as they waited to edge out into traffic. He was dying to talk about the film, ached to find out what she thought about it, if she liked it as well as he did. Sometimes they could really get under your skin, films. Sometimes they could change the way you think, change your life even.

Maybe for the first time in his life Spandau had seen a film that might outlive him, that might be watched and studied by future generations. He wanted to know what she thought. Wanted to know if she was as pleased and confused by it as he was. Wanted to know if she too felt this was the one diamond found on top of a dunghill, the one shining thing that lived up to what a film could be.

"The bastard," she said quietly, and Spandau knew.

4

I T WAS LUNCHTIME, AND THE CAFÉ IN THE HOTEL MORONI
in Nice was full of people there for the festival—the ones who
couldn't manage the Majestic or the Carleton, anyway. There was
a worn look to the employees and the decor, as if somewhere a
line of retirees waited to grab the premises again when the inter-
lopers got bored. The building was listed as a national treasure,
but then so was Jacques Tati.

The driver desposited Spandau in front of the hotel. When
Spandau went into the café, Vignon was at a table drinking a cup
of coffee and staring wearily at the stony beach across the Promenade des Anglais. A few elderly waiters shuffled back and forth,
serving overchilled *fruits de mer* to B-producers who frowned
whenever their pneumatic girlfriends gravitated toward the loftier
side of the menu. Vignon looked up as Spandau walked over and
sat down, but his expression never changed. Vignon went back
to staring at the beach. A waiter asked Spandau in English if he
wanted something to drink. Spandau ordered a Budweiser, knowing they wouldn't have it, just to be difficult. Spandau hadn't said

a word and once again resented people assuming he was American. This was, of course, stupid because he clearly looked the part and had no idea why it irked him. He didn't mind being American and that made him even angrier. Maybe it had something to do with feeling like a saguaro cactus in Times Square. Sometimes you're just sick of not fitting in, sometimes you wouldn't mind just being a goddamn ficus. The waiter came back and suggested Löwenbräu and Spandau ordered an iced tea, which is what he'd wanted all along.

Some clockwork marionettes nearby whirled and came to life. Spandau watched them frolic for a bit, dancing to calliope music. He turned and looked at Vignon, who wasn't bothering to suppress a smile.

To Vignon he said: "You want to remind me what it is we're doing here?"

"It was Anna's idea. She wants us to get along. To bury the ax, I think she said."

"Hatchet," said Spandau. "I think she meant hatchet."

"She said ax," Vignon said firmly.

"Of course she did," said Spandau.

His iced tea came. He squeezed lemon into it. A spray hit Vignon in the eye. Spandau hadn't intended it but there was a small twinge of satisfaction. Vignon blinked and dabbed at his eye with a stiff cloth napkin.

"And you said?"

"I told her we were in perfect accord," said Vignon, alternately batting and popping his eye. "That we couldn't stand each other."

"Good for you," said Spandau. "Then why are we here, please?"

"It's important to act with professionalism," Vignon said.

"It's important," said Spandau, "to do what your employer asks when she threatens to fire your ass."

"Do you know why people don't like Americans?" Vignon said.

"We have more money?" said Spandau.

"You *had* more money," said Vignon. "The Chinese are currently taking care of it for you. And anyway the EU is kicking your ass now as well. No, it's because you never get past the emotional age of fifteen. You're like underage drivers in a Maserati. It's inevitable that someone gets hurt, but somehow it never turns out to be you."

"Surely you're not implying," said Spandau, "that God is on our side."

"If there were a God," said Vignon, "then the Americans would have never gotten the bomb and my ex-wife would never have gotten my real-estate holdings. Or perhaps the Catholics are right and God truly does prefer fools."

The waiter returned. Vignon said he wanted nothing to eat but ordered a cognac. Then he said in French, Give the stupid American whatever he wants. Spandau had been hungry but suddenly lost his appetite. He too ordered a cognac.

"When I was eighteen and fresh out of high school, I decided to go into the army. I suppose I could have gone to college then, but there wasn't really enough money, my father didn't think much of colleges or education in general for that matter, so I decided on the army."

"How fascinating for you. I did two years with the paras in North Africa."

"And how proud you must be of that. Anyway, I joined the army. I was, as they say, full of piss and vinegar—"

"What?"

"Piss and vinegar. Stubborn. Full of myself."

"You've changed?"

"Full of piss and vinegar. I hated taking orders, got into trouble most of the time, and I was running away from a German father I hated. Taking all this carefully into consideration, the United States government sent me to Germany as a military policeman. They reasoned that if I couldn't take orders I was probably better at giving them, and that if I hated my *mein Deutsche vater* I'd be less inclined to fraternize with the natives. And I was big. The U.S. Army really likes big."

"Where are you going with this? I'm getting a headache."

"Just be patient, it will all make sense," said Spandau. "So they made me a military policeman, and I spent two years in Wiesbaden trying to stop enlisted men from fraternizing with the local high school girls or driving military vehicles through potato patches on Saturday nights."

"Yes, yes . . ."

"The military were wrong, of course, as they so frequently are. I did hate my father, the miserable old Kraut, but it turned out not to be transferable. I didn't hate the Germans, I actually liked them. In fact, I generally liked them better than the American enlisted men I was hauling off to the stockade, and I definitely liked them better than the officers who kept making me take them there. I fraternized like a bastard. My best friend was a German guy named Klaus, an optician. In fact I, lost my virginity to his sister, Magda."

"Please . . ."

"Klaus was a nut about World War One. Kept yammering about how it was the turning point for Germany, for Western civilization in fact, and was amazed how little Americans thought about it. So whenever I got a few days leave, Klaus and Magda would drag me on the train through Luxembourg into France to stomp around in the shitty weather around Verdun and the Argonne. I can see what the doughboys were talking about, a truly lousy spot to go on a picnic, much less fight a war. That place could export mud, let me tell you."

"I'm going to need another cognac." Vignon motioned to the waiter.

"Two, please," Spandau said to the old man when he managed to get there. "Anyway—"

"Don't you ever breathe? Do Texans all inhale from their asses?"

"I'm from Arizona, so I wouldn't know, but it's a common speculation in the southeastern part of the state. You'll appreciate this tale in the end, trust me."

The waiter brought two more cognacs. Vignon's first was already gone, and he took a healthy drink of the second. Spandau drained the last big swallow of his current cognac and moved the next one within reach.

"Aside from the mud, the place wasn't half bad. Klaus didn't care for the French—didn't think they were friendly enough—"

"And the Germans are, of course," said Vignon.

"But I got to like them. Klaus got married and Magna got knocked up—no, no, it wasn't me, it was the commanding officer's pastry chef, she'd been fraternizing with him too—and I discovered you could hitch a ride into Paris on transport planes ferrying troops back and forth from Desert Storm along with the Maine lobsters for Colin Powell's dinner. It was a great setup. You could leave on Friday night, spend the weekend in Paris, and still manage to show up—sober or otherwise—for mess on Monday morning. That's where my whole love affair with cooking and French food began. All those little mom-and-pop bistros tucked away in corners of the Left Bank. Hanging around at the Place du Tertre in Montmartre, chewing on a baguette ham-and-cheese sandwich, watching the artists con the tourists while I hit on big-boned girls from the English midlands. Ah, that was the life."

"Yes of course," said Vignon. "A bottle of rough *vin rouge,* accordion music under streetlamps at the foot of the Pont Neuf, the unread paperback of *Being and Nothingness* in your backpack, an eight-dollar cup of coffee at the Deux Magots for the honor of warming your ass where Hemingway sat. Please tell me you bought a beret and thought about becoming a painter after the obligatory ten minutes in the Louvre." He took a pull at the cognac. "You come here, you never learn a word of the language, you're afraid to venture ten feet away from the Hard Rock Cafe, and you walk around thinking you've somehow penetrated the subtleties of culture. You can't even drink the coffee without having it watered down for you, for God's sake."

"Well," said Spandau, "there is that attitude. I mean, the attitude of the Americans who visit and the French who assume we're so goddamned stupid we don't know how much we're missing. I was in a bistro once, one of those prix fixe lunch places. I walked in and the girl sat me at a table with some of the locals, which I didn't mind. But the manager told her, You can't sit him there, they don't like that. 'They' being, I guess, Americans. So she moved me to a table on my own, when I'd just as soon have sat with the other guys who were having their lunch. Then the waitress brought my salad. Actually it wasn't my salad, it was the wrong salad. The other waitress said to her, That's not the one he ordered. And the waitress with the salad replied, Oh, he won't know, he's American. Everybody had a good laugh at that one."

"I'm surprised someone told you."

Spandau took a sip of his cognac, smiled. "Well, see, that's just the point. Nobody did. Nobody had to. They just assumed."

Vignon stared at him. As the realization hit him, he became uncomfortable and found it difficult to look Spandau in the face.

"I'm sure you misunderstood," said Vignon. "It sounds as if you've simply interpreted it wrong."

"No," said Spandau. "I was nineteen years old, they made me take two years of language in high school. I refused to take German, I was sick of hearing Spanish, the likelihood of ever bumping into a Roman soldier seemed thin so I opted out of Latin. French was all that was left. You're always surprised how much of it comes back. I'm still shy about trying to speak it, though."

"We should be getting back," said Vignon.

"You've been riding my ass ever since I got off that plane," said Spandau. "I've never seen you in my life and you insult me literally within three minutes of hitting the ground. I'll give you credit, though, you're consistent. The entire time I've been here you've never missed a moment to get at me. I bit my tongue, in spite of your contention—contention, by the way, means 'your opinion' in my language—that I'm no professional. I also did it out of respect for Anna, when all my basic instincts were to take you out in the back of the villa and beat the shit out of you with something. I suppose I really did have some useless hope that you dragged me here as some sort of friendly gesture. But no, you bring me to this fun house with the dancing marionettes to laugh at me and insult me in front of the waiters and anybody else in the room who speaks French. Maybe we're barbarians in my neck of the woods, mister, but we got something to say to a man, we have the balls to say it to his face and not laugh at him behind his back."

He threw half a glass of cognac across the table and into Vignon's face. There was a collective gasp in the room, and Spandau couldn't tell if people were offended or just surprised it had taken him so long. Vignon was cool enough not to flinch, simply closed his eyes and let it rain over him. He slowly mopped at his face and chest with a stiff cloth napkin.

"You're right," said Vignon. "It was ill mannered of me and I apologize for insulting you. But I'm going to kick your ass anyway."

"Let's do it," said Spandau, and started to get up.

"You have to wait," Vignon said. "If we leave now they'll call the police because they'll know we're going to fight. If we wait, they'll just think we're homosexuals."

"You fuckers really do complicate things over here, don't you?"

"Do you want another drink? You wasted that one."

"Sure. What the hell."

Vignon called the elderly waiter over and ordered two more cognacs. "It will give us time to cool down. You should never fight when you're angry."

"This is apparently a continuing thread in French history," said Spandau. "Just when the hell are you supposed to fight, then?"

"You make mistakes when you're angry. That's why we got out of Indochina just before you moved in. We had sense enough not to stay just because we were angry at losing. You didn't."

"Cartesian logic?"

"Common sense. Descartes wasn't often that logical. If you've read him."

"Kiss my ass," said Spandau.

They drank their cognacs in silence. People glanced at them occasionally, wondering if the lovers were going to have another tiff. Vignon drained his glass, Spandau drained his. They both reached for the bill.

"I'll get it," said Spandau.

"No," said Vignon. "You came as my guest."

"I ruined your jacket."

"I deserved it. I publicly insulted you. Not once but whenever I could."

"Pay the goddamn bill, then."

"Thank you."

"Where can we do this?"

"Follow me out back. There must be some place."

There was a clochard sitting on a milk crate in the alley behind the hotel. Vignon asked him if there was a place they could be alone.

"Sex, then?" asked the clochard.

"I'm going to beat his brains out," Vignon said to him.

"All one and the same," said the clochard. "There's a place a few yards down where no one from the hotel can see you. Mind the dogshit."

They found the place, a blind spot where they'd be hidden but large enough to move around.

"This looks good," said Vignon. "What do you think?"

"I don't see any broken glass," said Spandau.

"I didn't think about that," said Vignon, "but it's a good point."

They both took off their jackets and it was a minute or two before they could find someplace clean to lay them. They squared off.

"I haven't done this for a while," said Vignon. "At least not fairly. As a cop, I clubbed criminals but it's not the same."

"No," said Spandau, "not really."

"I suppose I should tell you," said Vignon, "that I'm in very good shape."

"I'm not exactly a ninety-pound weakling myself."

"I climb. I exercise every day."

"Good. You can climb your way back to the car when I finish kicking your ass."

"I also studied savate," said Vignon.

Spandau was trying to remember what the hell savate was when Vignon kicked him high inside his left thigh. His leg went numb and sickly weak from hip to toes.

"Shit," said Spandau, stopping to massage his leg.

"I warned you," said Vignon, dancing back and forth.

Spandau was massaging his leg and Vignon danced in for an easy square kick to the chest to finish him off. The blow came but Spandau had suckered him into it and was ready. Spandau was bent over but swung his arm in a backhand that caught Vignon at the ankle just before it reached his chest, spinning his leg off to the right. Vignon was balanced on one leg at the time and it caused him to do an unnatural pivot at the knee.

"Merde!" said Vignon. He regained his footing but limped backward a few paces.

Spandau was rubbing his bruised thigh and Vignon limped in a small circle, trying to work the pain out of his knee. They regarded each other. Spandau, anticipating a slight advantage, quickly hobbled toward Vignon, who half hopped on his good leg to meet him halfway. Since neither man could kick the other without falling over, they started swinging. Vignon swung at Spandau's chin but lost his balance and hit him instead in the shoulder and fell forward. Spandau had aimed for Vignon's nose but Vignon tilted down and Spandau hit him very hard on the top of the head. There was a loud dull crack and both men emitted pathetic yelps simultaneously.

"Jesus!" cried Spandau, nesting his throbbing right hand in the safety of his armpit.

Vignon grabbed at his head with both hands, bent over, and made a hissing noise like a teakettle.

Both men walked around like this for a bit.

Vignon was bent over and dizzy but thought he would hit Spandau with his shoulder in a low tackle.

Spandau saw this coming but his right hand was useless and his left hand had never been much good. He moved quickly to sidestep Vignon like a bullfighter but slipped on something and went down. Vignon arrived but there was nothing to tackle and went flying over Spandau to land on his backside a few feet away.

Both men just sat there.

"Give me a minute," said Spandau, sniffing. "I think I've landed in dogshit." He checked and he was right.

"I've got you beat," said Vignon, holding up the remains of a bottle. "I believe I have seriously cut my ass."

Spandau got to his feet and hobbled over to Vignon, offering him his left hand. Vignon took it, smelled Spandau, then waved him away. Vignon pulled himself to his feet by holding on to a recycling container.

"See," said Spandau. "Your climbing paid off after all."

The two men inched back down the alley. The clochard was leaning against the hotel wall, watching them, where he'd been the whole time.

"Pathetic," the clochard said as they passed. "Perhaps you'd have been better at the sex."

They came up to the street. Vignon's car was around the corner.

"Will you check my ass?" he asked Spandau.

Spandau checked.

"It's bleeding," he told Vignon. "Not too badly, I think."

"Now the pants are ruined too."

"Do you think honor is satisfied?"

"It will have to be," said Vignon. "Unless you're prepared to finish this in wheelchairs."

"We could joust," said Spandau.

"Rolling forward, tilting at each other with our crutches. And me sitting on an inflatable donut. There's a certain romance to it. How are we going to explain this to Anna?"

"We'll tell her the truth. She'll laugh her ass off. Anyway she'll be glad it's over."

"Is it?" said Vignon.

"I can't imagine we'd care to repeat this anytime soon, do you? Pax?"

Spandau extended his hand, the bashed one. Then the other one, the one reeking of dogshit.

"Perhaps," suggested Vignon, "that might be pushing things a bit."

Vignon pulled the bloody trousers away from his anguished posterior and did a kind of Chaplinesque walk toward his car. Spandau thought this was amusing and rejoiced in another small bead of triumph, until he found himself confused over which hand he could use to phone the driver.

5

PEREC ARRIVED IN NICE EARLY IN THE MORNING, AND BY
late afternoon he was still walking the streets looking for a place
to stay. It was the same everywhere he went: I'm sorry, we're filled
because of the festival, this time of year Monsieur must make
reservations well in advance. No, once again we are sorry, we
cannot think of any hotel where there might be rooms. Perhaps
Monsieur would be willing to try the less popular neighborhoods?

Now Perec was tired and hot and hungry and facing a night
in the streets. He'd worked his way from the beach in toward the
train station, where the streets were smaller and dirtier and the
people were racially mixed. Perec went into a café and ordered a
coffee and a sandwich.

"Do you know where I could find a room?" he asked the waiter,
who laughed.

"Are you joking? It's festival. Even the shitty rooms are filled.
Good luck."

Perec ate and then launched himself back into the search,
stopping at *tabacs* and cafés to ask. No luck. It was after 6 p.m.

and he was ready to go to the train station and sleep there, when he went into a small backstreet café where a few men sat drinking and playing cards. They glanced up when he came in, then went back to their game. Perec sat at the bar and ordered a Coca-Cola.

"I'm looking for a room," he asked the bartender.

"Ha! You and everybody else."

"I've been looking all day. I'll take anything."

"I can't help you."

"There's Debord," one of the cardplayers volunteered.

The bartender shook his head. One of the men laughed.

"Where's that?" Perec asked the man who'd mentioned it.

"Not a where, a he. Sometimes he rents rooms. But they're illegal, see, and they aren't much. And he's, well . . . You could try it if you're strapped."

They gave him directions. Perec thanked them and dragged his suitcase the few blocks to Debord's street. It was a narrow alley that smelled of piss and desperation. Perec found the gray building they'd described. A young woman in her midteens was washing puke off the sidewalk with a hose. She was small, with short dark hair and large dark eyes. Perec waited to work up the courage to speak to her. The girl kept glancing up at him nervously, as if she too were afraid he'd speak. Perec approached her.

"I . . . I'm looking for a room. Someone told me I might find one here."

The girl nodded, avoiding his eyes. She went into the foyer to turn off the hose, then came back out, wiping her damp hands on her dress. She motioned with a small nod for him to follow into a dingy hallway. There was an open door and inside a middle-aged man sat watching a soccer game on television. The girl seemed frightened to disturb him, and finally the man noticed her.

"What is it?"

"He's looking for a room," said the girl.

"I'm not a hotel," said the man.

"I was told—" began Perec, but the man cut him off.

"I don't give a damn what you were told."

"Monsieur, I've looked all over and it's—"

"There's the attic room," said the girl.

The man gave her a dark look.

"Fine, then," said the man. "Show it to him. It's two hundred euros a week."

The girl was surprised. "Papa . . ."

"If he doesn't want it, he doesn't have to take it. Do you want it or not?"

"Let me see it."

The man ignored him and turned back to the soccer game. The girl led Perec up two flights of stairs to a tiny landing. She took out a key and unlocked the door. The room was hardly larger than a closet. There was space for a small bed and a table with a pitcher and washbasin on it.

"I'm sorry," the girl said to him when she saw the look on his face.

"No, no. I'll take it."

"He'll want a week in advance."

Perec took out his wallet and counted out the money. He saw the girl notice the amount of money he had and regretted this.

"I'll bring you some clean towels and some fresh sheets," the girl said. "The shower and toilet are on the floor below."

The girl handed him a key and left to get the linens. Perec sat on the bed and a small cloud of dust wafted up. There was a small round window above the table and Perec went over and wiped the dirty glass with his sleeve and looked down at children playing in the street below. The girl returned and knocked at the still-open door. When he looked up she darted in and placed the linens on the bed. She smiled at him nervously and went away.

Perec pulled off the blanket and the existing sheet and checked the mattress for bugs. He tried to forget the stains on the mattress and put on the clean sheets and gave the blanket a good shaking, which made him cough. He opened the window to let the air clear. He was hungry and sad and on a neighboring street found a small bistro where the food smelled. He ate the prix fixe menu, which came with wine. Perec rarely drank and had only sometimes tasted the cheap red wine he bought for his mother. Wine was the only alcohol she permitted since it was sanctioned by God.

Perec now drank the tiny carafe of wine and felt a bit light-headed and sleepy after the meal. On his way to his room he passed the landlord's door and could hear the man belittling his daughter. Perec climbed the stairs to his closet room and closed the door, where the walls suddenly moved in to crush him. He put his face to the window and drank in the fresh air that tasted of the nearly sea. He lay down on the bed in his clothes and fell asleep.

Sometime during the night he woke to hear the old man beating the girl. He remembered the beatings his own father gave him and lay there rigid and listened to her cries and the sound of the blows. At one point Perec found he had tears in his eyes but had no idea why.

6

HE WOKE LATE THE NEXT MORNING AND CAME DOWNSTAIRS
to find a café in which to breakfast. The door of the Debord flat
was open and the girl was sitting on the floor, cutting things out
of a magazine with a pair of scissors. She looked up as he went by.
Her left eye was very dark and swollen but she gave him a wide
smile. In spite of the eye her face seemed lighter and she seemed
almost happy. There was no sign of the old man.

"Did you sleep well?" the girl asked him.

Perec wasn't sure if she meant, did he hear the beating. "It
was a bit close," he said.

"There isn't much air," she admitted.

"What are you doing?"

"Would you like to see?"

"Where's your father?"

"He's at work. He won't be home until this evening."

Perec stepped into the room. The floor was littered with pictures and articles she'd cut out. They were all about Japan. She
was happy to be sharing these things and thoughtlessly took his

hand. Perec nearly pulled it away. She led him to her room, only a little larger than his own. It was covered with images of Japan she'd cut from magazines and old books.

"It's beautiful," said Perec, though it struck him as a silly waste of time.

"Do you think so? It's all Japan. I love Japan. It's the most beautiful place in the world."

"Have you been there?" Perec asked her.

"No. Have you?"

"No," said Perec.

"I ask everyone. I met a man once who was there. He was a sailor. He stayed here for a few days and told me all about it. Look."

She handed him a children's book containing photos of geishas.

"Are they the most beautiful women you have ever seen?"

"They're very . . . pale," Perec said.

"Oh, they're supposed to be. That's beautiful in Japan. They dance and they sing, and they play these little guitars with only a couple of strings . . . You're not interested."

"I just don't know anything about it."

"Oh, I know all about it," she said. "I'm an expert. You can ask me anything."

He pointed to a photo on the wall.

"What's this?"

"That's Mount Fuji. It's the highest mountain in Japan, only it's not really a mountain, it's a volcano, and some people here call it Mount Fujiyama, but that's wrong because *yama* means 'mountain,' so that's the same thing as calling it 'Mount Fuji Mountain.' See? I know a lot."

He motioned to another photo.

"And this?"

"It's a Zen garden."

"A garden? There's nothing but a lot of rocks."

"Sometimes they have gardens made out of rocks in Japan. See this? This part is supposed to be water. And see these rocks? These are islands. And it all has to be arranged in a certain way. There are a lot of rules. The Japanese have a lot of rules about things. You have to bow a lot."

She bowed.

"Now you try."

Perec gave a short bow.

"You have no respect for me," she said.

"What?"

"I gave you a deep bow," she said. "That means I respect you. The deeper the bow, the more respect. You hardly bowed at all."

Perec gave another bow, lower this time.

"That was much better," she said to him. "I don't feel so insulted now. I won't make you kill yourself."

"Why would I kill myself?"

"Have you ever heard of the samurai? They're the Japanese warriors. They cut off the heads of their enemies with swords, and they're not afraid to die. If they bring shame on themselves, they take a knife and zip"—she demonstrated a knife being drawn across her stomach—"all their guts fall out. Or else they just—whick!" and demonstrated cutting her own throat. "Isn't it just wonderful?"

"It sounds complicated."

"Oh, of course it's complicated. That's the point. That's part of why it's all so beautiful. All these rituals. And so gentle. The Japanese admire tranquillity, but they can be very fierce. I'll show you how to have tea."

"Everybody knows how to have tea."

"Not like the Japanese. They have a whole tea ceremony. I'm teaching myself how to do it. It's very serious."

"I have to go," said Perec as the discomfort of talking to a woman began to sweep over him. He needed to get away from her.

"What's your name?" she asked him.

"Vincent," he said.

"Mine's Amalie."

She held out her hand. Perec reluctantly took it. It was small and cool and felt like a wounded sparrow he'd found once. He felt himself getting ill. He let go of her hand and fled.

Perec managed to avoid her the rest of the day. He ate breakfast and then bought newspapers and magazines, anything that referenced the film festival and might tell him something about Anna. There was much about the festival but little about her. He bought a map and walked toward the beach, and when he reached the bay he stopped and sat on a bench and looked at the boats and yachts. Such wealth was beyond Perec's imagination. He walked down the Croisette all the way to the Palais and stood there for a while watching cars pull up and people going into the cinema. He wondered if Anna was among them. The streets and shops were crowded and he often heard people speaking English. Everyone was loud and it was very disorganized and Perec didn't like it. He was happier when he moved away from the beach and back into the small warrens of neighborhoods. The sky was clear and crisp and in the neighborhoods people sat in small corner cafés, drinking and talking. Lovers held hands and stopped to kiss in doorways. Children played football in the streets but no one bothered

Perec as he walked by, no one stopped to stare or toss insults at him as he passed. It seemed like a gentler world, though just as poor as the one he'd left.

He was going into the Debord house when he heard someone shushing him. Amalie beckoned to him from the alley next to the house.

"Come with me," she said.

She took his hand and led him down the alley past trash bins and through a hole in the fence. They emerged into the tiny courtyard of the derelict building behind Debord's. Rubble and trash had been pushed aside and in this clearing a blanket had been spread on the concrete. On this there was a wooden crate covered with a flowered cloth and a pillow on either side. A tea-kettle steamed on a small hibachi burning a few pieces of sticks and charcoal. On the table crate was a soup bowl and a jar of tea and a kitchen whisk and a soup ladle. Amalie went over and turned on a cassette player. The tinny sounds of Japanese music hung in the air. She pulled on a cheap kimono-like housecoat.

"I don't have a kimono for you, but I've got this."

She took out a homemade samurai rising-sun headband and tied it round his head. She sat on her heels at the table. Perec sat across from her. Using simple non-Japanese household imple-ments, she made the tea, mimicking the Zen tea ritual. She care-fully spooned green tea into the soup bowl and poured water into it from the kettle. She whisked the tea around until it made a soft pale froth. With both hands she handed the bowl across the table to Perec, who didn't know what he was supposed to do with it.

"You drink it," she said in a whisper.

Perec brought the bowl to his lips. The tea was horrible. He pulled a face.

"This isn't tea," he said.

"It's green tea," she said. "*Matcha*. It's what the Japanese drink. Anyhow the taste of it doesn't matter. It's what it means."

"What does it mean?" Perec asked her.

"I'm not sure," she said. "But it's supposed to be important."

She took the bowl from Perec, gave it a half turn then sipped from it, unable not to make a face herself. She put the bowl down and looked at him.

"What do we do now?" asked Perec.

"I don't know," she said. "I've never done this with anybody else before. Usually I just stop here." She giggled. "I suppose we could talk."

Perec shrugged. He didn't want to talk to this girl.

"I'm sure you're very interesting," she said to him.

"No I'm not."

"Your accent is funny. Are you from Canada?"

"The U.S. My mother was French and so am I. I was born here in Nice."

"So you have relatives here?"

"I suppose."

"We should find them."

"No."

"Why not?"

"I don't know them. I haven't seen them since I was a baby. And they didn't like my mother."

"Family is important."

"No it isn't."

"How can you say that?"

"Is your father important? He beats you. I heard him. Look at your face."

"You're not supposed to talk about anything ugly while we're having tea."

"It's all ugly. Family. People. I don't need anyone. I hate them all."

She covers her ears.

"I don't want to hear it!"

He stopped talking. She uncovered her ears and pretended as if nothing had happened.

"We should meditate."

"I have to go."

"I'll teach you. It will help you find tranquillity."

"I don't give a shit about tranquillity! I don't give a shit about your stupid tea! It tastes like piss!"

He got up and ran away from her, still wearing the headband she made. He was lying on his bed a few minutes later when she knocked at the open door.

"You forgot your papers."

She put them at the foot of his bed.

"I'm sorry I made you angry," she said.

"I'm sorry I said your tea was like piss."

"I know, it's awful, I think I must do it wrong."

"No, it was nice."

"Do you really think so?"

"Yes."

He looked around the room at all the papers he'd been reading.

"You like to read newspapers."

"I'm looking for something. I can't find it. I miss my computer. You don't have a computer, do you? The Internet?"

She shook her head. "I knew where there's an Internet café. I could show you."

"Now?"

"Amalie! Where are you, damn you!" came Debord's boozy voice from the bottom of the stairs.

"I'm coming!" she shouted back.

"Where the hell are you? What are you doing?"

"Tomorrow," she said quickly. "He goes to the racetrack."

She hurried down the steps.

"What were you doing up there?" Perec heard Debord say to her.

"I was taking him clean towels."

"How many towels does the little bastard need? I want you to stay away from him, do you hear me?"

The following morning after Amalie finished her chores, she and Perec were walking to the Internet café. Her eye was not as swollen and she had washed her hair and was wearing a light summer dress. She was wearing makeup on her eyes and lipstick. Perec was relieved she didn't take his hand again, but as they walked sometimes her hand brushed against his.

"Do you mean what you said?" she asked him. "Do you really hate everyone?"

"I don't know," said Perec. "Yes. Sometimes."

"Is there anyone you don't hate?"

"Yes," he said, thinking of Anna.

"Do you hate me?" Amalie asked.

"Not so very much," Perec said honestly.

Amalie laughed.

"I suppose that's a good start," she said. "I don't hate you very much either."

There were a few people in the cybercafe when they got there. Perec was nervous. He'd never used a computer other than the one in AnnaWorld.

"Bonjour, Yves!" Amalie said to the young man who worked there.

"Bonjour, Amalie! How are you?"

"I'm well, thank you. This is my friend Vincent."

Yves held out his hand. Perec took it with the greatest reluctance.

"We'd like to use a computer," Amalie said to Yves.

"Of course."

Perec paid Yves, then he and Amalie went to a computer terminal.

"You've never done this before? I mean, a cybercafe?"

Perec shook his head.

"It's easy, just like at home."

She was very patient in showing him how to use the computer.

"What should we look up first?"

"Movies," said Perec.

"Do you like movies? I love the movies! We have a DVD player but the discs are so expensive. We'll see what movies are playing."

She typed it in and they read the screen.

"Do you see anything you like?"

"No."

"Me either. I like Audrey Hepburn movies. Do you like Audrey Hepburn?"

"No."

"That's right, I forgot. You don't like anybody."

She looked at the clock on the wall.

"I have to get back. He'll be home soon. And probably drunk already. Can you manage?"

Perec nodded. She rushed out.

Now that she'd gone, he searched for Anna on the Internet. There were a bunch of hits.

Finally he landed on an article about where the movie stars were staying during the festival. Anna's real-estate lady (Mrs. May) had given an interview, since she was renting to several stars. Though she declined to say where they'd rented, another article, an interview with Anna held at "her grand rented villa in the hills above Cannes," gave him a clue.

Perec went back to the rental site, looking for houses that fit this description. There was just one.

Perec took a bus up into the hills and then began to walk. He found the house but didn't go as far as the front gate, where he knew there would be a camera. The old winery sat on a level patch of ground at the foot of a steep hill and at the end of a drop-off. Perec took a long walk around, went up the hill from the other side, and worked his way around until he was hidden in the trees but could see the comings and goings of the house. He climbed a bit higher and now could actually see over the walls and inside the compound. Perec saw the long black car and the driver waiting and saw Anna and Spandau come out and get in. He watched as the gates opened and the car drove through and turned out onto the road and disappeared.

He eased his way down the hill and came out where they could not see him. He walked around as much of the perimeter of the house as he dared. The house backed up to the ravine. He walked a few feet down the lip of the ravine, picked his way along the steep slope. The gates began to open again and he scurried forward to hide but tripped and fell off balance down the hill.

He bounced and rolled a quarter of the way down, finally stopped by one of the clumps of scrub trees that dotted the hillside. He lay there for a while, scratched and out of breath. Nothing was broken. He got up and started to look for a route back up when he saw, covered by a dense overgrowth of scrub, a metal grate in the side of the hill. He pulled brush away to get a better look. The grate was rusted and bound with an old chair and padlock. It covered a hole perhaps two feet in diameter. Perec pushed aside the bushes and peered in. He could only see a few feet, but it looked like some sort of old drainage tunnel. It was directly below the winery and could only come from there.

He tripped over a rock and moved it with his foot. Scorpions scrambled angrily from underneath. He kicked the rock aside and saw a nest of them, climbing nervously over one another, feeling vulnerable in the open. A few feet along he moved another rock and found the same thing. They were all over the hill. Perec squatted and watched them for a while. Sometimes he took a stick and touched their backs, wondering if they stung themselves. They never did. It was one more lie his *maman* had told him.

He covered the grate with brush then followed the edge of the ravine a ways and made his way back up to the road.

Perec found a hardware shop, where he bought a flashlight and a bolt cutter. These he put into a small knapsack and by nightfall was making his way to the grate again. By moonlight he cut the chain on the grate and forced it open. He climbed in and turned on the flashlight. There was barely enough room for him to inch along. A larger man couldn't have managed even to enter it. It was a tunnel cut roughly through the limestone rock, like a cave that had been widened. It sloped up toward the winery. Perec wriggled along until he was blocked by a cave-in where the tunnel widened a bit. He thought about giving up but he could feel air moving past him from behind the rockfall. He moved a few of the rocks and the air moved faster, and pushing aside a little more rubble, he was through. He climbed over the rocks and entered a low cave just high enough for him to sit upright. The floor was damp from water that dripped into it from the continuation of the tunnel that led up toward the house. Perec rested for a bit and tried not to think of the things he heard scurrying in the darkness around him.

Perec climbed into the continuation of the tunnel. After a while the texture of the tunnel changed and he realized he was climbing through a thick stone wall, the foundation of the winery. After a few feet the tunnel ended at a wooden wall covering its mouth. Light from his flashlight shone through chinks in the ancient board and fell on something smooth and solid beyond. Perec pushed at the boards and they came away and he found himself inside some sort of cavity between a rough, older outer wall and a smooth concrete inner one. The cavity was as wide as the tunnel, about two feet. The cavity ran a dozen feet to a concrete buttress pressing against the outer, older rock. He was at the base of the foundation, and the cavity went upward thirty or forty feet and disappeared in darkness. Above he could see a matrix of pipes and wires and ducts running back and forth. He was inside the walls somehow. He looked for a way to climb, and found that by wedging his back against the smooth inner wall, he could pick his way up the outer wall with his hands and feet. He climbed this way until there was a ladder coming down and a small ledge to give access to whoever built and maintained this. Perec moved along the ledge and thought he heard voices. He stopped and listened and moved slowly and silently toward them. A man and a woman were talking in French on the other side.

"My God," said the man, "they'd eat pasta every meal if I'd let them."

"Well, it's easier work for you, isn't it?" said the woman. "Why are you complaining?"

"A challenge would be nice, every now and again."

"Why don't you help me do the laundry? There's a challenge."

The voices faded. Perec waited until he was sure they'd gone, then he began to climb again. The entire structure was some sort of inner shell to the winery. The small access ledges appeared to circle at each floor, which gave complete access to the surface of the place. As he moved around and up and down in the hollow wall, he could hear snatches of conversations or television or music, which became even clearer if he put his ear to the pipes and air-conditioning ducts that fed into the rooms. Perec climbed higher until he reached the upper lip of the wall and climbed onto a flat subroof three feet below the original winery ceiling. The roof stretched out like the lid of a box, like an attic, thick layers of insulation punctuated by ducts and pipes and wires that entered the rooms below. He made his way carefully, from joist to joist, and could hear the sounds of the rooms below and sometimes the shadow of movement that filtered up through the ceiling light fixtures. Anna was not there. But soon she would be, and soon he would be hovering close above her, like an angel.

7

WHEN HE GOT BACK THE HOUSE WAS QUIET. THE DOOR TO the Debord room was ajar but no one appeared to be home. Perec was tired and dirty and his hands and back were scratched from the climb. He wanted to shower and go to bed. He unlocked his door and flipped on the light and saw her on the floor, in the corner of the landing. Her knees were drawn up and she was facing the wall.

"Amalie? What's wrong?"

He went over to her and knelt next to her. He tried to turn her face but she pulled away and he tried again. Debord had beaten her badly this time. The right side of her face was a purple-engorged mass. Perec wondered if her jaw were broken. Her eye was closed and her lips were swollen at odd angles and did not quite meet. Oddly, she wasn't crying. He led her into his room.

"Where is he?"

"He won't be back tonight," she said thickly.

"Do you have some medicine? I could go down and get it."

He made a move to the door, to go out.

"No! Don't go. Please."

He stopped, looked at her. Shut the door. He went over and stood looking down at her, unsure what to do now. She reached up and took his hand. Still holding it, she lay down on the bed.

"Hold me."

Perec thought about just running and leaving her there. Instead, never letting go of her hand, he climbed onto the bed with her. She turned and curled herself into him, bringing his arm around her. Perec had never held a woman before. He felt the usual sickness sweep over him. Part of him wanted to kick her out of the bed, run her off. He felt violated, as if she'd pulled him from the shallows into deep and uncomfortable water. She held his hand against her cheek and he could feel the rise and fall of her breathing and smell her hair and the scent of her skin. Then it began to happen Down There and he pulled away from her in horror, but she said softly, "It's all right," and pushed herself closer into him. In a few moments she felt his body quiver against her and then rest and she gently squeezed his hand. Perec buried his face in her hair and went to sleep.

They were woken sometime before daylight by Debord pounding on Perec's door.

"Are you in there, you little whore? Open up, damn you!"

They heard his key in the lock. Amalie rushed to the door, leaning her weight against it to keep it closed. Debord gave a great shove and it flew open.

"I'll kill you this time! I'll kill you both!"

Debord slapped her and threw her against the wall. She slid to the floor and Debord took off his heavy thick belt and began to whip her. She covered herself, whimpering.

Perec watched this for a few moments, as if he were merely a
spectator and it had nothing to do with him. Then it sank in and
he leaped at Debord, trying to pull him away. Debord shrugged
him off and hit him, knocking him off balance, then began on
Amalie again. Perec felt helpless, then remembered the razor.

He picked it up and slashed at Debord's back. The man roared
and turned on him, stepped forward to attack, but Perec moved
inside the man's arms, as if encouraging an embrace, and reached
up to slash his throat. Debord stopped and stared at Perec for a
moment, as if unsure of what had just happened, and put his
hands to his throat.

It was only when he felt his own blood pouring through his
hands that a look of panic swept across his face. Amalie screamed
and Perec put his hand over her mouth. She struggled but Perec
kept his hand there as they watched Debord turn very pale and
fall to his knees, then to the floor, where he lay twitching and
gurgling in a widening crimson pool.

Perec felt nothing but watched in fascination. Debord stopped
twitching and lay still. Amalie broke free of Perec and fled out of
the room and down the stairs. Perec followed her downstairs and
went into the flat, where Amalie was trying to dial the phone. She
was shaking and could not remember the number, couldn't quite
recall what it was she was supposed to be doing. Perec took the
phone away from her and replaced it.

"Get away from me!" she cried. "Don't touch me!"

Perec wondered why she thought he might hurt her. It
wounded his feelings and actually made him a little angry. Amalie
stood there shaking and glaring at him in fear. Perec pulled the
phone from the wall. Amalie thought, Now is my turn, but Perec
turned and went back upstairs to his room. He poured water from
the jug into the washbasin and cleaned the blood from his hands.

Debord's blood had sprayed over his shirt and pants, so Perec took those off and put on clean ones. He put some things in his knapsack and came back down the stairs. Amalie was sitting at the foot of the steps with her head in her hands. Perec stopped and looked down at her. He wanted to say something but could think of nothing. Amalie looked up at him.

"Go," she said. "Now."

She buried her face again in her hands. Perec reached out and laid his hand on her soft hair. If she felt it she did not say. Perec went out into the dark morning and did not look back, not once.

It was at least three hours until daylight and Perec made his way on foot through the backstreets of the city to the edge of town. Day was breaking when he reached the tunnel. He pushed his knapsack into the tunnel ahead of him then climbed in himself, pulling the metal grate shut with his foot, careful to bring the freshly cut chain and lock with him. He climbed the rest of the way into the wall space then climbed up into the attic. He moved to the edge behind a low wall where he would not be seen and fell into a deep sleep.

8

THE NICE-CANNES AIRPORT IS ABOUT AS ARCHITECTURALLY
exciting as a VD clinic. Occupying acres of some of the most
beautiful and expensive coastland in the world, it was apparently designed by the Amish, with the intention of purging it of
as much sinful beauty as possible. They were successful, and
rather than feeling as if you've landed on the Riviera, you have an
uncomfortable sensation the pilot may have wildly overshot and
dumped you in Bognor Regis.

Things do improve a bit when you get out the other side.

Though sophisticates turn up their noses to hear it, Cannes and
Nice are actually the same town. The two thriving and aggressive
cities hug the rugged Mediterranean French coast, with poor quiet
Antibes wedged in between them like a puppy in a bridal bed.

It is never clear where one ends and the other begins, either
geographically or culturally. It's helpful, then, to think of them as
a kind of urban Abbott and Costello: one is far more amusing but
it's the duller one that ends up holding all the money. Cannes,
host of the infamous film festival, has a reputation for Vegas-like

flash and excess. But rest assured that when a flashbulb pops in Cannes, a cash register dings somewhere in Nice. Cannes is small and snooty; Nice is larger and appears more welcoming. There are just so many wealthy actors and jet-setters you can force into Cannes during those two weeks in May. The rest are forced into potluck farther down the road, where Nice triples its prices, turns storerooms into B&Bs, and suddenly learns how to speak impeccable English.

The men are bronzed and the women go topless. But given the range of ages this includes, the reality isn't nearly as delectable as it could be. World-class restaurants hide amid the flyblown and the merely mediocre, and when the crowds arrive in May, it's often hard to tell the difference until the botulism hits.

As for the Cannes Film Festival itself, it is the largest movie marketplace on the planet. People come to buy and sell movies the way bedouin gather at an oasis to barter goats, though with marginally less honesty or tact. Nor is it truly a festival, unless you consider desperation festive, since fortunes and reputations are lost at the place even more easily than they are made. All this roiling along under the jaundiced eye of the French, who throw the shindig each year simply to relieve their existential boredom by causing trouble and paying back old international scores either real or imagined. It's been rumored that people who actually like movies have sometimes attended. If so, they are placed on a list and never allowed back into the hotels.

Special came out of the Nice airport terminal into the middle of all this with his rolling suitcase and his iPod blasting Aida. He was looking for a taxi. There were several and Special went over to the one closest.

"You speak English?"

"Yes," said the driver. "I lived for five years in Chicago."

"How much to take me into town?" Special asked.

"Nice?" said the driver. "Cannes? Antibes? Juan-les-Pins?"

"Nice," said Special, who already did not like him.

"What part?"

"What do you mean, what part?"

"It's a big place," said the taxi driver.

"Okay then, goddamn it," said Special. "The middle of Nice."

"Thirty euros," said the driver.

"What's that in real money?"

"You mean," said the driver, "real American dollars instead of the imaginary euro? About forty-five dollars."

"Well, shit," said Special, "I didn't ask for no guided tour."

"If you can't afford it, monsieur, then would you let this other person in?"

"All right, all right. What about my suitcase?"

"I have a bad back," said the driver.

"Yeah, and I'm fixing to develop a tight wallet."

Special climbed into the cab.

"And . . . ?" said the driver.

"I'm looking for a hotel."

"Which hotel?"

"Can we not do this again?" Special asked him.

"Contrary to what your guidebook may tell you, monsieur, there is more than one hotel in the area."

"Can you recommend someplace to stay?"

"*Oui*, monsieur. Many places."

"A decent, clean hotel? Someplace not too expensive?"

"*Oui*, monsieur. Several."

"Can you take me to one of them?"

"*Oui*, monsieur," said the driver, who made no attempt to get the car moving. They sat there for a while.

"Is there a problem?" Special asked him.

"*Oui,* monsieur."

"And that is?"

"Is monsieur acquainted with the Cannes Film Festival?"

"Yeah . . ."

"And perhaps monsieur is also acquainted with the number of people who attend it?"

"You want to get to your point?" said Special.

"The festival begins today, monsieur, and unless monsieur has made reservations, it is unlikely monsieur will find a hotel that has a room."

"You're shitting me," said Special.

"Non, monsieur," said the taxi driver, "that would be most unlikely."

Special stared at the back of the driver's head for a while.

"Why don't we," said Special finally, "try this a different way."

"Whatever you prefer."

"I need a room somewhere. Can you—would you—be able to help me find one?"

"I fear that isn't my job," said the taxi driver.

"But you could find one," said Special, "if you felt like it."

The driver smiled. "It's a great deal of trouble."

"Aha."

"And I would have to charge you extra while we looked."

"Aha."

"God knows how long it will take."

Special thought for a moment.

"How do the French say, 'If you're getting fucked you may as well enjoy it'?"

"I'm sorry, monsieur, it would never occur to the French not to find it pleasurable."

* * *

After driving around for an hour, the driver took him to a small B&B in the Old Town of Nice. The driver went in, checked on the availability of a room, then came back out with a positive report.

"How much is it?" Special asked him.

"Two hundred euros a night."

"What? What is that? Goddamn, that's"—Special did a hasty calculation—"over a thousand goddamn dollars a week! This ain't exactly the Hilton."

"We could keep looking, but you won't find better. Also, my meter is still running."

"Yeah, yeah, okay. And how much do I owe you?"

"I regret, monsieur, that in our haste I neglected to turn it on."

"This is bullshit. You scamming my ass."

"Monsieur is welcome to file a complaint."

"How much?"

"I should have turned on the meter, so I feel obliged to give monsieur a discount. Shall we say two hundred euros?"

"We can say that, but I ain't giving it to you. I look to you like I just fell off a turnip truck? Ain't my fault you didn't turn on the meter, Jack. Seventy-five euros."

"Monsieur is joking, of course."

"Monsieur is dead fucking serious."

"In France it is a very serious offense to refuse payment."

"I ain't refusing payment, I'm refusing to let you hang it in me, you goddamn frog extortionist. You want to call a cop, go ahead. We can check your last meter reading against the mileage on the car. 'Course, you're going to waste all evening, but me, I got all the time in the world. I'm here on vacation."

"Monsieur leaves me with no choice. Here in France we uphold the law. I shall have to report this. Monsieur will wait here."

"Knock yourself out, Charlie. I'll be inside."

The driver went to the car, where he pretended to radio his garage. Special went inside, where he booked a room for three days. He paid the old lady who owned the place and she showed him to his room. It was a nice enough room with a toilet and shower but no TV. The wallpaper, carpet, furniture, and bedcover were flowered. There were paintings of flowers, and there was a vase of flowers on the desk.

Special opened up his suitcase and took out a pint of vodka. He sat in the chair and took a few drinks and thought until the driver knocked on his door.

"I fear I must relinquish my position," said the driver.

"No shit."

"One hundred and fifty euros."

"Here's ninety. Use it to get some therapy on that bad back of yours." Special handed him the money and shut the door in his face.

The truth was, he didn't have any idea where to begin. He didn't speak a word of the lingo, and he had no idea about the festival or what the hell went on with it, except a bunch of goddamn movie stars and rich producers showed up once a year to party. Driving around, he could see the place was packed—they weren't joking about that—and he'd expected something a little quieter. He'd also never been to France before, didn't know a thing about the culture, and he felt helpless. This worried him.

He went out walking around the Old Town, which was nice enough. A lot of old buildings, a lot of people running in and out of bars and cafés. Special knew nothing about the place, didn't want to know anything about it. All he wanted was to find that crazy little bastard and get his money back before Jimmy Costanza sent two or three more goons to inflict pain and suffering on him.

He was hungry and went into a café, where the waiter gave him a menu in French. Might just as well have been in Chinese.

"You speak English?" he said to the waiter.

The waiter shook his head.

"Then you won't mind me saying how bad I hate this goddamn country so far. You parlay-voo 'hamburger'?"

(In French) "Yes, monsieur would like a lousy hamburger."

"All I want is a cheeseburger, french fries, and a Coca-Cola."

The waiter stared at him. Special launched into a humiliating mime: "Hamburger, right? *Oui?*"

"*Oui.*"

Special held out one hand to represent the burger. "Hamburger, then . . ." He laid his other hand on top of that. "Cheese. *FROMAGE,* or whatever the fuck it is, on top of it. Fromage-burger, you got that?"

"*Oui,* monsieur."

"And fries."

"Pardon?"

"Fries," Special repeated. "Ah, fuck the fries, I don't care. Just give me a goddamn Coke." Special mimed drinking a soda. "Glug glug glug. Coca-Cola. Jesus Christ."

The waiter scribbled it all down and went away. Special tried to will his blood pressure back down to a safe level when he noticed some students at a table, looking his way and sniggering. Goddamn French, the whole fucking country is ganging up on me. There were two girls and a faggy-looking guy, all speaking

French. One of the girls, the plain one, got up and came over to him.

"The hamburger comes with fries," the girl said. "They never put cheese on it even if you ask because they don't have Velveeta and it's too much trouble, and it might be fairly raw, which is how they like them here, except he knows you're an American, so they might burn it to a cinder. So be prepared."

"You speak English!" Special was delighted.

"So does the waiter, for that matter."

"What the hell is it with these bastards."

"Oh, they're all right. You were rude. They're into all that good-morning, good-bye, please, and thank-you stuff here. And they like it if you at least try to speak the language. Where are you from?"

"L.A."

"How would you like it if thousands of people who didn't speak the language invaded your city every summer?"

"Baby, you ain't been to L.A., have you? You American?"

"From Manchester, New Hampshire. I'm taking a language course here."

"My name's Eduardo. What's yours?"

"Patsy."

"Nice to meet you, Patsy. I appreciate your help. Even if I wasn't being rude."

"You were," she said. She gave him a quick smile and went back to her friends.

Special took out his iPod and listened to a collection of Pavarotti arias. He looked over at the girl every now and then and caught her looking back.

9

Special took a cab east into Cannes and to the Croisette and spent a while walking up and down, taking in the sights, watching all the people. They all appeared to be incredibly busy, but as far as Special could tell they weren't doing anything. There were a hell of a lot of people, though, and the idea of finding Perec in all this—if he was still here at all—began to look pretty slim. He thought about having dinner in one of the restaurants but they were all packed. He took a cab back and had dinner at a bistro near the place he was staying. Bought a bottle of wine and took it back to his room and drank half of it while listening to *La Traviata*.

In he morning he awoke early and went back to the café on the corner. He'd bought a phrase book the night before and read to the waiter that he wanted American coffee and some scrambled eggs. *Oeufs brouillé*. What a goddamn language. He sipped his coffee. His stitches itched and he tried not to succumb to a sizable anxiety attack, fending off visions of what Locatelli's people were likely to do if he came back without the money. He needed some sort of systematic way of finding the little fucker, but so far none had revealed itself to him. The *oeufs* came and they were runny and there was no toast, just some pieces of god-damn baguette. It was easy to understand why so many people lined up at McDonald's over here. These people couldn't even get their eggs to hold together, much less take their place as a world power.

The girl from the previous day came in alone. She ignored him and sat at a table inside, ordering something in her rapid Froggish. She took out a notebook and began scribbling. Special went over to her.

"Can I buy you a coffee?"

"I've got one, thanks."

"You know, when I say, 'Can I buy you a coffee?' I don't actu-ally mean 'Can I buy you a coffee?' It's more along the lines of saying, 'You mind if I sit down?'"

"Why?"

Special looked at her. "Tell me you're not one of those people who, when they go abroad, try to pretend they're not Americans."

"That would be me, okay."

"You don't like me."

"I don't actually know you, so there's nothing to dislike yet. I could work on it."

"You let me sit down and it'll give you a chance."

"I could learn to dislike you while you're still standing."

"It would be more convenient over a nice plate of *eefs*."

"*Eu,*" she corrected.

"What?"

"That's actually the way it's pronounced."

"Hell of a language, ain't it?"

Special went over and got his own *eu* and coffee and brought them to her table. He called the waiter and ordered *eu* for the lady as well.

"See how jolly this is," Special said to her.

"Oh yeah," said the girl. "What do you want?"

"Who said I want anything?"

"You're hitting on me."

"The hell I am. I ain't hitting on you."

"Then what do you want?"

"Well, okay, maybe I am hitting on you just a little."

"You're wasting your time."

"Why?"

"I'm frigid. I think sex is overrated. I'm trying to rechannel my energies. To transcend the whole sexual thing."

"Jesus," said Special, shaking his head and smiling.

"What?"

"The only people who talk that shit are old people who can't get it and young people who haven't had it."

She turned red. "I'm not discussing my sex life with you."

"Why not? You got anything better to do?"

"Why don't you just take your *eefs*," she said, "and go back to your own table."

"A good-looking girl like you, it's hard to understand. You don't look queer."

"Not that it's any of your business, but I'm not queer. And you can save that good-looking bullshit for somebody who'll fall for it."

"You are."

"I'm not. I'm twenty pounds overweight, my teeth are crooked, I've got hair like steel wool, and if I took off my glasses you'd dissolve into Jell-O. These are not qualities designed to have men swoon."

"You got one hell of a bod on you, you don't mind me say-ing so."

"Well, I do mind. You don't even know me. It's insulting and it reduces me to the level of a side of bacon."

"Your problem is, you don't know a goddamn thing about men. How the hell do you know what a man likes?"

"I've been told often enough."

"Shit," said Special, "people never know what the hell they want until they finally come face-to-face with it. A man goes on and on about how he'd like to fuck Marilyn Monroe, and even he knows that shit ain't never going to happen, he ain't going any-where close to no Marilyn Monroe. But a man's got to talk about something and that's what they talk about. You put that same man next to a woman with an ass on her and a face that ain't going to win no awards, and he don't give a shit as long as she's willing to make him happy. Confronted with the choice between riding that woman or going home to pull his pud, he'll take the ride every time. Trust me on this one."

"You make it all sound so romantic."

"You got your romance," said Special, "and you got your down and dirty. They hardly ever in the same room together. That's the mistake people make. Both of them got their place, you just got to keep your timing straight, is all."

The eggs came. The girl buttered a baguette piece and smeared jam all over it and took a healthy interest in the eggs. Took long gulps of the coffee before it got cold. Damn, but Special liked to see a woman eat. Special was of the philosophy that people usu-ally fucked the way they ate. You see a woman dain'tily moving grub around on her plate, it ain't worth bothering. This one fin-ished off the bread and that tongue darted out for a crumb she'd missed at the corner of her mouth. Oh yeah, this one will do.

"Your French pretty good, is it?" he asked her.

"I studied in school. I'm over here on vacation for a couple of weeks so I get to use it."

"What do you do?"

"I'm a secretary at an insurance firm. Pretty exciting stuff."

"I'm a movie producer."

"Yeah, right."

"They got black ones."

"That's not what I meant."

"Nothing big, little independent films. Low-budget stuff so far. I'm looking to expand, though."

"You done anything I'd know?"

"You ever see a film with Mario Van Peebles? Called *Posse*? I produced that one. There were a lot of black cowboys but nobody ever talks about them. Me and Mario, we just felt the story needed to be told. I'm here for the festival."

"You got a film here?"

"Nah, but you got to go where the money is. Lots of rich bastards around. I'm trying to put together a new project. You know how it is."

"Yeah, sure I do," she said. "I saw you yesterday listening to your iPod. What kind of music?"

"Opera."

"Opera?" she repeated.

"Yesterday it was Pavarotti. Today it's José Carreras and tomorrow it's Placido Domingo. The Three Tenors. You like opera?"

"My mom listens to Andrea Bocelli."

"Bocelli, if you'll excuse me for saying so, is shit. That ain't opera, that's just some blind guinea trying to make out like he's singing opera. Irritates the piss out of me. I mean, I'm sorry he's blind and all, but the man got no voice control, no projection. You want opera, I can show you some opera."

She stared at him. "You're not like I thought."

"You see?" he said. "You're coming around now."

"I still think you're a bullshit artist, but at least you're an interesting bullshit artist."

"I'm pretty sure you mean that as a compliment," said Special. "I got an idea. How about you teach me some French, and I teach you some opera?"

"I'm leaving in a couple of days."

"Hell, you can learn a lot in a couple of days."

"Sure."

"We can start with you teaching me how to order dinner. Not here. Why don't we go find someplace nice later on tonight? We can meet here, if that'll make you feel more comfortable."

"Sure, why not?"

He watched her walk away, stood there letting her know he admired that fine ass of hers. She turned to look back at him a couple of times, smiled at him.

Oh, Special, he thought, just look at you. You got to keep that mojo rolling and it will roll you, baby, right on home.

10

HE MET HER THAT EVENING AT THE CAFÉ. SHE SHOWED UP wearing a nice dress that proved he wasn't wrong about the body. He ordered drinks and they sat at the café for a while talking. He wanted to take her somewhere good but didn't know where and couldn't have arranged the reservation if he did. She knew of a little place not far away she'd passed and thought interesting. It was a small bistro in a backstreet, and even then they had to wait. They weren't kidding when they said the town got full. Special and Patsy stood in the street leaning against the stone wall talking. She was easy to laugh, which was another good sign. She was smart, too, though Special normally didn't like to have much to do with smart women. They were more trouble than they were worth; you spent most of your time just trying to convince them of shit. Life was hard enough without having to explain every goddamn thing you were trying to do.

Patsy didn't ask a lot of questions, she just seemed fine to let things happen however they were going to happen. In the bistro she guided him through the menu and helped him order in

French when the waiter came. She was having a good time and even Special nearly forgot she was one more bitch he needed to use. They drank champagne while they waited for the meal, and by the time the food came she was touching him on the arm when she talked. They had wine with the meal, and by the end of it she was a little drunk.

"You have me at a slight disadvantage," she said, leaning her head on his shoulder. "I'm tipsy."

"Hot damn," said Special, and she laughed.

They left the bistro and walked toward the beach. She put her arm through his. As they walked he was humming, though he didn't realize until she mentioned it.

"What is that?"

"An aria from *Tosca*," he said. " 'Vissi d'arte.' You never heard it?"

"No."

"Here, listen to this."

He took out the iPod and thumbed up the aria, putting one bud in her ear and the other in his.

"Maria Callas," Special told her. "It don't get no better than that."

They walked arm in arm listening to the music.

"It's beautiful," she said. "I wish I knew what she was saying."

" 'Vissi d'arte, vissi d'amore,' " he said. " 'I lived for art, I lived for love.' Ain't that some shit?"

They crossed the Promenade des Anglais out onto the rocky beach and walked down to the water. They stood with their arms around each other, listening to the music and looking out at the lights from the boats in the bay. Patsy had tears in her eyes. Special had sense enough not to say anything. Instead he kissed her and she in turn devoured his mouth. There was an unlocked bathing hut nearby and Special took her inside. He pushed her up against the wall, lifted her skirt, and shoved his hand into her panties. She moaned and moved against his hand. He pulled off her panties and unzipped himself and slid it partway in. She gasped in pain and he stopped moving and instead let her lower herself onto him.

"You okay?"

"Yes, don't stop, please."

He put his hands beneath her ass and raised her up, held her there while he pushed in and out of her. She wrapped her arms around his neck and her legs around his hips, and if she'd never done this before, she was, thought Special, a goddamn prodigy. Special came but she didn't.

"It gets better after the first time," he said, lowering her to the ground.

"This may be the beginning of a beautiful friendship," she said. "Sex, I mean. Not you, necessarily."

She was sore when they got back to her room, but could they do it again if he was able? Hell yeah, he was able. They did it three more times by dawn, and when the sun rose on the Bay of Angels, Patsy had made a very long list of the entertaining things she wanted him to teach her.

"It should be pretty simple to find her," said Patsy. "If she's a judge, then she'll be seeing the films, right? So all you have to do is get a list of the screenings. They're listed in the papers, or you could probably get a list through the festival office."

"You see? I knew you were going to be my lucky charm."

It was nice, thought Special, to watch her do the grunt work. He'd bought a cigar and a brandy and they were sitting at one of the café's sidewalk tables as she shuffled through the pile of newspapers and magazines, then followed up with phone calls on her mobile. Lovely young women moved past them in an endless stream. The cognac was good and the cigar was a genuine Cuban you couldn't get in the States, and he could afford it now that Patsy was paying for nearly everything. She was grateful for a whole new world of naughtiness being opened up for her, and the way she'd taken to it, Special felt he was earning his money. He puffed on the cigar. Took a sip of the brandy. The sun was out. He was finally beginning to see what all the fuss was about. Life was good.

"Here," she said, and handed him a list. "She's on the committee judging the main films in competition. They're all being shown in the Palais. These are the names and the times they're being shown."

"And?"

"And nothing. The films are being shown three times a day at the Palais, which means she has to show up for one of them. There's no way of knowing which one it will be."

"So we have to show up and stand around all day waiting for her?"

"What is this 'we' business? You got a mouse in your pocket? The place is going to be lousy with people. It seems like a pretty lame idea to me. Isn't it easier just to call her agent? Or try to see her back home? It strikes me as a perfectly good waste of copulation time."

"I'll never get past her agent. You know how goddamn snobbish they get. I need to see her here. And I need you with me, because of the language thing. It'll be fun. Anyway, just how bad can it be?"

He was to discover just how bad that afternoon. They got to the Palais for the second showing of that day's film. Here it was nearly three in the afternoon and the place looked like goddamn Times Square on New Year's Eve. Didn't anybody work in this goddamn country? Then he looked at the faces and listened to the voices and realized that at least some of them weren't French. They were tourists, people who'd come from all over to stand on a sidewalk in the sun with a few thousand others, waiting to get a glimpse of a movie star. Or maybe not a glimpse—you had to elbow to get through for a chance at a sighting, and even then your timing had to be damned good.

Security was tight and you couldn't get anywhere close. You clawed your way to the front of the crowd and struggled to remain there while the cars pulled up and disgorged the famous and the beautiful onto the red carpet. They stopped every few feet and waved and smiled, then shuffled on while you got your ears repeatedly clipped by the elbows of arms shooting out to wave autograph pads or simply just, stupidly, to wave blindly.

It made no sense to Special. There was some sort of insanity possessing these bozos that he didn't get. Anyway it looked pretty hopeless. Not because he was actually trying to get to Anna Mayhew—hell, that would have been just plain dumb—but because there was a snowball's chance in hell of finding Perec in a crowd like this. The maddening thing is that Perec was there, somewhere. If not now, then this morning, or tonight, or tomorrow.

"This is useless," he shouted to Patsy. "There's too many goddamn people."

"I tried to tell you," she yelled back. She reached over and tweaked his crotch, causing him to make an undignified jump—her subtle way of reminding him of his true obligations.

They went back to the Old Town. Special was in a bad mood. Patsy kept trying to fondle him and he kept pushing her wandering hands away. She wanted to go immediately up to the room, but Special couldn't be bothered and thought another brandy and cigar might grease his thinking process. He needed another plan.

"What's wrong?" she asked when they sat down at the café. "Have I done something wrong?"

"Just order me a brandy, will you?"

"Don't you want to go to the room for a little while?"

"Look here," said Special, a little less than patiently. "I know you enthusiastic and I know you taking to the dick like a koala to eucalyptus, but I got other things on my mind just now. Let me get this settled and I'll ride you raw from now til doomsday, but at this point just order me the goddman brandy."

He plugged in the iPod and listened to Ramón Vinay do Verdi's *Otello*, thinking what a goddamn shame it was that nobody remembered who the hell Ramón Vinay was. There were clearly no guarantees in art, which is why he took to the far more practical job of pimping. In a few minutes he felt the muscles in his neck unlock and the brandy went down his gullet like soft-warmed lava. He closed his eyes and the terrible world melted away as he pushed Patsy's exploring fingers from his fly and thought about his life's only great dream, a season ticket to La Scala in Milan.

"Well, damn," said Patsy, removing one of the buds to complain in his ear. "You're turning out to be pretty unreliable, if you ask me. It really is unfair to get all this started if all you're going to do is just stop in the middle of it. I have to go home one of these days, and I can't see you coming to Manchester, New Hampshire."

The mood was broken. Special thought about hitting her. He didn't usually hit women unless they required it and this one surely did.

"Anyway," she went on, "you're going about getting to this actress all wrong. You can't get to her, but you could probably get to her chauffeur. Just write her a letter and give it to him to give to her. That's as close as you're going to come."

Which of course didn't help worth jackshit, since it wasn't actually her he was looking for. Special opened his eyes and was about to give Patsy fair warning to leave him in peace when he saw the newspaper the guy at the next table was reading.

"What's that say?" he said to her.

"What?"

"That, goddamn it. That."

She looked at the small headline on the bottom half of the front page.

" '*Sweeney Todd* in Nice,' " she said, reading the headline.

"Shit," said Special. "Tell him I want to borrow his paper for a minute."

Patsy shrugged and translated. The man said something back.

"He says he's reading it."

"Well, please tell the asshole I can see he's reading it, I just want to look at something."

She relayed this and the man pulled a sour face but surrendered his newspaper.

"Read this," Special said to her, pointing to the article.

" '*Sweeney Todd* in Nice,' hum hum, hum hum . . . Some guy cut some other guy's throat over a girl. They're looking for him."

"What did he use?"

"Why?"

She was desperately close to getting bitch-slapped all over half of Nice, and apparently this was conveyed well enough in the way he looked at her.

"A barber's razor," she said. "A cutthroat, poetically enough."

"Praise be to Jesus," said Special.

"You want to tell me how come," Patsy said, "you get excited about this but not about me doing that thing again with the Nutella?"

"Give the nice man back his paper," Special said to her, "and prepare to bump uglies to your heart's content. I have an idea."

They went back the following day. They hit the morning showing and lucked out—she came up, the driver let her and the big guy out, and drove off.

Patsy said it made sense that the drivers wouldn't wander off too far. They'd been watching where the cars went after they dropped people off and found there was a parking area in back of the Palais.

"There he is," said Patsy. "What'd I tell you?"

"Yeah, yeah, you practically psychic. Now take this note over to him."

"Why me?"

"Because you ain't no big ugly nigger fixing to scare the shit out of somebody, that's why."

Special waited out of sight until she came dancing back with a smile on her face.

"He flirted with me," she said.

"See, this giving you a whole new lease on life. He take the note?"

"He said he'd give it to her. He asked me who I was and I told him my name was Teresa, that I was a fan."

"He some kind of actor?"

"Who knows?" said Patsy. "But it'll get him to read it."

*　　*　　*

Anna and Spandau came out of the theater and got into the car.

"There's a note for Anna," Thierry said to Spandau. "From a fan, an American girl."

Spandau opened the note and read it. *I have information about your sharp little friend.* And gave a phone number. Spandau showed Anna the note.

"What does it mean?"

"I think it means he's here," Spandau said. "The crazy little guy from L.A. He's here."

11

When Spandau arrived, Special was sitting at a back table in La Palme d'Or in the Hotel Martinez on the beach. He was eating what appeared to be lamb and it looked remarkably good. There was an open bottle of Haut-Brion and Special was drinking a glass of it and looked profoundly happy with the world.

"I won't ask how you knew it was me," Special said to him. "Not too many of us gentlemen of color in here."

"You mentioned that we had a mutual acquaintance."

"Oh yeah," said Special. "You already had one run-in with him, didn't you? He cut a friend of yours too."

"How do you know all this?"

"I got special insight into our little pal. You want some of this? It's pretty damn good."

"What is it?"

"Lamb with cucumber, smoked eel, garbanzo beans, and some sugary mushrooms. They speak English here in case you have trouble. Here, have a glass of this wine anyway."

He poured Spandau a glass.

"What's your interest in this? What do you want?"

"The little bastard has something that belongs to me. Or, rather, something that belongs to some people who are very angry at me. When we catch him, all I want is five minutes with the little fucker and then you can do whatever you want with him."

"Why do we need you?"

"Because I know how his twisted little mind works and exactly what he has planned. That's how I was able to follow him here."

"So he is here?"

"Oh yeah, he's here okay, and making friends already."

Special took out a copy of the newspaper article and gave it to him. You didn't need a hell of a lot of French to see what it was about.

"What's to stop me from calling the police and telling them all this?"

"Why on earth would you do that? They pull me in, ask me a bunch of questions, none of which am I going to answer. What are they going to do? I ain't broke any French laws I can think of. They got to let me go and you right back where you started. Anyway, I think you ought to talk it over with Anna. She the one in the middle of all this."

"So he is looking for her?"

"He a real dedicated little bastard, I give him that. You got my number. Just give me a ring."

Special took a last gulp of wine, wiped his mouth, stood up, and walked out of the restaurant. Spandau sipped his own glass. The waiter came over, asked if there would be anything else. Spandau thought about ordering the lamb, but he was already confused about how to put this on his expenses. He said no thank you and the waiter gave him the bill. There was half a bottle left and he was damned if he was going to waste it.

*   *   *

Vignon was angry.

"You met with him and you didn't tell me?" he yelled at Spandau.

"You would have handled it differently?"

"You have no idea what you're doing here," Vignon said to him. "Of course I would have handled it differently. I'd have done it in a way that made sense. I saw the article in the paper this morning and I've already made some phone calls to my pals at the *commissariat*."

"Guys, hey, sorry, it's my ass we're talking about here, remember?" said Anna. "I think we should bring him here."

"Here?" Vignon wasn't sure he'd heard correctly.

"We've obviously got to talk to him," said Anna. "What better place? That way we can keep an eye on him until this thing is over."

"It makes a weird kind of sense," Spandau admitted. "We can put him in the guesthouse."

"Before we do anything, I'm going to check this out," Vignon said.

"Where are you going?"

"To see the girl. I'm sure she knows more than she's telling. You stay here."

"The hell I will."

"Why don't you listen to reason? Would it kill you to cooperate for once in your life? We don't need any cowboys here."

"Just shut up and take us there, Tonto."

"You know, for the first time I actually dislike Americans more than I do the British. I wasn't sure this was possible."

"Just drive," said Spandau as they climbed into the car. "Hi-yo, Silver."

*   *   *

They drove along the coast road, then turned to zigzag inland, picking their way through the streets from the fine shops and apartments to the poorer quarters, the older and narrower passages where the scents of Africa, India, Asia, all combined to fill the air with a spicy perfume that barely hid the stink of the bad sewers and the garbage that piled up faster than the city could gather it. These were the homes of the people who swept out the fine shops, who cooked and cleaned for the people in the fine apartments overlooking the yachts in the Bay of Angels.

"It looks different here, doesn't it?" Vignon said to him. "Well, you've got to put them somewhere. So here they are, and we hope they'll be so busy robbing and killing each other they forget about all that money just a bit farther toward the water."

At Amalie's, they knocked at the door but there was no answer.

"Hello?" Vignon called into the house.

Amalie appeared at the top of the stairs. She wore rubber gloves and was holding a scrub brush. She was a small, thin girl, almost pretty in a way, thought Spandau.

"What do you want?" she asked.

"We'd like to speak to you for a few moments."

"Are you from the newspapers? Or cops?"

"I used to be a cop but not anymore," said Vignon. "We'd like to talk to you about Vincent."

"They've found him?"

"Not yet."

"I've already told everything I know."

"Just a few questions and then I'll leave you alone."

Vignon and Spandau went upstairs. She was in Perec's room on her hands and knees, cleaning up her father's blood.

"We're sorry to intrude," Spandau said as Vignon reluctantly translated. "I know it must be difficult for you."

She kept on scrubbing.

"I've read the statement you gave to the police," Vignon said, "and I spoke to both the officers who interviewed you. Do you know Vincent well?"

"I've gone over all this, for hours and hours . . ."

"Just once again, please," asked Spandau.

She stopped scrubbing. She sat in the middle of the floor and pushed her hair out of her eyes.

"He rented this room. No, I did not know him well. I don't even know his last name."

"You were friends?" asked Vignon.

"Yes. No . . . I don't know . . . He was trying to help me."

"Your father beat you often?" Spandau asked her.

"Sometimes. When he was drunk, which was often."

"You hated him?"

"My father? Yes, I suppose so. I sometimes wished him dead. But he was my father."

"But you're not sorry he's dead, are you?" said Vignon.

"No. But I'm sorry Vincent killed him. More sorry for Vincent than my father. They think I may have encouraged him, talked him into it, don't they?"

"Did you?" Vignon asked.

"No. But I don't care what they think. It doesn't matter."

"You were lovers . . ."

"No, that's a lie," she said quickly. "That's what they think, but it's a lie. I would have been, if Vincent had asked me. But it wasn't like that."

"You say your father found you together . . ."

"My father came home drunk and beat me, then left. Vincent found me at the top of the stairs, just outside his room. I was hiding there. He took care of me and let me lie on his bed. I asked him to hold me. That's all."

"And that's the way your father found you."

"Yes."

"And began to hit you again . . ."

"We were asleep, he pounded on the door, unlocked it, and burst in. He knocked Vincent down and started beating on me. Vincent tried to stop him, but my father is a big man and Vincent is, well, he's small and kind of frail."

"Do you think your life was in danger?" Spandau said.

"From Vincent or my father?"

"Your father."

"He's a big man. He was beating me. Look at my face and tell me what you think."

"And Vincent? Were you ever afraid of Vincent."

"No. Never. Vincent wouldn't have hurt me."

"He loved you?"

"No. I'm not sure he was able to. I don't think it was something he understood."

"But you loved him."

"He needed to be loved, and he needed to love. One couldn't get in, and the other couldn't get out. Do you understand?"

Spandau nodded.

"Did Vincent ever mention Anna Mayhew, the American actress?" he asked her.

"No."

"Never mentioned her? Never spoke about wanting to see her, to talk to her?"

"No."

"Miss Debord," asked Vignon, "do you know where Vincent is?"

"No."

"If you did know, would you tell us?"

"No. I won't help you hurt him."

"All we want is to stop him from hurting anyone else. If he comes back or contacts you, you must phone the police."

"He won't. I'll never see him again. He'll be dead soon. Like my father. There are worse things than death."

"Such as?"

"When you find Vincent, you should ask him," she said.

"Thank you for your time," Spandau said to her.

She shrugged, went back to her scrubbing. They heard the *wish-wish-wish* of the scrub brush until they reached the bottom of the stairs, when it stopped and was replaced by the sound of her crying.

12

SPECIAL ARRIVED THAT NIGHT IN THE LIMO. THIERRY DROVE him into the compound and Special stepped out as if he did this sort of thing all the time.

"If you'll come this way, please," Vignon said to him. Special followed him into the guesthouse. As Special was surveying his new environment, Vignon closed the door and put a gun to the back of his head.

"I would like to go on record as saying I'm not in favor of this," Vignon told him.

"Yeah, I can feel a certain lack of enthusiasm."

"I could blow your brains out right now and there are a hundred places I could hide the body and it would never be found. Put your hands against the wall."

Vignon patted him down, took his passport and his wallet. Spandau came in.

"Getting acquainted?"

"He always like this?" Special asked Spandau.

"He's French," Spandau told him.

"That must be it."

Special continued to look around and appeared to be satisfied. He sat down on the sofa and crossed his legs.

"Okay, you're here," Vignon said to him. "Now talk."

"I'm feeling a little peckish," Special said. "You all got any of that Haut Brion stuff? And some of that goose-liver pâté. And a fresh baguette. I can't get over how much better it tastes over here."

"The French take bread pretty seriously," Spandau said.

"You ever try the stuff back home at La Brea Bakery? That's some damn fine shit."

"Their focaccia is pretty amazing."

"Who are you now? Escoffier?" Vignon said to Spandau.

"Just making small talk."

"You're trying to irritate me," Vignon said to him, "and it's working."

"It strikes me there are better ways to warm somebody up than threatening to shoot them in the head."

"We could break something," Vignon suggested.

"Like what? A vase? Oh, you mean him."

"Guys, guys. I hate to interrupt this whole good cop/bad cop thing—which is pretty entertaining, I have to admit—but I really am getting hungry."

"I told you this was a mistake," Vignon said.

Special was chowing down. He was having such a good time with the pâté and the bread that Spandau was tempted to join him. Vignon came in and tossed Special's passport and wallet onto the table.

"Your friend Eduardo here is a classy guy. He's a pimp. One

conviction in L.A. for pandering, some petty theft as a teenager. Other than being part of the dregs of humanity, he's clean."

"You know, I don't like this as well as I like the Haut-Brion. Is this the cheap stuff?"

"This is a Calon-Ségur. It needs to age a little longer," Vignon put in before he could catch himself. He glared at the two men. "Now you've got me doing it."

"What's his name?"

"His name is Vincent Perec," Special began. "He's a hair-dresser. He's got one or two little bad habits, like slicing people up with a straight razor. Him and his mother owned a little beauty shop down off Western near Koreatown. I say owned, because Vincent's here and he ain't going back, and I saw his mother hanging upside down like a sugar-cured ham in their attic."

"She was cut?" Vignon asked.

"Looked like her neck was broken to me, 'cause I didn't see no blood. But he did it okay. He wrote all about it in his diary."

"You have the diary?" Spandau asked him.

"Hell no. It was on his computer. I found it and old granny when I went looking for the little son of a bitch. I erased the whole thing."

"Why?" asked Spandau.

"Because I didn't want to take a chance on the cops finding him before I did. He stole nearly a hundred and fifty thousand bucks of the Mob's money that I'm responsible for. I got to find out where he hid it or me and old granny going to be strung up somewhere like a matched set of earrings."

"How do you know he didn't spend it? Or put it in the bank?" Vignon asked.

"He didn't need it," Special told him. "His old lady was liter-ally sitting on maybe thirty thousand—it was in the chair cushion under her ass. Perec didn't need any more than that to do what he wanted. He just took my goddamn money because he was mad at me. That boy is stranger than a bag full of hair. Nah, he didn't spend it and it ain't in no bank. He's weird but he ain't stupid. The bastard hid it somewhere and I got to find it. Probably somewhere around the house, which is why I got to find him before the cops come across the old lady."

Special smeared some pâté on a slide of baguette, ate it, then washed it down with some of the wine.

"It's better, it's starting to open up a little," Special said. "Anyway, Vincent ain't interested in money, Vincent's in love."

"Anna," said Spandau.

"Oh, big-time. That diary was some interesting reading, let me tell you. Vinnie's idea of lovemaking is likely to be a little messy."

"He intends to kill her?"

"Oh yeah. Among other things," said Special. "You got any more of that pâté?"

13

ANNA WENT OVER TO THE GUESTHOUSE CARRYING A BOTTLE of wine. One of Vignon's men stopped her at the door.

"I'm sorry, I don't think—"

"Who the fuck pays you?" Anna asked him.

"Vignon," said the op.

"And who do you think pays Vignon?"

He had to mull this over a bit.

"While you're chewing on that, get the hell out of my way."

She knocked on the door. Special was on the couch, watching TV and peeling an orange with a paring knife. He slipped the knife into the back of his belt and answered the door. He was surprised to see Anna standing there.

"Don't tell me. You come to borrow a cup of sugar?"

"May I come in?"

Special stood aside and waved her in with a gallant flourish. He started to close the door, but the op prevented it.

Anna looked around.

"This is the first time I've been in here," she said. "Not too shabby."

"You should have called. I'd have put out some tea and cookies or something."

"You know who I am?"

"Sure I do," he said. "You're little Vincent's girlfriend. I'm surprised the cowboy and the frog let you anywhere near me. But they don't know you're here, do they?"

"I usually get what I want."

"Oh, I don't doubt that."

She handed him the wine.

"A housewarming gift."

It was, of course, Haut-Brion.

"Well, at least somebody else around here got some taste."

He got two glasses. Opened the wine. Gave her a glass. They clinked glasses, drank.

"Very nice," said Special. "Now, you want to tell me what the fuck you're doing here, before them two come rushing in and rip my arms off?"

"You mind if I sit down?"

"You pay the rent."

"I want to know about him," she said.

"Who? Vincent? Why? What difference does it make?"

"I want to know."

"This just kinky movie-star shit, or you feeling some kind of guilt?"

"Why me?"

"He's a crazy fucking little psychotic pervert. I figure that's enough."

"Was it a particular role I've played? Something I said in an interview? Why me? You read his diary. He must have talked about it."

"He never went into it. Look, you're giving him too much credit. He's just your everyday garden-variety crazy motherfucker. Guys like him don't need to make any sense. That what makes them crazy."

Vignon and Spandau came bounding in.

"What the hell are you doing?" Spandau asked her.

"I wanted to talk."

"This is why it was a bad idea to bring him here," Vignon said. "The less you're associated with all this, the better."

"I think I'm already associated with it, don't you? I'm the one he wants to kill." She turned to Special. "Thank you."

"Drop by anytime."

Vignon accompanied her out.

"What was all that about?" Spandau demanded.

Special poured himself some wine.

"Nothing. Just us girls having a little get-together."

Spandau grabbed him by the shirt, pulled him from the chair, and slammed him against the wall.

"I ask you a straight question, I want a straight answer."

"You don't get your motherfucking hands off me, all you're fixing to get is three straight inches of shiv in your gut."

Spandau saw the knife, backed away.

"She come looking for me. I didn't set no goddamn mousetrap for her."

"What did she want?"

"She wanted to talk."

"About what?"

"What do you think? Same thing you'd want to talk about, why some crazy motherfucker she never met wants to kill her."

"What did you tell her?"

"Not much."

"Keep it that way. The less she knows, the better."

"Unless you don't catch him."

"We'll catch him."

"Like I said, he's crazy but he ain't dumb. I made the same mistake you're making and he nearly gut me like a fish. He don't think the way you think. There's no way you going to be able to predict him. I got a better shot because I read his diary, but that don't mean he ain't changed his mind a hundred times by now."

"Maybe he's given up."

"He ain't going to give up," Special said. "That's one thing that won't change. You not going to tell her why?"

"It wouldn't change things one way or the other."

"You can't blame her for wanting to know why the man wants to kill her."

Special went back to work on the orange with the knife.

"So it's true? Her old man cut his throat, just like his?"

"Just leave it alone."

"I mean, it is a little weird, isn't it? Both their daddies cutting their own throats, both kids finding them, both of them the same age. I mean, you can see how he might make something out of it. Gives me the willies just to think about it."

14

Special and Anna were in deep conversation on the patio. They'd spent a couple of hours talking, a real heart-to-heart, and Anna had even broken into tears a couple of times. At one point she'd gotten up, went into the house, and came back with a small box which she gave to him. A goddamned present, thought Vignon. It was disgusting. These Hollywood types and their emotional slumming, they had no idea what real life was like.

"They getting along rather well, don't you think?" Vignon asked Spandau.

"What's that supposed to mean?"

"Elena is offended."

"She doesn't like cooking dinner for a black?"

"She doesn't like cooking dinner for a pimp. We have them in France, as well."

"What about you?"

"I don't like pimps. Other than that, I have no opinion in the matter."

"You can tell Elena the last bit of conversation I overheard, they were talking about Baz Luhrmann's film of *La Bohème*. It doesn't sound much like the first step on the rocky road to prostitution. He's an unusual man and she's curious."

"He could dance like Nijinsky in *The Rite of Spring* but he'd still be a pimp. We'd all do well to remember that."

Vignon went inside. Anna came over to Spandau.

"What a fascinating guy," she said. "He's not who you think he is."

"I'm pretty sure he's not Mahatma Gandhi," Spandau said to her. "Be careful. It's a bad idea to get too chummy with him."

"Are you jealous? There is something charismatic about him. I could see how some women might fall under his spell."

"I'm serious. He may be charming and intelligent, but he's still a crook, and he makes his living sending women out to have sex for money. This is not a nice guy, Anna, in spite of the opera and the smooth talk. He can't be trusted."

"I work in Hollywood. He's not the only flesh peddler I know."

"Yes, but he's probably the only one you know who's liable to beat the hell out of you if you don't turn over at least five johns a night. He pulled a knife on me last night and he didn't learn that at La Scala. He's used it before."

Anna turned on a Texas twang. "Why, my daddy used to say the same thing when he caught me talkin' to the Negroes who used to come in the summer to harvest our peaches. I declare, I didn't like it then and I don't like it any better now. Kiss my magnolia-scented ass, Mr. Spandau."

She smiled sweetly and fluttered her eyelashes at him, gave him the finger, and went into the house. Spandau looked over at Special, who was laughing his ass off.

"You got your hands full with that one."

"Whatever it is you think you're doing, stop it," Spandau said to him.

"I got a theory why you white guys are so convinced us niggers just can't get enough of your women. Aside from the legend that our dicks are bigger—which I have to admit is true—we don't waste so much time talking about what we're going to do, we just do it. I ain't hitting on your woman. If I was, there'd be a whole lot less talking going on."

"She's not my woman, and all I'm trying to do is keep her safe. From Perec, from you, from anything that might hurt her. That's what I'm paid to do."

"Which brings me back to my original critique, that you ofay pale-assed motherfuckers spend so much time overcomplicating shit that you forget to take care of business. No question that she finds me utterly goddamn irresistible, because I am, but she's also getting bored to death in this kennel and I'm an interesting distraction. The real bonus, however, is that she knows it irritates the piss out of you. Since I like her and I don't like you, I find it amusing to play along. How fucking stupid are you?"

15

THE ATTIC WAS HOT WHEN PEREC WOKE. HE WAS SWEATING and he needed to pee. He looked around then shuffled over to the edge and pissed down the side of the wall. He moved back to his spot and opened his knapsack and took out a couple of energy bars and ate them, then drank some water from a plastic bottle. He could hear voices below him. The people he'd heard before and one other.

"I've made sandwiches," said Elena. "They're in the kitchen."

"Thank you, that's very kind," said François, one of Vignon's ops.

"And there's coffee."

"Thank you. I'll tell the rest of the boys."

A door closed and Perec heard the sound of the man pissing. He moved closer to the overhead light and could see the man standing at the toilet, then saw him go over to wash his hands. The man walked out of sight and Perec heard the door open again and the man went away. Perec moved a few yards over and now he could hear Elena again, now on the phone.

"Is she better? . . . No, no, she's seen the doctor already, he says it's her kidneys . . . Yes, she's old. I can't help it that she's old. She's my mother, your grandmother, what do you want me to do? Strangle her? . . . I don't care . . . I don't care. I'll be there later tonight. Good-bye."

Then, some distance toward the front of the house, Anna's voice.

"Did you call Harry?"

"I got his assistant," said Pam.

"Is he going to meet with Cheryl?"

"He says he is."

"Just keep on her about it, will you? She doesn't want me to do it and I think it's a good part. Maybe it's time to change agents."

"You have to be patient. She's always come through."

"I don't think she gives a shit anymore."

"Now you're just being paranoid."

"I'm going to take a shower. Just call her, will you?"

Pam left and in a minute Perec heard water running. A flexible air-conditioning pipe ran down into the room and Perec cut it with the razor and opened it a bit. He could see half of the bedroom through the ceiling grate. Perec anxiously looked around but couldn't find a way of seeing into the bathroom. Instead he waited with his heart pounding and imagined the scene. The water stopped and after a bit she came out of the bathroom naked and drying her hair with a towel. It was far better than the photos and he wanted to cry out, but instead bit his hand until he tasted blood in his mouth. She passed out of sight again, and when she came back she was in a terrycloth robe. Perec had wanted it to go on and on, but of course nothing good ever did. Still the thing was happening to him and he felt as if his body would explode.

There was a knock at the door.

"It's me."

"Come on in."

Pam came in. "I just talked to Cheryl. She called him. They'll set up a meeting when you get back."

"Good. About goddamn time."

"Elena wants to know what you want for lunch?"

"A salad, maybe? Ask David what he wants. You guys work it out. I don't care."

Perec lay on his back, trying not to moan. The words from below were just meaningless sounds since all his mind could do was embrace the image of her naked. He felt the universe attempting to dissolve. He kept biting his hand, his own blood tricking along the edges of his tongue and into the back of his throat. He turned quickly onto his side and his body stiffened and shook and he came into his hand.

"Did you hear something?" Anna asked Pam.

"Oh God. Rats?"

"These fucking old buildings, of course there are rats, fucking Italian rats the size of quarter horses. Thank you for reminding me."

Perec lay there, unable to move.

"Franz was talking about some kind of seafood. A seafood salad? That sounds good," said Pam.

"Yeah, yeah. Let's go for that."

He began to silently curse himself.

"About an hour?" asked Pam.

"Yeah. I've got to do my eyebrows. I look like fucking Oscar Homolka."

"You could sand wood with my legs right now," said Pam.

They laughed.

Perec wiped his hand on his pants, curled into a ball, and continued to cry.

Anna was alone in the living room when Spandau came down.

"It's quiet around here," he said.

"Pam's at a party. Elena's mother is sick, so I sent her home. I told her we'd get something out. Wine?"

"Sure."

She poured him the wine.

"I've been trying to figure out what to eat, which has started me thinking about how much time I spend on that," she said. "When did deciding what to eat become such a goddamn time-consuming activity? I'm sick of people asking me what I want to eat. Don't you miss the days when you just showed up at the dinner table and ate whatever they fed you?"

"I remember eating a lot of pork. The German thing."

"You know what I'm craving? Chili. Here I am in the gastronomic capital of the universe, and all I want is a bowl of chili. Good luck finding that."

"Real chili or froufrou chili?"

"Cubed beef, maybe some peppers thrown in. And a cold beer to go with it. Oh man."

"Beans or not?"

"Common wisdom says that beans are for homos and intellectuals, unless you make them separately and with corn bread. I'm from Texas, remember."

"We got any beef? I happen to be the chili king of the San Fernando Valley."

"What's your secret?"

"More cumin than anyone thought humanly possible."

"What's the French word for 'cumin'?" she asked. She dug out an English-French dictionary and looked it up. *"Cumin,"* she said.

"It's an omen," Spandau said.

It took a while to gather the ingredients, then Spandau set to cooking while she worked on a salad.

"How hot you like your chili?" he asked her.

"Hot."

"You sure?"

"I can outpepper your candy ass any day of the week, son."

He diced a handful of peppers and dropped them in.

"You miss Texas?"

"I miss the lack of bullshit. I miss the presumption that some things in life actually are black-and-white, even when I know that's mostly crap in itself. I miss coffee before Starbucks and Dan Rather reading the news. I miss riding around in old pickup trucks and men who don't wax their asses."

"You know men who wax their asses?"

"Honey, I know men who tweeze their goddamn balls. In case you haven't heard, there's a war on testosterone in Hollywood. I'm surprised they haven't dragged you out somewhere and shot you."

"It's been suggested more than once."

"You handle that knife right well."

"Been a long time since I cooked for anybody."

"All the cowboys I ever knew were pretty good cooks."

"Cowboys got to eat. No Wolfgang Puck on a cattle drive."

"You cook for your ex-wife?"

"Sometimes. She liked hers with ground chuck and beans."

"I can see why it didn't last. I was married once, about a thousand years ago. To a rock musician."

"How'd he like his chili?"

"With a gram of cocaine on the side. He preferred the coke to food, and in the end he preferred the coke to me. It was not, as they say, a marriage made in heaven. Who left who?"

"She did."

"How come?"

"She didn't like my job. She said it was all based on deception and betrayal, and that it was fucking up the guy she married."

"Was it?"

"Nah. I was fucked up before, it just took some time for her to notice."

"What does she do?"

"She's a schoolteacher."

"You ever think about trying to make it work again?"

"She's married to a guidance counselor named Charlie."

"Yeah, boy, that sounds like a world of excitement. He collect stamps too?"

"She probably made the right decision."

"I've never made a logical decision in my life that amounted to anything."

"You happy?"

"Hell no. I'm a has-been movie star who's going to end up living with a thousand goddamn cats or something. I'd do it all over again, though."

"Even the fucked-up parts?"

"Yeah, even the fucked-up parts. Certain kinds of people—of which I am one—require getting hit upside the head before they notice anything. I learned mostly from the fuckups. I won't say they've made me a better person, because I'm a shit-ass most of the time. But I've survived in a world where lots of people don't. Like your pal Bobby. The difference between him and me is that my expectations are lower. I don't need to be loved, all I've wanted to do is just stay in the game awhile longer. I'm tired, though, and I don't even think it's worth it anymore, to be honest."

"Is there life after Hollywood? Come on, Anna. You're smarter than that."

"It has nothing to do with Hollywood. All I ever wanted to do was act. It's all I've done since I was eighteen. I gave up everything for it, and I'm not bitching about it because I knew what I was doing. Now I'm watching it all disappear. There's a saying in Hollywood that your career follows the same path as your tits. So what do I do with my drooping tits and sagging ass when the phone stops ringing. And it is soon going to stop. The fatal flaw, see, is putting your identity, your entire life, into something that isn't yours to begin with. That's what nobody ever tells you. The whole fame thing, you're only there on sufferance. The movies giveth and the movies taketh away. They give you the attention and the money, but nobody explains that one day they're going to take it all back from you again."

"Nobody can stop you from acting."

"You think doing a fucking sitcom is acting? I started out in a sitcom, remember, and I swore I'd never go back to that again. It's the fucking anteroom to hell. I'll just go ahead and snuff myself, thank you. Oh, don't give me that look! You never thought about the big good night after your old lady left you?"

Spandau didn't reply.

"Besides, offing yourself is one of the great Hollywood career moves. I'm not kidding. Look at George Saunders. George Reeves. Pier Angeli. Bobby Dye. Suddenly every shit role you

ever did gets forgotten and all anybody talks about are your suc-
cesses. The night I won my Oscar, I should have tied it to my
ankles and jumped off Santa Monica pier."

"Jesus, you really know how to kick off a party, don't you?"

"Yeah, that's the worst of it. The self-pity seems unavoidable.
Even I'm fucking bored with it. I think that's the really dangerous part, though. When you're just completely sick of the whole
goddamn thing. People don't fucking kill themselves out of pain.
That's why so few terminally ill people ever do it. You can live
with pain. What you can't live with is feeling nothing at all, the
belief that this is what the rest of the road is going to be like."

Anna drained her beer. "How long has this Pecos Red got to
cook?"

"Normally it should simmer for about six months. I figure
we'll let is cook for an hour."

"Well, there's a pool table downstairs. Meanwhile you can
gaze at my ass while I line up shots. How's that sound?"

"This takes me right back to high school."

"Too bad there's no pickup truck. We could listen to the radio
and make out. Second base guaranteed, and third base too if you
brought a joint."

"Ah, youth."

They were downstairs in the game room, shooting eight ball as
they ate the chili and sucked at more beers. Spandau lined up a
shot and made it.

"Don't get cocky. I can still whip your ass."

"It's a done deal, sweetheart."

"Twenty bucks says you choke."

He shot and missed.

"Ha. I told you. It's all about character."

"Thank you, Minnesota Fats."

Anna lined up a shot. In the pocket.

"Eight ball, corner pocket."

She shoots. It's in.

"That's the game, cream puff. Where's my twenty?"

He took a twenty out of his wallet and laid it on the table. She picked it up, kissed it, and stuck it in her cleavage.

"Why do I have the feeling I just got hustled?"

"Well, gosh, could it be because you were? My daddy was the best pool player in East Texas. He'd sit me on a stool in a pool hall and I'd watch him play for hours. He said I was his good-luck charm."

"Apparently you're not mine."

"All the chickens ain't home yet, cowboy."

"I'm not even going to try to fathom what that could mean."

"It means rack 'em up, loser. I'm giving you one more chance."

He was in his room, standing at the open window and smoking a cigarette. There was a knock on the door and he opened it and there was Anna.

"Come to my room."

"What are you doing?"

"Admit it, you were staring down my sumptuous cleavage all night."

"I was."

"What's the verdict?"

"Why do you think I kept losing?"

She put her arms around his neck.

"Anna," he said.

"Just shut up, will you. You're liable to put me right out of the mood and neither one of us really wants that. You can wring your hands all you want to in the morning and tell everybody I raped you. They'll all believe that."

She hooked her finger in the front of his belt, pulled him gently through the door.

When they reached her room she said: "Well, this place is no '65 Ford short bed, but I guess it'll do."

Just a few feet directly above them, Perec hovered like a dark angel.

Through the ceiling light fixture he'd watched the room, saw them moving back and forth, heard them talk. It disgusted him— not that there was a lot of talking to be heard. He saw them kiss, saw her begin to undress, then they moved out of sight toward the bed. Perec shifted to the spot just above them, put his ear close to the ceiling, and listened to the sounds of their rutting. Like pigs, disgusting grunts and moans. What the man was doing pleased her, and Perec found himself despising her for it, though he despised the big man far worse. He wanted to kill the man. He wanted to see him hurt and humiliated, then he wanted him to die, and he lay there above them, listening to them speak softly to each other afterward, the disgusting little voices, and thought of ways to do it.

"It wasn't that bad," she said to him. She was resting in the crook of his arm, her hand on his chest. She could feel the scars, long and short, that peppered his torso. "Jesus, no wonder you got out of the business. Do all stunt people look this way?"

"Sooner or later," he said to her.

"You're awfully quiet."

"You almost killed me."

"Not disapproval, then?"

"It was great. Couldn't you tell?"

"I thought I was pretty good but I don't know about you. I think you need more practice. I have this regimen planned for you. It involves sex eighteen hours a day and us marooned on a desert island for two weeks. We'll whip you into shape in no time."

"Thanks."

"You're supposed to tell me now how the earth moved for you, because it hit a fucking nine-point on the Richter scale for me."

"It was wonderful." He turned her face toward him, looked into her eyes. "Look at me. You know how it was for me."

"But you feel guilty."

"Now isn't the time to talk about this."

"It's simple. Do you want to be here? Do you want to be here with me?"

"Yes. You know I do."

"That's all that's important." She sat up, reached for her cigarettes. Gave him one. They sat up in bed and smoked. "What a cliché."

"What?"

"Fucking and then smoking in bed. I've never been able to figure out why a cigarette tastes better after an orgasm. The better the orgasm, the better it tastes. Is it the same for men?"

"Men tend to like the orgasms better, though the cigarettes don't cause nearly as much performance anxiety."

"You were nervous?"

"What do you think?"

"I was petrified."

"I could tell by the way you knocked me down and jumped on me."

"That's just me being shy yet overcompensating."

"It's effective."

She kissed him, said: "Look, if you're going to go, go now. Another day or so and I won't be able to deal with it. I can just about manage to hang on to my dignity for another day or so, but after that it's going to get humiliating."

He said nothing. She pulled away from him, moved to the edge of the bed to reach the ashtray. She remained there.

"Thierry has told me about this great little place in Cannes, on the rue d'Antibes. Le Vent Provençal. Authentic Provençal, he says, cooked by somebody's grandmother. He's made reservations for us at eight tomorrow night. Just us, you and me. It's supposed to be romantic. You can gaze into the limpid pools of my eyes across the garlic. The bodyguards wait outside."

"I'm supposed to be a bodyguard," he said.

"You're my squeeze," she said. "You get to guard my body in a whole different way."

A small pale scorpion moved along a joist not far from his head. Perec saw them often, the scorpions, though he didn't mind them much. He actually rather liked them, admired their aloofness and their ability to strike so rapidly and deadly, without hesitation. And unlike people, they left you alone unless you bothered them.

Perec killed it angrily with his hand, before the tail had a chance to strike. He watched it twitch and then lie still, and he now he felt bad about it, they were so much alike.

Scorpions, he thought.

Yes, that would be just the thing.

16

THE RUE D'ANTIBES CUTS THROUGH THE MIDDLE OF CANNES
a few blocks inland from the Croisette and the beach. It's a long
and narrow street and runs behind the famous hotels, provid-
ing shopaholic succor to all the elegant visitors who have more
money than they know what to do with. Imagine Rodeo Drive
in Hollywood, stretch it out, yet cram in enough shops to make
it look like a Hong Kong bazaar, and you begin to get the idea.
Walking those few blocks roughly behind the Hotel Carleton
is like running a commercial gauntlet, and it's been said the
street has more ways to relieve you of money than a Somali pi-
rate. You can find practically everything on the rue d'Antibes,
from a decent kosher corned-beef sandwich to an emerald-
encrusted chastity belt for your Russian mistress, but don't expect a bargain. Especially during those crazy two weeks in May.

The restaurant Le Vent Provençal sat wedged in the rue
d'Antibes between a jeweler's and a perfumery. Le Vent Provençal had sat there for as long as anybody could remember, handed
down in the Cotas family from generation to generation like a

sacred mission. From the outside, positioned between the two shining and upscale modern businesses, and indeed on the increasingly modernized street, the restaurant looked like a brown shoe in a line of spats. This was part of its charm, and the Cotas family knew it was worth at least eight hundred thousand euros a year not to paint the place. The jeweler's and the perfumery were mere upstarts anyway, having only been there a few decades. Like every other business in the rue d'Antibes, they existed side by side in a mutual ambush of the tourist trade. The jeweler's and Le Vent Provençal traditionally got along well, though there was occasional enmity between Le Vent Provençal and the perfumery. Once in a while the *poulet roti* came out with an ever-so-slight taste of Égoiste, and the Acqua di Parma samples exhibited just a soupçon of Acqua di Frogslegs.

Le Vent Provençal had for nearly a hundred years served traditional Provence cuisine. It was the sort of place that wouldn't serve bouillabaisse because it was more than thirty feet from the ocean, while there were restaurants that served it right on the beach. Those few hundred yards made a difference, as far as Le Vent Provençal was concerned. Michel Cotas, the owner, bought his seafood—as did his father and his father's father—from the Sangiovese family, whose boats had snuggled up to the Antibes harbor since the storming of the Bastille. The chickens were flown in twice a week from Brest; their corpses had little medals on them and they were granted all the respect of tiny heroes of the Republic. The lambs spent happy lives not far from the Brest chickens, noshing on grass in the salt marshes of Brittany, while the beef grazed like Latin American dictators in the rolling fields outside of Limoges. Even the vegetables had faces and a pedigree. Small farmers contracted with the restaurant to deposit *des légumes,* still damp and smelling of earth, on Le Vent Provençal's doorstep. The Cotas family had a deep-running love of money, but this was more than outdistanced by the pride they took in their heritage. Slow Food Movement be damned, and Alice Waters, eat your liver.

Thierry pulled the black Mercedes up in front of the restaurant. Vignon got out first, went inside to check that the arrangements had been made, then came back out to get Spandau and Anna. Spandau could see that Vignon was seething. With Perec now somewhere around, Vignon thought all this a dangerous whim. Nor was he happy that Spandau ate with Anna at a table while he was forced to sit waiting out front in the car with Thierry. The restaurant was fully booked, there were no free tables, and even Anna's was fitted in at the last moment. Anna would send something out for them to eat. It was humiliating.

Cotas greeted them effusively at the door, and led them back through the dining room to a table hidden by a large folding screen. A few people recognized Anna, but Vignon gave them enough of a scowl to discourage any autograph seekers.

"If you need anything, I'll be outside," said Vignon needlessly, gave Spandau an icy look, and left them.

A faded Provence cloth covered the table where they sat. The table itself rocked gently on the uneven wooden floor, and the chairs moaned sharply whenever their weight shifted. The plates had aged with a fine *craquelure* inside the porcelain, and on the wall just above their heads was a pigeon box for the napkins of regular guests long since departed. Cotas recommended a local rosé, regardless of whatever the hell they were going to eat. It came before they even ordered. Neither Spandau nor Anna particularly liked rosés, but this one was chilled and sharp and had the desired effect of leveling the playing field for any food that came after it. Anna ordered the lamb, Spandau the chicken.

"I don't know about you," said Anna, "but this gets my vote as about the most romantic place I've ever been in."

"It's up there."

She inhaled deeply. "You smell that? The herbs? My God, you think I'm the last woman alive who thinks garlic is sexy?"

"You think everything is sexy."

"Damn right. All the best things, anyway. Somebody cares about what they do, takes the extra time and effort, cares about pleasing you. Hell yes, that's sexy. That's exactly what lovers are supposed to do, isn't it? Somebody explained to me once that food and sex are both things you put inside someone else to give them pleasure. How's that for a turn-on?"

More rosé, as the mouthwatering smells drifted in to them from the kitchen. And they talked. The wine helped, dulled the edge of their nervousness, and they talked. About their childhoods. About their hopes, both past and gained. About their careers. And carefully about old loves, the ones that mattered least, anyway. Anna and Spandau did what men and women have always done when they are falling in love. They joined hands and carefully strolled through the minefields of each other's history.

The chicken, when it arrived, smelled of thyme and the scent of a distant field of lavender. Anna's lamb was trapped inside a casing of clay, baked there in its own juices, and when Cotas cracked it, the heady odors rose and engulfed the table. They ate, trading bites, making delighted noises. She was right. It was like love. It excited him to see her pleased, realizing now that she ate the same way she made love, slowly and a bit shyly at first, primly careful of the napkin and the falling crumbs, then allowing herself to be overtaken by the tastes and smells and textures. In spite of her facade, she needed to take things slow, to learn to trust them and to ease herself into them. Then came the passion.

"You know what Elizabeth Taylor once said?" She swallowed a sip of rosé, looked Spandau in the eye, smiled like a schoolgirl with a secret crush. "That the sexiest thing is the world was a man who could laugh in bed."

"At the appropriate time, one imagines," said Spandau.

"Ever since I heard that, that's what I've wanted. A man who could laugh in bed. Somebody who could put the whole thing in perspective. Guys take fucking so seriously."

"What about a guffaw?" said Spandau. "Would a man who guffawed in bed still work?"

"Is a guffaw like a snort? I couldn't do a snort."

"I think a guffaw is more like a huh-huh-huh."

"No, God, not a guffaw, then. I like the way you laugh."

"I don't guffaw?"

"You're maybe a little wheezy but it's a good laugh."

"I'll try some epinephrine next time."

"No, don't change your wheezy laugh, I like it. Reminds me of a little congested lamb I raised in 4-H. I get all warm and fuzzy thinking about it."

Two bottles of wine and a world-class meal does wonders for the libido. By the end of dinner it was like the food seduction scene in *Tom Jones*. She was licking the crème caramel off the spoon with the tip of her tongue, and letting Spandau watch her take her time doing it. Spandau teased her with a bite of warm chocolate macaroon, and when she finally took it into her mouth, he felt that light spinning sensation all men feel just before six million years of reproduction kick in. Both began thinking of the shortest distance home. He put his arm around her as they walked out into the night and Anna hoped there were reporters there, hoped there were flashbulbs, because for once in her life she wanted the bastards to see her happy. Instead, a small group

of fans had gathered, tipped off by an earlier guest. Anna stopped
to sign a few autographs.

Perec had been waiting in a doorway across the street, huddled in the shadows and wearing a pair of dark glasses. When
Anna and Spandau came out, he crossed the street into the light
and stood behind Thierry's parked Mercedes. He watched Spandau and waited for him to look his way. When he did, Perec took
of his sunglasses and smiled.

Smiled.

The big man barked something at the French bodyguard and
pushed his way through the crowd after Perec. Just as Perec had
known he would. People are so stupid, they're so predictable.
Hadn't this been exactly what he'd done in Los Angeles, when
he'd chased Perec into that Mexican restaurant? And hadn't Perec
outsmarted him then too? Of course he'd chase Perec. That's
what he'd done before in a situation like this, that's now what his
brain was wired to do. A neural pathway, I think it's called. I read
about it in Wikipedia. The mind wants to follow the path of the
things it's done before. Wikipedia, like Google, was wonderful.

Perec ran. He was small and light and fast. The big man was
taller, but he was heavy and less agile and he'd just eaten. The
sidewalks of the rue d'Antibes were still busy with people pouring out of the clubs and restaurants. Perec zipped in and out,
whipped between them like an eel. The big man crashed into
people, stumbled in and out of groups talking in the street. Perec
kept his pace, made sure not to lose him.

Then: left. Down a side street. Glance over the shoulder, yes,
he's still seeing me.

And: right. A short sprint, quick left again. He's following,
following, left again. And then right, and another right . . . Come
on, come on . . .

Spandau followed. He was short of breath and the wine and the food churned in his stomach. How far had he run? He pushed ahead, following the little man up and down dark streets, until he turned a corner into an alley, a cul-de-sac between two ancient warehouses.

And there he was. The little bastard was cornered.

There was a door. Perec pushed it, and was gone . . .

The door was half open when Spandau hit it, heard the dried wood crack as it bounced off the stone wall. Spandau tripped at the bottom of a flight of stairs. It was dark. There was an overwhelming sour, rancid smell and it burned his heaving lungs, made him sick, and the food in his stomach wanted to escape. He looked up. Perec was at the top, a shadow looking down at him. Then he disappeared.

Spandau stumbled up the stairs, half blind in the darkness. At the top the stench was even worse, seemed to rise up after him from both sides. He realized he was on some sort of catwalk. Felt motion behind him, started to turn.

Then Perec hit him. It was something like a heavy oar, swung through the darkness, and it caught Spandau across the chest. He went backward and kept falling into the sour mouth of darkness.

Landed in a thick, fetid stew of water and something else. The disturbed liquid gave off great quiet belches of noxious smell that was still somehow familiar.

"You okay?" Perec called down to him. "You're not dead, are you? That would be a real disappointment."

Spandau moved slowly knee-deep through the ooze. Thicker at his feet, then watery, then a thin crust floating along the top. His hand touched wall: wood, he could feel the cracks and splinters. Oak? Like a giant barrel.

"Stinks, doesn't it? They used to make vinegar here about a thousand years ago. I spent half the morning just looking around. Interesting. When it rains I guess the vats fill up and soak the smell out again. Of course, some of that stuff you're wading through is probably rat and pigeon shit. I wouldn't get any in my mouth if I were you."

Perec sat at the edge and looked down at him. A flashlight played around until it found Spandau.

"I bet you feel really dumb now," said Perec. "Hey, aren't you going to talk to me?"

Spandau felt a piece of wood hit him on the shoulder.

"I'll talk to you pretty good when I get out of here," Spandau said.

"Big talk for a man who got himself trapped in a vinegar barrel," said Perec.

Spandau leaped toward the light. Not high enough, his hand never came within two feet of the top. When he landed the water churned and the smell thickened again.

"I wish you'd stop that. It just makes it worse. You don't want me to vomit on your head, do you?"

"You sick little fuck."

"Be nice to me. I gave this a lot of thought. I wandered around all day, looking for a place. I never really expected to find something as nice as this. I just stumbled across it. I was just going to find someplace and like hit you and tie you up or something. Do it that way. This is just perfect."

"In about five minutes half the cops in Provence will be looking for you."

"Well, it won't do them much good, will it? They don't know where you ran off to. We ran for maybe half a mile, they have no idea in what direction. No, they won't find me and they won't find you in time either. In fact, I'll bet they have no idea even why you ran off in the first place. You just took off running, didn't you?"

"I suppose you have a point to all this."

"Oh sure," said Perec. "I'm going to kill you."

"Well, seeing as I'm down here and you're up there, you fucking lunatic, what are you going to do, talk me to death?"

"I bought a tape recorder. I want you to beg. I want to record it so I can play it for Anna. I want her to hear what a big baby you are. I want her to know you're not what she thinks you are."

"You're never going to get anywhere near Anna, no matter what happens to me."

"Oh, you don't know anything. You are so dumb."

Another bit of wood hit Spandau in the head.

"You want to beg now? Come on, start begging. Beggy-weggy."

A four-foot length of two-by-four rattles against the wall, bounces, and hits him. Settles floating on top of the mire.

"How much time have you got? There's water here and I could stay weeks without eating. There's nothing you can do."

"You think?"

Perec shuffling around up there. A pause. Something small and light hits Spandau on the head, sticks to his hair. He jumps, swipes it off.

Then another on his shoulder. Swipes at it, sends it into the void.

"You've got company."

The flashlight plays around the bottom of the vat.

"Found him."

A scorpion rests on the layer of crust not two feet away from Spandau's knee.

"I can't find the other one. Oh, there he is, over by the wall."

The light goes away. Then another one hits his shoulder, Spandau thrashes about. The next one clings to his jacket, he flicks at it, the waving tail, flicks at it until it sails off and hits the wall.

"I can't hear you begging."

Another.

Another.

Perec shines the light around. A few have gone into the water. Some are clinging to the walls or picking their way across the thick scum toward Spandau.

"They're really mad at you, you know. They've figured out you're there. Won't be long now. They sting you yet? I guess not."

Another . . . Another . . .

One lands on his shoulder, at the base of his neck, he can't knock it off fast enough. Feels the hot needle sink into his flesh. Cries out.

"Oh, good, finally. I was starting to have my doubts about them. Are you begging yet? I'm not hearing it."

On his head.

One on his shoulder again.

Get them off, get them off . . .

"I've got about seventy-five of these guys. You can find them all over the place. Under rocks, in old tin cans. I just gathered them up with a pair of tongs, put them in a plastic bucket. They can't crawl on plastic. Dish them out like meatballs. How many meatballs do you want? Do you feel it yet? The poison. I read about it. One sting won't kill you, probably, unless you're allergic. But a bunch of them . . ."

Again . . . again . . . again . . .

Just above the left knee, the sharp pain, little bastard climbing up the leg, got me through the pants.

He was right, one sting probably wouldn't kill him. He'd been stung as a child in Arizona. His leg had swollen but he hadn't

died, got sick, the doctor who gave the anivenom said they sel-
dom killed if you got help soon enough . . .

The hand. The hot pin going through it. The scorpion had
clung to his jacket and walked down his arm until it found flesh.

Spandau's heart pounded. How much longer before the poison hit? How bad would it be? The faster the heartbeat, the faster
the poison pushes through the veins. The one in my neck, I'll be
feeling it soon. The neck is starting to stiffen and swell . . .

Some way out of this, has to be a way out of this . . .

If he passed out they'd swarm all over him . . .

I won't die. I won't die this way.

Please don't let me die this way.

The sickness began to creep upward through his body.

Oh God, oh God.

"Are you dying yet? Sing out, everybody who's not dying.
Hands up, people who aren't stung by scorpions."

A way out, there's a way out . . .

Phone.

Oh, you blessed idiot, the phone!

Reaches into his pocket, feels the cell phone in his fingers.
Takes it out. Please God, don't let me drop it in the water.

"What are you doing? What is that you've got?"

Vignon's number, the speed dial. What is it? What's the number?

Presses buttons.

The poison buzzing in his ears now, running around in his
head like strong drink.

"Where the hell are you?" Vignon. Lovely, lovely Vignon!

"In trouble . . . Perec . . . Help me . . ."

"Where are you? It was Perec you were chasing? What's
wrong?"

"Find me . . . In trouble . . ."

"Where are you? Tell me where you are!"

"Trace the phone . . ."

"What are you doing?" cried Perec. "Stop that! You can't do that!"

A board, something, hits Spandau on the head and shoulder. Falls into the muck.

"Who is that? Who is that yelling?"

"Trace the phone!"

"Hold on, hold on . . ."

Vignon goes away. The longest pause in history of the world. Perec screaming.

"They won't find you! They won't find you in time! You'll be dead, dead, dead!"

A rain of scorpions, all down on Spandau. The stings don't hurt so bad now. He writhes against the oak wall, can hear them crush beneath his back.

Knocks them away, over and over.

"Are you there? David, are you there?"

"Here . . ."

"Hang on, they're tracing the phone. It will take a few minutes. Can you hang on, David?"

Voice a croak. "Please find me, please . . ."

Hands getting weak. Put the phone in the pocket, dumb bastard, before you lose it in the water. Do phones work in the water?

Throat swelling.

Stay alive, stay alive. Don't pass out.

They're all over the place, he dumped in all of them. They're on the walls. Crawling around on the scum.

Spandau picks up one of the boards Perec threw. Spandau churns the water. The crust sways, splits, separates. Some of the bastards go down like the *Titanic*. Go down like Eskimos on ice.

They crawl toward Spandau. Using the heaviest stick in the universe, a stick the weight of a grown man, Spandau pokes at them and pushes them through the crust into the water.

Can scorpions swim?

Takes the stick, swings it, swings it, killing them on the walls, knocking them into the water, crushing them into bug mush, crushing them to pulp.

How many did I get? How many are left?

He felt himself slide down the rough oak wall and into the muck, into oblivion.

Vignon yelling, screaming angrily in French.

Someone lifting him. A man. Like a fireman. Lifting him up.

Vignon saying, You're going to make it, David, you're going to make it.

The lights in his face, lying in the ambulance. The sirens. The jostling. A pretty young face looks down at him, puts a cuff on his arm. A man with a serious face gives him a shot.

Sick, sick, I'm going to be sick . . .

Into a bucket, all that lovely meal.

Where's Anna? Will I see Anna again?

And then the darkness one more time.

The doctor with the French accent says, "People hardly ever die from it. If we get two cases a year, it would be a lot. Mainly babies."

The doctor says, "Five times. I've seen people stung as many as nine or ten. Stuck their hand somewhere they didn't belong, weren't careful. With adults it usually involves boots. One must check."

The doctor says, "On the other hand, they tell me there were quite a lot. So you were very lucky."

"Really," said Spandau. "Nine or ten times?"

"Well, they died," said the doctor. "And you're a big healthy man. That helped. Strong as a moots."

"What?"

"A moots," said the doctor. He put his thumbs to the sides of his head and extended his fingers in a very realistic imitation of antlers.

"A moose," said Spandau from the emergency-room bed. "You mean a moose."

"A moots," repeated the doctor. "Yes, that's what I said."

17

THERE WAS A SMALL WINDOW HIGH UP IN THE ROOF. THIS was how Perec could tell if it was day or night. That and the house got very quiet when people went to bed. He heard running water a lot and toilets flushing and sometimes people said good night. And then the quiet and lights went out below. Not that it mattered to Perec.

It had gone badly with the big man in Cannes. He'd almost managed to kill him. It was dumb about the phone. He should have thought of that. Perec was sure they'd sting him quicker. They must have been disoriented. Of course, the police were looking for him, but he'd come back here, long gone by the time they found the man. Climbed back in through the drainage pipe and collapsed it behind him. He wouldn't be leaving again. This was it now. There was no place to go. Perec had hoped the big man had died anyway, but no, he could hear when they brought him back to the villa, hear Anna running around, fussing about him in a disgusting way. The man was even walking. Perec had hoped maybe an infection, dead tissue, an arm or leg would fall off. The least that could be hoped for.

But no. Here he was still alive.

Perhaps once he got to Anna, after that, maybe he'd get to kill him.

It was time now, and Perec lay there thinking about how he would get down into the house. There had to be a trapdoor somewhere. He looked around and found one. When he was sure no one was up, he inched it open. It led down into a linen closet. He heard someone coming and he closed it, leaving a small crack to look through. It was Pam, she'd come for a blanket. She got the blanket and left. Perec shut the trapdoor.

He crawled back to his hidden corner. For some reason he felt safe here. It's strange, he thought, how something so small can almost turn into a home. He curled up and went to sleep. Perec sometimes worried about the rats, which he'd seen. Not so much that they'd bite him but about the rat shit. It bothered him he might fall asleep or put his hands in rat shit and then you could get the plague or something, that's how it spread in the olden days. Rats were filthy.

Perec was tired. He curled into a ball and slept, his hands folded beneath his head. Thought of Anna, thought about her hard, and hoped he could force himself to dream about her. Sometimes that worked. He fell into a sound sleep.

He didn't, for instance, feel the small pale scorpion that inched its way into his pant leg while he slept. It rested there for a long time, appreciating the moist warmth coming from Perec's body but clearly understanding that Perec was a living thing. The scorpion could hear Perec's blood moving beneath his skin as clearly as humans listened to the wind, and the scorpion was aware that if the thing moved in a suspicious way, the scorpion would have to kill it.

Meanwhile, though, the scorpion was content.

Sometime in the middle of the night the scorpion moved and Perec felt the tickle against his calf and in his sleep reached down to scratch it. The scorpion felt fingers push down against the cloth and the scorpion did the sensible thing. It got the hell a few inches out of the way, and when it could move its tail, it stung Perec. Perec cried out and sat up, clawing at his pants as the scorpion stung him again before he slapped at the cloth and crushed it. He pulled up his pant leg and the dead scorpion fell out. It was small, but Perec knew nothing about scorpions. He was thankful, though, it hadn't been a big one. He looked at the bites on his calf. They felt like wasp stings, but Perec had been stung by wasps before, and though it hurt it wasn't serious. A small scorpion, he'd get a little sick. He wasn't allergic and it barely hurt.

He tucked his pant legs into his socks and went back to sleep.

Anna knocked on Spandau's door.

"Come in."

He was lying on the bed, smoking a cigarette.

"How do you feel?"

"Like shit."

"I'm glad you're alive."

"Well, that makes two of us."

"I want you to go home," she said. "None of this is worth it. Go home, and when I get there we'll talk about it."

"Come here," he said.

She climbed onto the bed with him. Lay against him for

the longest time, tried hard not to cry, and failed miserably. He touched her, kissed her eyes, her lips.

"We'll see what happens," he said, but she never knew if he meant him going home or them being together.

How much longer was it? An hour? Two hours? A few minutes? Perec woke and his leg was hurting. He sat up and looked at it. Swollen badly. He was sick too, felt as if he'd eaten some bad food. Then he remembered the scorpion. Perec curled into a ball and waited for sickness or death or whatever it was that was coming for him.

He soon went to sleep, but it didn't feel like sleep. His body was hot and heavy, and when he opened his eyes he was shivering and sweating. He closed his eyes and then opened them again because his mother was hanging right there above him, in her plastic cocoon. She opened her upside-down eyes and glared at him through the plastic and said, *Cochon*. He closed his eyes and opened them when Amalie stroked his hair, sat there next to him and stroked his hair, how nice it was that she'd found him, come all this way to keep him company and make him feel safe. He did feel safe with her. Felt safe that night she'd slept in his arms, waited for her to do it again, but no, he heard Anna's voice, and he looked up and there was Anna, sitting naked on the far side of the attic, saying to him, *It's time* . . . and he worried that Amalie might be jealous and looked and Amalie wasn't there and then looked again and neither was Anna, and Perec was horribly cold and hot at the same time and the loneliness, oh, the loneliness, was more terrifying than anything he'd felt in his life.

*   *   *

Early in the morning Spandau was outside by the pool, smoking, and drinking a cup of coffee. Anna came out, tying a nightgown around her.

"You're really leaving, then, aren't you?"

"I think that makes the most sense."

"It was the lack of foreplay, wasn't it?"

Spandau laughed.

"I don't suppose my throwing a hissy fit would do any good, would it?"

"Just make it harder for me, but it's not going to change anything. I can't do my job, Anna. I've thoroughly fucked this up. All of it."

"Well, some of the things that were thoroughly fucked aren't making any complaints."

"I don't go now, I won't be able to go."

"I guess that's some sort of compliment."

"It is."

"You are making a big mistake here, bub, and I'm not just saying this because I'm one step away from asking for a pity shag. I don't get a chance to say this very often—in fact, goddamn it, I don't think I've ever said it—but I'm the one you need. I'm your girl, lack of foreplay and all. I guess I could say I won't wait for you, but we both know I'd be lying."

She moved from under his arm and walked back toward the house. "You'll figure it out sooner or later. Dumb-ass cowboys, I swear to God. Now I remember why I left Texas in the first place."

She went inside.

Vignon was talking to Special by the pool when Spandau came out.

"She told me you were leaving," Vignon said.

"You don't want to hang around and see the fireworks?" Special asked.

"There's no indication that the guy is coming," said Vignon. "The police are looking for him now. It's only a matter of time before they catch him. Assuming he could find us, why would he risk coming here?"

"Because he's a crazy little fuck and he don't think the way you do," said Special. "That's the problem. Look, I read his goddamn diary. He ain't worried about getting caught. Hell, he ain't even worried about living. He knows he's not going back. He's got nothing to lose. As far as he's concerned, he's a walking dead man already."

"I think it's a ridiculous idea," said Vignon, "but to be on the safe side, we'll check the grounds again, and have a closer look outside the compound. I've checked the architect's drawings. The place is like a fortress. The only way in is through the gate or over the wall. That isn't going to happen."

"You still think he's coming?" Spandau said to Special.

"Oh, I know he is. Until you hear they done shot and killed his ass, I'd set another place for dinner."

Vignon and Spandau were checking the property outside the walls. The walls themselves were, as Vignon had said, like a fortress. Nobody was coming in that way. The property line extended down the hill and they slowly picked their way down the hillside. Before long Vignon spotted the old grate.

"Look at this."

They pulled aside the brush and opened the grate. Vignon pulled a flashlight from his back pocket and shined it up into the tunnel.

"It look like a drainage tunnel," he said. "Probably a way to drain the caves of the old winery. These hills are full of little limestone caves that are perfect for storing wine. It's too small for anyone to use."

"Perec is a small guy."

"Now you are truly being paranoid. Anyway, it's caved in maybe twenty feet up. There's no way to get through. Have a look."

Spandau checked it and agreed with Vignon. They looked around the property for a while longer, then went back to the house, satisfied that all was well.

"You're still leaving?" Anna asked him that night.

"I have a flight out first thing in the morning."

"You think maybe, once I get back . . . ?"

"I'm pretty much of a train wreck these days."

"You'll say good-bye before you go? Promise?"

"If you're awake."

"I'll be up with the chickens," she said.

18

D ID NOT DIE. No, DID NOT.

Lay there for hours or days or perhaps weeks and years and didn't die, shook and tossed and muttered silently to himself (they'll find me, said his brain, they'll find me) and puked as if in a silent film down the edges of the wall into the darkness then pulled his pants down and lying on his side put his ass to the edge of the wall and shit thin gruel down his cheek and into the void. The smell seemed to fill the attic. How long did he lie there with his pants down too weak to move? He pulled them up again thinking about the filth now dried on his bottom but was beyond caring. He moved back to his spot, where he felt safe. Yes, it was important to feel safe.

But did not die.

Time passed or did it. Perec slept and woke and slept and woke and it occurred to him that he still might die. He didn't care about dying except he had not done what he had come to do. After that he could die. The thought of doing what he had to do, what he realized he had been waiting his entire life to do, kept him alive.

It's time, Anna said to him. Sometimes she came to the far side of the attic and called to him, reminding him. He crawled to the spot above her room and lay there as she slept in the dark below him. He listened and he thought, yes, he was sure of it, he could hear the soft whisper of her breathing. He was filled with a great love for her, a great understanding of Anna's heart that no one else could ever attain. They were soul mates, he had always known this. Twinned spirits connected by a ritual of blood and sacrifice. Perec moved to the spot directly above her bed and lay on top of her and felt her body beneath him and kissed her face, her eyes. Told her, *I love you I understand you,* and waited for her to say it back but she didn't, she wasn't there, he was kissing the back of his hand. He had to tell her now, before it was too late.

He opened the trapdoor and dropped to the ground in the darkness. His leg buckled and he fell, but he caught himself and made no sound. He was quiet as a mouse. He would move like a mouse in the darkness. He opened the door a little and looked down a hallway. No one there. Her room was—where? He counted the closed doors, tried to remember. How far did I crawl? He looked at the ceiling, imagined himself crawling the distance. Yes, it would be that door there. Quiet as a mouse he moved, out into the hallway, along the wall. His leg shook beneath him, weak. Mustn't fall, I will not fall. And to the door. Listened. Turned the knob, and opened oh just so very little. Listened, listened. The sound of her breathing in the darkness. Yes, hers. She was there! Only a few feet away! Opened the door just enough to slide through, quiet as a mouse. Eased it shut again. Stood by the closed door in the darkness and heard her, her breathing, the rustle of the sheet as she moved. A dark black-blue figure on the bed in the darkness, she turned and her face was illuminated in the pale red spotlight of the clock on the nightstand.

"David?" she said.

She said nothing as he came at her through the darkness, but then when her eyes widened and her lips opened to scream, Perec was on her with his hand over her mouth, saying, "Don't make me hurt you I have a knife don't make me hurt you."

Perec laid the cold flat side of the razor against her throat and felt her shudder, but she went still in his arms.

"Don't make me hurt you, I don't want to use this." Anna nodded. "If you scream, I'll have to kill you. I don't care about myself. They're going to kill me anyway, but I don't want to hurt you. I just want to talk. Okay?" He waited. No response. He shook her, put the razor to her cheek. "Okay?"

Yes, she nodded. He put the arm holding the razor around her neck so that the edge of the blade rested just beneath her chin. He took his hand away.

"You don't have to do this," she said. "You can put it away. We can talk."

"No, I have to have this. It's what keeps you here with me. Even I know that. I'm not stupid."

"How did you get in here?"

"Oh, I'm a ghost. I've been haunting you. I can go anywhere. Quiet as a mouse."

"Let me go. We'll talk. I swear we will."

"No, stop talking, please. Let me think. I don't feel well."

"You're ill. We'll get you a doctor."

"No. I need to lie down."

He pulled her down on the bed next to him, her head resting in the crook of his arm, the razor nearly touching her ear. He curled up against her. Just like Amalie, he thought. He smelled the fruity shampoo in her hair. Moved his lips to her bare shoulder and found himself kissing her flesh. The thing didn't happen, though, and he was glad about that. It would have been so awful if that had happened with her now. He'd worried seriously about that. Thank you, Mr. Scorpion. It was, Perec well understood, all part of a divine plan.

"We'll just hold each other." he whispered to her. "This is nice. So much I want to say, tell you."

"What do you want to tell me?"

"It's all inside me. It doesn't want to come out now."

"What do you want to say?"

"Touch my arm."

In the dark Anna ran her fingers along the arm that held the razor, feeling the many small scarred ridges.

"You've hurt yourself."

"Those are for you. Each one of those, when I had a bad thought about you. Men are pigs. We're all pigs, all dirty. I never wanted to think bad thoughts about you. I just wanted to hold you. Talk to you."

"I'm here now. You can tell me."

"Blood cleans everything. You let the blood come and it washes the dirt inside you away. Did you love your father?"

"Yes. Very much."

"He purified himself, didn't he? That's what I want to say to you. Yeah, that's it. Don't be angry at him."

"You know about my father?"

"You found him, didn't you? I found mine. All that blood. He loved you so much."

"Yes, I believe so."

"I loved mine, I think. I don't know. I'm not sure. I don't remember. Maybe he loved me. He must have loved me. That's why he did it. He was a pig, he was dirty, he killed himself to be clean. That's what you do for people you love. You try to be clean."

"My father killed himself because he was sad. Your name is Vincent, isn't it? He killed himself because he was unhappy, Vincent, not because he was unclean."

"No, no. His body was filled with dirty thoughts and he did it to be clean for you, that's why. It's like Jesus, but I don't believe in Jesus, I don't believe in God. I used to. But you can still be clean. You've done things with men."

"Vincent . . ."

"You have. I've read about them. You let men look at you, you let them touch you. That big man, the one who's here. Do you let him touch you?"

"No."

"You're lying to me. I know you're lying to me. He's a pig. He should have his throat cut. I should cut his throat and hang him up and watch him bleed like a pig."

"What do you want from me, Vincent?"

"I . . . I don't know. I can't remember . . . My leg hurts . . ."

Anna moved herself closer to him, deeper into his arms.

"Hold me, Vincent. Do you like this?"

"Yes . . ."

"This is nice like this."

"I'm so tired . . ."

Anna lay there waiting for a thousand years. Perec didn't move and the hand with the razor fell slowly to her breast. The razor was still only inches from her neck, and if she moved, if she startled him, he might kill her simply out of reflex. She waited and waited, then she moved closer into him. He seemed to wake for just a moment and the razor moved, but when the arm relaxed it fell away from her onto the bed. She moved by millimeters toward the panic button on the nightstand. Her fingers nearly touched it when the edge of the mattress gave a bit under her weight and lurched just enough to wake him. He grabbed at her, the hand coming back around her neck, and this time the razor grazing her cheek, she felt the cold burn of the cut as he pulled her back to him. But she had the panic button in her fingers and she punched at it frantically.

"Don't make me kill you," he said. "There isn't anything at the end of it. It's all just nothing, just emptiness, like sleep. There's no badness, no goodness. Just nothing. It's where your father is. Mine too. In the nothing. You don't want to die, do you?"

"No," Anna said. "I don't want to die."

"You have so much to learn," he said. "It's not your time."

Footsteps down the hall to the door. Knocking. Vignon.

"Anna? Are you okay? The panic button keeps going off. Anna?" He rattled the doorknob. "Anna?" Pounded at the door. "Anna, answer me! Open this door!"

"Tell him to go away!" Perec whispered hoarsely in her ear.

"I'm fine," Anna said to the door. "I'm okay."

"Come to the door, Anna."

"Go away!" cried Perec. "Leave us alone! I just want to talk, just to talk, that's all . . ."

Vignon nodded to Yves, who quickly dialed the police on his cell phone. Spandau was coming down the hallway now. Vignon stopped him.

"Perec is in there. I've called the police. The question is, will he really kill her?"

"Yes, there's no question about it."

"Then there's not enough time. You go to the door, talk to him. I'm going to try from outside."

Vignon ran off down the hall.

"Vincent?" said Spandau. "This is David Spandau. You remember me, right?"

"Go away!"

"Let her go, Vincent. Let her go and no one will hurt you."

"I'm going to die," said Vincent. "I have to."

"You don't. Just open the door and let her come out and everything will be fine. The police are coming, Vincent, and if you wait until they get here, it will be worse. Right now it's just us. You need to let her go."

"Stop talking," Perec said to him. "If you keep talking you'll make me kill her. Tell him," he said to Anna.

"David, oh God, David . . ."

"You need to let her go, Vincent. You wanted me, now you can have me. She comes out, I come in. You get to finish what you started."

"Stop talking! I mean it! I can't think!"

Perec nicked her ear with the razor. She screamed.

"Anna!"

"I'm fine, I'm fine! Don't talk, David, please, we'll just sit here. You'll be good, won't you, Vincent? You're not going to hurt anyone, you just want to talk, don't you? We can talk, we can talk all you want." The hot blood from her ear ran down her neck and her voice quivered until the words hardly came out.

Yves appeared at the end of the hall and motioned Spandau over. "You think you can break down the door? They're not heavy."

"Sure."

"Vignon is going to try to get a clear shot at him from the window. One way or another, when you hear him, you hit the door, right?"

"It's two floors off the ground! By the time he gets a ladder—"

"Oh, Serge doesn't need a ladder. Trust me on this. Just hit the door when you hear him, right?"

Spandau nodded.

Perec said: "They made me cut your ear. I'm sorry. Does it hurt?"

"A little," she said.

Perec began to cry.

"It's fine," she said. "Just a little scratch is all."

"It isn't what I wanted," Perec said. "It isn't at all."

Vignon was sitting on the ground untying his shoes when Special came out of the guesthouse.

"Why everybody running around? What the hell is going on?"

"Perec's in Anna's room. He's got her."

"Shit," said Special. "I told you that little fucker was persistent."

"The police are on their way."

"Old Vincent hear the sound of police coming and he'll panic and kill her for sure. He's nervous, is Vincent, and he's shit-scared of the police."

"We're going to try something else."

"What the hell you going to do?"

"Just stay back here out of the way."

Vignon stood up in his socks and tucked a 9mm automatic into the back of his pants. He moved to the winery wall and then edged his way against it, out of sight from above, until he was directly below her window. Special wondered what the fuck he was going to do. He watched Vignon touch the rough stone wall for a moment with his hands, as if caressing it. Then Vignon started to go up the wall. Special couldn't believe it. The goddamn Frenchman was going up the goddamn wall like a spider. Special didn't see how it was possible. Vignon eased his way upward a few inches at a time, stopping, then feeling the wall with his hands and his toes, finding some invisible spot, somehow taking hold of it, and moving on a few mores inches. Special had never seen anything like it.

"Was your father alive when you found him?"

"No," answered Anna. "He'd been dead for a couple of hours."

"Mine was alive," said Perec. "I watched him die. It was messy. I sat there next to him and he didn't move but his eyes were open. We just looked at each other. Then he closed his eyes. It was a good way to die."

"There aren't any good ways to die," she told him.

"The Japanese, you know, they know how to die," he said.

It took Vignon a very long five minutes to get up to the window. The window was closed. He slowly eased his head over the sill and dearly hoped Perec wasn't looking in that direction. The sun was coming up and in the soft light he could see them sitting on the bed, Perec with his arm resting on her shoulder, like a pair of lovers. Perec's back was to him, and had the window been open, it would have been a clean shot. He pushed firmly at the window but it didn't move. He couldn't fire through it, the bullet was liable to go anywhere. He'd have to break the goddamn thing.

* * *

"You're going to kill me, aren't you?" Anna said.

"No," said Perec. "Why would I want to kill you?"

"Then what is all this about? Why did you do all this, come all this way?"

"I love you," he said. "I thought you knew that. You can see it, can't you, how we're so much alike? I've always loved you."

"But why all this?"

"To give you the one thing I can give you," he said quietly. "Like your father did for you and my father did for me. I can die for you. I've always known I have to die and I wanted it to be for you. It's my gift," he said. "It will make everything okay."

Perec let Anna go and stood up in front of her.

"All that about Jesus, all that stuff my mother told me all my life. She never understood what it meant. I didn't either until I found you, read about you and your father. It was like me, it was so much like me that it couldn't be an accident. And I knew what it was all about. It's like the samurais," he said. "You need something to die for."

He looked down at her and smiled and brought the razor up toward his own neck.

Vignon broke the glass with the barrel of the gun.

It was, sadly, not a successful move. The heavy pane of glass broke into thick wide shards and fell on his hand like a guillotine. He pulled it back as the glass threatened to lop it off, dragging it and the pistol back through the raining shards, tearing the flesh of his hand. It threw him off balance and he felt himself fall. Perec turned at the crashing sound and saw Vignon for a split second before he disappeared into space.

At the sound of the glass breaking, Spandau hit the door with his shoulder. It cracked and flew open. Perec saw the big man and the anger in his eyes and he leaped at Anna, grabbed her

again, rolling her in front of him on the bed as he put the razor to
her throat. Spandau hovered there with his fists clenched and his
face red and Perec thought, We've done this before.

"Let her go," said Spandau.

Already they could hear the police sirens through the broken
window as they got louder and came screaming through the gate
into the compound.

"You don't understand," Perec said to him. "You've ruined everything, you've messed it all up."

"The police are here, it's over, just let her go."

Perec thought: I can't do it now not here they've ruined it. If
I can get her out. If I can get her into the room and then up into
the attic where she called to me. He was very dizzy. If I could
just get her to another room I could do it there. Perec stood up,
holding Anna.

"Go over by the window," he said to Spandau.

"Let her go, Vincent. It's all over."

"I'll kill her," he said. "I'll cut her throat right here. You can
watch her bleed."

Spandau hesitated. The police would be coming into the
house now, they'd appear at the door any second. Spandau moved
to the window. Perec turned to watch him, keeping the razor at
Anna's throat. Spandau later thought how odd it was that he saw
Perec's head explode before he actually heard the gunshot. The
great crack itself was almost like an afterthought. The top quarter
of Perec's head disappeared into small white pieces and a fine
spray and the hand with the razor fell away from Anna's throat
and Perec's body just stood there for a moment and then it fell
too. Anna was screaming.

Spandau turned to the door to see Special standing there
pointing the 9mm automatic he'd picked up off the ground next

to an unconscious Vignon. Special waited for a moment then lowered the gun. He looked at Perec and then a pained look swept over his face.

"Well, there goes my goddamn money," he said. "Son of a bitch."

Spandau went over to the still screaming Anna and took her in his arms. The back of her own head and shoulder were covered in blood and gray matter. Down the hallway the police had arrived and were shouting something in French.

"Stop!" they cried. "Put down the gun now or we'll shoot!"

Of course nobody knew what the hell they were talking about, there were other considerations. Anna was screaming, for instance, and Special had just shot the only motherfucker who could save his own life. Sometimes not a goddamn thing works right. Special was angry about it.

He turned to the cops at the end of the hallway and said: "Goddamn it, motherfucker, can't you see I have just lost my motherfucking mon—"

Large angry black man swearing and holding a gun.

We have seen this before.

They fired at least six times, three of them hitting Special square in the chest.

19

Vignon, his hand swathed in bandages and his broken leg in a cast, hobbled with his crutches down the hospital corridor.

"The doctor's coming out now," he said to Anna and Spandau.

"Will he be okay?" Vignon asked the doctor in French when he came out of Special's room. "This is the woman he saved."

"Yes," said the doctor in perfect English. "I've read all about it. He's quite the hero. The French government is actually talking about giving him a medal. Can you imagine? He'll live, I think, but he must have the constitution of a gorilla to have survived this long. Shot right through the lung. His chest looks like an abattoir inside and out. Do you have any idea where all those cuts on his body came from?"

Vignon shook his head.

"May I see him?" Anna asked.

"He's heavily sedated. I doubt if he'll even know you're in the room. Don't stay too long."

Anna went inside.

"A medal, for God's sake," said Vignon. "They're afraid if he lives he'll sue the cops for plugging him. Better a dead hero."

"Yes," said the doctor. "It's the French way."

Special lay in the bed, lost in a mass of bandages and tubes. He was alive but hadn't opened his eyes or spoken for two days.

"Thank you," she said. "I knew I was right about you."

She took his lifeless hand in hers and held it for a long time, tears streaming down her cheeks. When she came out of the room, Spandau was waiting and she threw herself into his arms.

"So what happens now?" she said to him.

They were back at the villa, sitting in the living room.

"We go home," Spandau said to her. "I go back to work and you become the darling of the media once again."

It was true. Since the incident she was world famous again, her name and image pasted across every newspaper and TV in the world. Even now the media huddled outside the villa gates, waiting for a chance to see her. The phone rang continually. Poor Special too. The police had guards in the hospital to keep the paparazzi from shooting him as he lay dying in the bed. It was a hell of a way to be famous, though few people cared anymore how it happened, just as long as it did.

"I mean about us," she said.

The festival was over for her. The managers had gracefully relieved her of her duties. Andrei had called a dozen times. She hadn't answered any of the calls.

"I don't know," said Spandau.

"You," she said to him, "are taking this Gary Cooper shit just a little too far. This is it, bub. You are finally going to have to make some sort of real decision in your life, instead of hiding under the bed like you've been doing. I've been chasing you around like Wilma Flintstone with a fucking club, but now it stops. You know as well as I do we're good for each other, and that's saying a lot, considering what a couple of royally fucked-up goobers we both are. It's the end of the picture, kiddo, and it's your call whether you get to kiss me or your horse."

"You've never seen my horse," he said.

"Just how many people," she said, "do you get to have this kind of banter with?"

"Banter is important," he said.

"You bet your ass it is."

"We're like Nick and Nora Charles," he said. "We're like Burns and Allen. We're like Ben and Jerry, like Sacco and Vanzetti, like—"

"Oh, shut up," she said. She went over to him and sat in his lap.

"I was going to say Tom Mix and his wonder horse Tony."

"Oh yeah?" she said. "Well, ride off into the sunset on this, cowpoke."

Vignon on crutches navigated the steps up to Amalie's door. He knocked and waited. He'd phoned to say he was coming but she'd sounded distant, distracted, and he wondered if she'd even be there. But she opened the door.

The flat looked different now. Cleaner, certainly, and lighter— as if the absence of Debord allowed sunlight to enter the place. She'd set out all her Japanese things.

"Would you like some tea?"

"No, thank you. I can only stay a moment. I thought you might want this."

He took out the samurai headband she'd made for Perec and handed it to her.

"It was in his pocket."

"He wouldn't have killed her, you know."

"Anna doesn't think so either. But it's hard to know what people will do."

"You don't think people can change."

"No. I don't."

"Then I feel sorry for you. How can you understand anything until you understand that everything changes. Change is all we have."

"I think he was a madman. I feel a little pity for him, but it's better he's not still in the world."

"And you don't think he knew that?"

A beat.

"Perhaps I will have that tea."

"Good. I have a treat for you."

He followed her through the flat out into the small enclosed garden. She'd set up the tea things on a low table and there were pillows on either side. A metal Japanese teapot was heating on a brazier next to the table. There was a lovely bowl of crackled stoneware, a long-handled bamboo spoon, and a delicate-looking whisk. Vignon struggled to sit down on his pillow. Amalie seemed to levitate onto hers.

"Do you know anything about the Japanese tea ceremony?" she asked him.

"No," he said. "Not much."

"They say if you do it right, it's like a little bit of enlightenment."

"Well," said Vignon, "I can use all the help I can get."

Amalie smiled at him and bowed deeply and poured the scalding water over the powdered green leaves of tea.

Special lay there in the hospital bed in the middle of the night, unmoving, lost in all the tubes and beeps and blinking machinery. Just after 3 a.m. the door opened and a figure came in and sat down in the chair next to his bed. The figure stared at Special for a few minutes.

Then said: "You owe me one hundred forty-seven thousand dollars and"—Locatelli took a piece of paper from his jacket pocket and looked at it—"fifty-three cents. I'm not going to hold you to the vigorish because you appear to be having some problems."

Locatelli waited for an answer but none appeared to be forthcoming. He got up with a small puff of effort and went over to a bowl of fruit and picked out an orange. He took it back to the seat with him, where he sat back down with a small grunt, and began peeling it with a tiny gold penknife.

"There are two ways we can do this. One way is that I have the two guys out in the hallway come in here and rewire some of this stuff."

Locatelli occupied himself for the next few moments with the process of peeling the orange in one long unbroken strip. He held it up, examined it proudly, then laid it on the table nearby. He began separating the orange.

"The other way," he said, "is that we do a deal."

Special's eyes fluttered and opened.

"In exchange for exactly one hundred forty-seven thousand dollars and"—he checked the paper again—"fifty-three cents, the exclusive rights to your heroic and heartwarming story go to my publishing company, Collateral Press, for whom you will write a book. Well, somebody will write it anyway. This book will, in turn, be sold to my movie company, Collateral Pictures, and you will sign a nondisclosure agreement where you do what we tell you and avoid being backed over by a garbage truck repeatedly. How is this sounding? You get to appear on *Oprah*, whoop-de-doo."

Special's hand was twitching, his fingers making motions like he was writing something. Locatelli took out a small leatherbound notebook and a maroon Montblanc rollerball pen. He put the pen in Special's fingers and the blank notebook page beneath it. Special scribbled quickly. Locatelli picked up the notebook and put on his reading glasses and looked at it carefully under the light. The handwriting was all over the place but still legible:

kiss my ass—exec prod cred + points!!!

"Now let me see," said Locatelli, "if I have this correctly. You're a miserable two-bit pimp from East L.A., sliced up like a goddamn loaf of mortadella, shot three times in the chest, on life support in some frog hospital—not to mention in hock to me for over a hundred g's—and you're trying to *negotiate*?"

Locatelli capped the Montblanc and folded the notebook and put them away. He sat back in the chair and ate a couple of pieces of the orange, wiping his fingers on a silk handkerchief.

He stood up, popped the remaining segment of orange into his mouth, and said around it: "Welcome to Hollywood, kid. You're a natural."

Locatelli went to the door, paused for a second and shook his head, made a short noise that almost passed for an appreciative laugh. Then he opened the door and was gone.

Special closed his eyes and smiled. He thought about Patsy and Haut-Brion and that lamb he had at the Martinez Hotel and how Cannes and France and all that shit wasn't half bad if you gave it a chance. He thought about how a man, if he don't lose his head and get all sentimental and just stick to his business, can pretty much get his ass through anything.

He closed his eyes and slept the sweet sleep, not of an innocent, but of a justified sinner.

Virtue may have its own rewards, but the crooked have sexier dreams.

SIX MONTHS LATER

DONNIE MASCALLARI SAT IN AN ITALIAN RESTAURANT IN the middle of the afternoon in Reno, Nevada. He was eating linguini with a very good clam sauce, though he always felt a little strange about eating clam sauce in the middle of the desert. But it wasn't, of course, as if the fucking clams had walked here.

There were only a couple of other people in the restaurant at this time of day, aside from Louis, the owner. There was an old guy Donnie had seen up and down the strip for years. Then there was this blond girl talking to him. She wore a tight leopard-print skirt and a tight black low-cut top. She was a little plump but Donnie didn't mind plump and she had great tits. Donnie had been watching the horses run on the TV above the bar. The race he'd bet on at Santa Anita came up and Donnie was yelling at Louis to turn the thing up. While he was yelling at Louis the blonde walked past him on the way to the bathroom. She gave him a big smile. He was still yelling at Louis, who was deaf as a post, to turn the goddamn thing up when the girl came back out

of the bathroom, broke her high heel, and lurched against Donnie's table, nearly falling into his linguini.

"Sorry, honey," she said. "These goddamn heels."

"No problemo," said Donnie. "The view was nice," meaning
he'd had a good chance to see down those knockers. The girl
caught what he meant. She slapped him playfully on the shoulder, winked at him, and swayed her ass nicely for him as she
left the restaurant. Damn, thought Donnie. He'd probably see
her again soon. He shoveled another forkful of linguini into his
mouth, chewed it, and started to yell at Louis again when all of a
sudden his voice just stopped.

A second later his breathing stopped.

Then, just after that, the rest of Donnie Mascarelli stopped.

He went facedown into the pasta, his last thought that, in
retrospect, he might have been right about the clams.

At a roadhouse just outside of Pocatello, Idaho, Sam Arness had
spent the last hour trying to pick up this redhead. She was a little
drunk and he didn't figure he had all that much longer to go.
She'd already let him kiss her and feel up her boob and at one
point he'd worked his hand pretty well up that skirt.

Sam was trying it again when she pushed his hand away and
said, "Baby, hold that thought, and when I come back you can
hold something else."

She slid off the bar stool and in reaching for her purse managed to knock over what was left of her beer.

"Hand me some of them napkins, will you, baby?" she asked
him.

Sam turned and reached for a pile of napkins and they mopped up the beer. "Shit," she said. "I figger I'm pretty drunk. Now don't you be taking advantage of me."

"Oh, I won't."

"Too bad," she said, giggling and lurching toward the restrooms.

Sam sat there on the bar stool drinking his beer, waiting for her to come back, thinking about all the fun they were going to have the rest of the evening. She was a pretty fun gal, it seemed. Sam liked fun. Yeah, it was going to be a good evening okay.

Or it would have been if Sam's autonomic nervous system hadn't shut down at that particular moment, stopping his heart and his lungs and pretty much everything else as well.

Sam keeled over onto the bar stool where the girl had been sitting, where he was to rest nearly an hour before anybody bothered to realize he was dead.

The redhead walked out the back door of the roadhouse and circled around to her car in the parking lot. She started the car and drove away. The roadhouse was well out of sight before she pulled off the auburn wig, scratched her brown hair, and dialed a number on her mobile phone.

"Daddy? Mission accomplished. Warm up the hot tub 'cause baby's coming home."

She reached down and turned on the CD player and cranked it up. Maria Callas singing "L'amour est un oiseau rebelle" from Bizet's *Carmen* spilled out of the car and along the highway back toward Los Angeles. Patsy sang along, then remembered the now-empty vial and threw it out the window, where it bounced to the side of the road and shattered harmlessly amid the tall grass.

Five hundred miles away, Special hung up the phone and found himself touching the thick scars beneath his shirt. He thought about Anna, about that day by the pool when she talked of finding out how badly she wanted to live and passed the vial to him in a small box for him to dispose of. Well, now he'd disposed of it okay. And there was Perec, the black angel, the psychotic little fuck who'd caused so much mayhem but somehow ended up changing everybody's life for the better. Now, there was some kind of weird-ass moral tale for you. It was damn near enough to shake your faith in morality, period, except Special had never believed in morality in the first place. Special believed in taking care of business and never letting your enemies off the hook. Locatelli fortunately understood, which is why he allowed Special his own private justice as an unwritten part of their contract.

Locatelli had never thought the two bastards were particularly useful anyway.

Yes, it was easy to overcomplicate the whole thing, and you could mess your head up pretty badly if you spent much time thinking about it. Screw that philosophy shit, we are all just a bunch of big goddamn monkeys with car keys. What's that line about music soothing the savage beast?

Which is precisely why he spent the rest of the afternoon in his wine cellar, listening to Verdi and trying to decide which of their *premier cru* Bordeaux to drink that night when his woman finally brought her ass back to town.